TO PLAY
THE KING

MICHAEL DOBBS

HarperCollins*Publishers*

HarperCollins*Publishers*
77–85 Fulham Palace Road
Hammersmith, London W6 8JB

Published by HarperCollins*Publishers* 1992

9 8 7 6 5 4 3 2

A catalogue record for this book
is available from the British Library

ISBN 0 00 223886 1

Set in Linotron Meridien by
Rowland Phototypesetting Limited
Bury St Edmunds, Suffolk
Printed in Great Britain by
HarperCollinsManufacturing Glasgow

Lucy and Andrei.
For Medford 1971. For Fiskardon 1981. For Villars 1991.
For everything.

ACKNOWLEDGEMENTS

My beloved Aunt started it all. In a midnight phone call after the showing of BBC TV's final episode of *House of Cards* she complained: 'They let the bastard get away with it!'

And wasn't that the truth? In the original book I had awarded the honour of survival to the delectable political correspondent Mattie Storin, believing in truth, justice and the triumph of good. But those sinister people who run the BBC's drama department are made of sterner stuff and, deciding that virtuous heroines are not to conquer the Nineties, reversed the ending to leave the evil Francis Urquhart triumphant and my poor, desirable heroine lying trampled on the cutting room floor. It was a wicked twist of fate which has brought me nothing but great good fortune and, long after the credits had finished rolling, left many people insisting on knowing what happened next.

So my thanks to Ken Riddington, Paul Seed and Andrew Davies, a team of unique talent whose abilities pushed me into the instant resurrection business while they deservedly picked up awards around the globe. And, most particularly, my gratitude goes to Ian Richardson. His electrifying portrayal of Francis Urquhart will live with me for a lifetime.

There are many others I want to acknowledge. John Hanvey held my hand through the murky parts of the opinion polling business while Tony Hutt also held it through some of the murkier drinking establishments of London. Benjamin Mancroft lent me his wisdom, Charlotte Morrison one of her bedrooms and Tracy Macmunn her wardrobe and three years of her life. Chris Sear of the Public Information Office at the House of Commons was imaginative, patient and immensely resourceful in answering my obscure questions, as were Ian Nimmo and Tim Walker in the City and Sergeant Ian

Allan in the firing ranges of Westminster. I am also indebted to Lord Callaghan of Cardiff, a Commander-in-Chief at Westminster when I was a foot-soldier in the opposing army. Many others, both high and humble, guided me through the labyrinthine passages of Buckingham Palace and Downing Street, but prefer to remain uncharacteristically coy. If anyone is to be taken to the Tower of London for extended incarceration, it shall be me alone.

Oh . . . And thank you, Auntie.

PROLOGUE

It was the day they would put him to death.

They led him through the park, penned in by two companies of infantrymen. The crowd was thick and he had spent much of the night wondering how they would react when they saw him. With tears? Jeers? Try to snatch him to safety or spit on him in contempt? It depended who had paid them best. But there was no outburst; they stood in silence, dejected, cowed, still not believing what was about to take place in their name. A young woman cried out and fell in a dead faint as he passed, but nobody tried to impede his progress across the frost-hard ground. The guards were hurrying him on.

Within minutes they were in Whitehall, where he was lodged in a small room. It was just after ten o'clock on a January morning, and he expected at any moment to hear the knock on the door that would summon him. But something had delayed them; they didn't come until nearly two. Four hours of waiting, of demons gnawing at his courage, of feeling himself fall to pieces inside. During the night he had achieved a serenity and sense of inner peace, almost a state of grace, but with the heavy passage of unexpected minutes, growing into hours, the calm was replaced by a sickening sense of panic which began somewhere in his brain and stretched right through his body to pour into his bladder and his bowels. His thoughts became scrambled and the considered words, crafted with such care to illuminate the justice of his cause and impeach their twisted logic, were suddenly gone. He dug his finger nails deep into his palms; somehow he would find the words, when the time came.

The door opened. The captain stood in the dark entrance and gave a curt, sombre nod of his helmeted head. No need for words. They took him and within seconds he was in the Banqueting Hall, a place he cherished with its Rubens ceiling and magnificent oaken

9

doors, but he had difficulty in making out the details through the unnatural gloom. The tall windows had been partially bricked up and boarded during the war to provide better defensive positions. Only at one of the farther windows was there light where the masonry and barricades had been torn down and a harsh grey glow surrounded the hole, like the entrance to another world. The corridor formed by the line of soldiers led directly to it.

My God, but it was cold. He'd had nothing to eat since yesterday, he'd refused the meal they had offered, and he was grateful for the second shirt he had asked for, to prevent him shivering. It wouldn't do to be seen to shiver. They would think it was fear.

He climbed up two rough wooden steps and bowed his head as he crossed the threshold of the window, onto a platform they had erected immediately outside. There were half a dozen other men on the freshly built wooden stage while every point around was crammed by teeming thousands, on foot, on carriages, on roofs, leaning from windows and other vantage points. Surely now there would be some response? But as he stepped out into the harsh light and their view, their restlessness froze in the icy wind and the huddled figures stood silent and sullen, ever incredulous. It still could not be.

Driven into the stage on which he stood were four iron staples. They would rope him down, spread-eagled between the staples, if he struggled, yet it was but one more sign of how little they understood him. He would not struggle. He had been born to a better end than that. He would but speak his few words to the throng and that would be sufficient. He prayed that the weakness he felt in his knees would not betray him; surely he had been betrayed enough. They handed him a small cap into which with great care he tucked his hair, as if preparing for nothing more than a walk through the park with his wife and children. He must make a fine show of it. He dropped his cloak to the ground so that he might be better seen.

Heavens! The cold cut through him as if the frost were reaching for his racing heart and turning it straightway to stone. He took a deep, searing breath to recover from the shock. He must not tremble! And there was the captain of his guard, already in front of him, beads of sweat on his brow despite the weather.

'Just a few words, Captain. I would say a few words.' He racked his mind in search of them.

The captain shook his head.

'For the love of God, the commonest man in all the world has the right to a few words.'

'Your few words would be more than my life is worth, Sir.'

'As my words and thoughts are more than my life to me. It is my beliefs that have brought me to this place, Captain. I will share them one last time.'

'I cannot let you. Truly, I am sorry. But I cannot.'

'Will you deny me even now?' The composure in his voice had been supplanted by the heat of indignation and a fresh wave of panic. It was all going wrong.

'Sir, it is not in my hands. Forgive me.'

The captain reached out to touch him on the arm but the prisoner stepped back and his eyes burned in rebuke. 'You may silence me, but you will never make me what I am not. I am no coward, Captain. I have no need of your arm!'

The captain withdrew, chided.

The time had come. There would be no more words, no more delay. No hiding place. This was the moment when both they and he would peer deep inside and discover what sort of man he truly was. He took another searing lungful of air, clinging to it as long as he could as he looked to the heavens. The priest had intoned that death was the ultimate triumph over worldly evil and pain but he discovered no inspiration, no shaft of sunlight to mark his way, no celestial salvation, only the hard steel sky of an English winter. He realized his fists remained clenched with the nails biting into the flesh of his palms; he forced his palms open and down the side of his trousers. A quiet prayer. Another breath. Then he bent, thanking God that his knees still had sufficient strength to guide him, lowering himself slowly and gracefully as he had practised in his room during the night, and lay stretched out on the rough wooden platform.

Still from the crowd there came no sound. His words might not have lifted or inspired them, but at least they would have vindicated. He was drenched in fury as the overwhelming injustice of it all hit him. Not even a chance to explain. He looked despairingly once more into the faces of the people, the men and women in whose name both sides had fought the war and who stood there now with blank stare, ever uncomprehending pawns. Yet, dullards all, they were his people, for whose salvation he was bound to fight against those who would corrupt the law for their own benefit. He had lost, but the justice of his cause would surely be known in the end. In the end. He would do it all again, if he had another chance, another life. It was his duty, he would have no choice. No more choice than he had now on this bare wooden stage, which still smelt of resin and fresh sawdust. And they would understand, wouldn't they? In the end . . . ?

A plank creaked beside his left ear. The faces of the crowd seemed frozen in time, like a vast mural in which no one moved. His bladder was going – was it the cold or sheer terror? How much longer . . . ? Concentrate, a prayer perhaps? Concentrate! He set on a small boy, no more than eight years old, in rags, with a dribble of crumbs on his dirt-smeared chin, who had stopped chewing his hunk of loaf and whose innocent brown eyes had grown wide with expectation and were focused on a point about a foot above his head. By God, but it was cold, colder than he had ever known! And suddenly the words he had fought so hard to remember came rushing back to him, as though someone had unlocked his soul.

And in the year sixteen hundred and forty-nine, they took their liege lord King Charles Stuart, Defender of the Faith and by hereditary right King of Great Britain and Ireland, and they cut off his head.

In the early hours of a winter's day, in a bedroom overlooking the forty-acre garden of a palace which hadn't existed at the time Charles Stuart took his walk into the next life, his descendant awoke with a start. The collar of his pyjama shirt clung damply and he lay face-down on a block-hard pillow stained with sweat, yet he felt as cold as . . . As cold as death. He believed in the power of dreams and their ability to unravel the mysteries of the inner being, and it was his custom on waking to write down everything he could remember, reaching for the notebook he kept for the purpose beside his bed. But not this time. There was no need. He would never forget the smell of the crowd mixed with resin and sawdust nor the heavy metallic colour of the sky on that frost-ridden afternoon. Nor the innocent, expectant brown eyes of a boy with a dirty chin smeared with crumbs. Nor that feeling of terrible despair that they had kept him from speaking out, rendering his sacrifice pointless and his death utterly in vain. He would never forget it. No matter how hard he tried.

PART ONE

December: The First Week

It had not been a casual invitation, he never did anything casually. It had been an insistent, almost peremptory call from a man more used to command than to cajolement. He expected her for breakfast and it would not have crossed his mind that she might refuse. Particularly today, when they were changing Prime Ministers, one out and another in and long live the will of the people. It would be a day of great reckoning and few could doubt that by evening he would have still more trophies to adorn his many mansions. She wondered if she were intended to be one of them.

Benjamin Landless opened the door himself, which struck her as strange. It was an apartment for making impressions, overdesigned and impersonal, the sort of apartment where you'd expect if not a doorman then at least a secretary or a PA to be on hand, to fix the coffee, to flatter the guests while ensuring they didn't run off with any of the Impressionist paintings enriching the walls. There was a Pissarro, a Monet and at least two Wilson Steers, all displayed ostentatiously at the whim of some interior designer rather than hung for the discerning pleasure of a true collector. Landless was no work of art himself. He had a broad, plum-red face which was fleshy and beginning to sag like a candle held too near the flame. His bulk was huge and his hands rough, like a labourer's, with a reputation to match. His *Telegraph* newspaper empire had been built by breaking strikes as well as careers; it had been as much he as anyone who had broken the career of the man who was, even now, waiting to drive to the Palace to relinquish the power and prestige of the office of Prime Minister.

'Miss Quine. Sally. I'm so glad you could come. I've wanted to meet you for a long time.'

She knew that to be a lie. Had he wanted to meet her before he would most certainly have arranged it. Something had happened to make him want to meet her now, and alone. He escorted her into the main room around which the penthouse apartment was built. Its external walls were fashioned entirely of toughened glass, which offered a magnificent panorama of the parliament buildings across the Thames, and half a rain forest seemed to have been sacrificed to cover the floor in intricate wooden patterns. Not bad for a boy from the back streets of Bethnal Green, he occasionally admitted, but the description was redundant. They had all been back streets where he was born.

With so much light the apartment seemed to hover in the air, suspended halfway between street and sky, gazing down upon the politicians and law-makers on the other side of the river and thereby diminishing them to the scale and significance of punctuation marks in one of his editorials, an effect she felt sure was intentional. It was Olympus, an eyrie which seemed to cut them off from reality, and Sally off from any means of escape. But that was why she had come, the challenge of meeting a man of power face-to-face, the opportunity to test herself, to prove she was as good or better than any of them, perhaps to beat them at their own game and to get her own back. It might end in disaster, of course, in a crass attempt at physical flattery and seduction or even coercion, but it was a risk she had to take if she were to stand any chance of getting what she wanted. Risk was all part of the exhilaration.

He ushered her towards an oversized leather sofa in front of which stood a coffee table laden with trays of piping-hot breakfast food. There was no sign of the hidden helper who must only recently have prepared the dishes and laid out the crisp linen napkins. She declined any of the food but he was not offended. He took off his jacket and fussed about his own plate while she took a cup of black coffee and waited.

He ate his breakfast in single-minded fashion; etiquette and table manners were not his strong points. He offered little small talk, his attention focused on the eggs rather than on her, and for a while she wondered if he might have decided he'd made a mistake in inviting her. He was already making her feel vulnerable. Eggs finished, he wiped his mouth and pushed his plate away.

18

'Sally Quine. Born in Dorchester, Massachusetts. Aged thirty-two, and a girl who's already made quite a reputation for herself as an opinion pollster. In Boston, too, which is no easy city for a woman amongst all those thick-headed Micks.' She knew all about that; she'd married one. Landless had done his homework; he wanted to make that clear, and to know what she felt about her past being pawed over by him. His eyes searched for her reaction from beneath huge eyebrows tangled like rope. 'It's a lovely city, Boston, know it well. Tell me, why did you leave everything you'd built there and come to England to start all over again? From nothing?'

He paused, but got no reply. 'It was the divorce, wasn't it? And the death of the baby?'

He saw her jaw stiffen and wondered whether it was the start of a storm of outrage or a move for the door. But he knew there would be no tears. She wasn't the type, you could see that from her eyes. She was not unnaturally slim and pinched as the current fashion demanded, her beauty was more classical, the hips perhaps a half-inch too wide but all the curves well defined. She was immaculately presented. The skin of her face was smooth, darker and with more lustre than any English rose, the features carefully drawn as though by a sculptor's knife. The lips were full and expressive, the chin flat and the cheekbones high, her long hair thick and of such a deep shade of black that he thought she might be Italian or Jewish. It was a face full of strength and passion, capable of defying the world or captivating it as she chose. Yet her most exceptional feature was her nose, straight and a fraction long with a flattened end which twitched as she talked and nostrils which dilated with emphasis and emotion. It was the most provocative and sensuous nose he had ever seen; he couldn't help but imagine it on a pillow. Yet the eyes disturbed him, didn't belong on this face. They were shaped like almonds, uplifted, full of autumnal russets and greens, translucent like a cat's, yet, while the nose was prominent and almost public in its emotion, the eyes hid behind oversized spectacles. They didn't sparkle like a woman's should, like they probably once had, he thought. They had an edge of mistrust, as if holding something back, and when she concentrated

19

her mouth turned down puckishly but defiantly at the corners. She was a woman who would not easily lose control, nor readily give of herself.

She looked out of the window, ignoring him. Christmas was but a couple of weeks away, yet there was no seasonal cheer in the air. It was a typical December scene for London, wet and dreary as if the day had not properly woken. Low clouds scudded across the sky, seemingly only feet above their heads. It was a day when Waterloo Bridge would be tap-tap-tapping to the sound of umbrella points as pedestrians hid inside their raincoats and tried to make it across to the other side before the next squall hit. Street traders would be cursing as they struggled to keep their Christmas stock from getting soaked while trying to entice customers out of the warm coffee shops and pubs. Another couple of pounds would be added to the fare of every mini-cab and to hell with the punter who argued. The festive spirit lay discarded in the running gutters, and somehow it didn't seem a propitious day for changing Prime Ministers.

A seagull beaten inland by North Sea storms cartwheeled outside the window, its shrieks and insults penetrating the double-glazing while it made repeated attacks on their position, envying them their breakfast and beating up against the window before finally tumbling away through the blustery sky. She watched it disappear into the greyness.

'Don't expect me to be upset or offended, Mr Landless. The fact that you have enough money and clout to do your homework doesn't impress me. Neither does it flatter me. I'm used to being chatted up by middle-aged businessmen.' The insult was intended; she wanted him to know he wasn't going to get away with one-way traffic. 'You want something from me. I've no idea what but I'll listen. So long as it's business.'

She crossed her legs slowly and deliberately so that he would notice. From her days as a child she had had no doubts that men found her body appealing and their excessive attention meant she had never had the opportunity to treat her sex as something to treasure, only as a tool to carve a path through a difficult and ungenerous world. She had decided long ago that if sex were to be the currency of life then she would turn it into a business asset, to open the doors which would otherwise be barred. While captains of industry drooled and got a tight sensation in their pants, she would put a contract under their noses and get them to sign. Men could be such dickheads. She saw Landless's eyes following her ankles. So, he was just like the rest of them and she had dressed for the part. A meanly cut black cashmere sweater which hugged those parts of her figure it didn't reveal and a Donna Karan skirt straight from Fifth Avenue which was tight and shorter than most professional women would dare to wear but not so short as to make her seem a tart. Anyway, she had the legs for it. And she wore a fashionable and expensive silk-cotton jacket from Harvey Nicks which hung loosely over her shoulders. She could shift around inside it and either expose her cashmere-covered breasts or hide them, as she chose. It was all part of the risk, of the tension of dealing with men and exploiting their weaknesses. She dressed to dominate and to be in control. Power dressing. And in the tight-assed business circles of London it seemed to work all the more effectively.

'You're very direct, Miss Quine.'

'I prefer to cut through it rather than spread it. And I can play your game.' She sat back into the sofa and began counting off the carefully manicured fingers of her left hand. 'Ben Landless. Age . . . well, for your well-known vanity's sake, let's say not quite menopausal. A rough son-of-a-bitch who was born to nothing and now controls one of the largest press operations in this country.'

'Soon to be the largest,' he interrupted quietly.

'Soon to take over United Newspapers,' she nodded, 'when the Prime Minister you nominated, backed and got elected virtually single-handed takes over in a couple of hours' time and waves aside the minor inconvenience of his predecessor's mergers and monopolies policy. You must've been celebrating all night, I'm surprised you had the appetite for breakfast. But you have the reputation of being a man with insatiable appetites. Of all kinds. So what's on your mind, Ben?' She spoke almost seductively in an accent that had been smoothed and carefully softened but not obliterated. She wanted people to take notice and to remember, to pick

21

her out from the crowd. So the vowels were still New England, a shade too long and lazy for London, and the sentiments often rough as if they had been fashioned straight from the dole queues of Dorchester.

A smile played around the publisher's rubbery lips as he contemplated his good fortune and her defiance, but his eyes remained unmoved, watching her closely. His humour seemed confined to the lower half of his face, not touching his eyes nor penetrating beneath the skin. 'There is no deal. I backed him because I thought he was the best man for the job, but there's no private pay-off. I shall take my chances, just like all the rest.'

She suspected that was the second lie of the conversation, but let it pass.

'Whatever else happens, it's a new era. A change of Prime Minister means fresh challenges. And opportunities. I suspect he'll be more relaxed about getting the wheels of business turning and letting people make money than was Henry Collingridge. That's good news for me. And potentially for you.'

'With all the economic indicators scooting downhill?'

'That's just the point. Your opinion-research company has been in business for . . . what, twenty months? You've made a good start, you're well respected. But you're small, and small boats like yours could be swamped if the economy gets rough over the next couple of years. Anyway, you've no more patience than I do in running a shoestring operation. You want to make it big, to be on top. And for that you need cash.'

'Not your cash. If I had newspaper money poured into my operation it would ruin every shred of credibility I've built. My business is supposed to be objective analysis, not smears and scares with a few naked starlets thrown in to boost circulation.'

He ran his thick tongue around his mouth as if trying absentmindedly to dislodge a piece of breakfast. 'You underestimate yourself,' he muttered. He produced a toothpick, which he used like a sword-swallower to probe into a far corner of his jaw. 'Opinion polls are not objective analysis. They're news. If an editor wants to get an issue rolling he commissions people like you to carry out some research. He knows what answers he wants and what headline he's going to run, he just needs a few statistics to give the whole thing the smack of authenticity. Opinion polls are the weapons of civil war. Kill off a government, show the nation's morals are shot to hell, establish that we all love Palestinians or hate apple pie. You don't need facts, just the blessing of an opinion poll.'

He grew more animated as he warmed to his theme. His hands had come down from his mouth and were grasped in front of him as if throttling an incompetent editor. There was no sign of the toothpick; perhaps he had simply swallowed it, as he did most things which got in his way.

'Information is power,' he continued. 'And money. A lot of your work is done in the City, for instance, with companies involved in takeover bids. Your little polls tell them how shareholders and the financial institutions might react, whether they'll be supportive or simply dump the company for a bit of quick cash. You can discover how opinion is running amongst the analysts and financial journalists, not over some wine-sodden lunch at the Savoy Grill with a company chairman but back at their desks, where it matters. Takeover bids are wars, life or death for the companies concerned, and your job is to tell them whose guts are most likely to be spread over the floor at the end of the day. That information has great value.'

'And we charge a very good fee for such work.'

'I'm not talking thousands or tens of thousands,' he barked dismissively. 'That's petty cash in the City. The sort of information we're talking about allows you to name your own figure, if you make it work for you.' He paused to see if there would be a squawk of impugned professional integrity; instead she reached behind her to pull down her jacket, which had ridden up against the back of the sofa. As she did so she exposed and accentuated the rounded curves at the top of her breasts. He took it as a sign of encouragement.

'You need money. To expand. To grab the polling industry by the balls and to become its undisputed queen. Otherwise you go belly-up in the recession. Be a great waste.'

'I'm flattered by your avuncular interest.'

23

'You're not here to be flattered. You're here to listen to a prop-osition.'

'I've known that from the moment I got your invitation. Although for a moment there I thought we'd wound up on the lecture circuit.'

Instead of responding he levered himself out of his chair and crossed to the window. The gun-grey clouds had descended still lower and it had begun to rain. A barge was battling to make headway through the ebbing tide beneath Westminster Bridge where the December winds had turned the usually tranquil river into a muddy, ill-tempered soup of urban debris and bilge oil. He gazed in the direction of the Houses of Parliament, his hands stuffed firmly into the folds of his tent-like trousers, scratching himself.

'Our leaders over there, the fearless guardians of the nation's welfare. Government is necessarily a secretive business, full of shared confidences, of information which is restricted because its public release would be sensationalized or abused. And every single one of those bastards would leak the lot if it served their purposes. There's not a political editor in town who doesn't know every word of what's gone on within an hour of a Cabinet meeting finishing, nor a general who hasn't leaked a confidential report about the nation's security before doing battle with the Treasury over the defence budget. And you find me the politician who hasn't tried to undermine a rival by starting gossip about his sex life.' His hands flapped in his trouser pockets like the sails of a great ship trying to catch the wind. 'Prime Ministers are the worst,' he snorted con-temptuously. 'If they want to rid themselves of a troublesome Minister, they'll assassinate him in the press beforehand with tales of drunkenness or disloyalty. Inside information. It's what makes the world go round. And it's not a matter to our masters of *if* you use it, but when.'

'Perhaps that's why I never went into politics,' she mused.

He turned towards her, to discover her seemingly engrossed in removing a stray hair from her sweater. When she was sure she had his full attention she stopped toying with him and hid once again inside the folds of her jacket. 'So what is it you are going to suggest I do?'

24

Once again his tongue rolled distractedly around his mouth, this time in search not of the elusive piece of breakfast but of inspiration and the appropriate words. He sat down beside her on the sofa and the proximity of his shirt-clad bulk squeezed any suggestion of levity from the air. His physical presence was, surprisingly to her fashion-conscious eye, indeed impressive.

'I'm going to suggest you stop being an also-ran, a woman who may strive for years to make it to the top yet never succeed. I'm suggesting a partnership. With me. Your expertise' – they both knew he meant inside information – 'backed by my financial clout. It would be a formidable combination.'

'But what's in it for me?'

'A guarantee of survival. A chance to make a lot of money, to get where you want to go, to the top of the pile. To show your former husband that not only can you survive without him but even succeed. That's what you want, isn't it?'

'And how is all this supposed to happen?'

'We pool our resources. Your information and my money. If there's any action going on in the City I want to be part of it. Get in there ahead of the pack and the potential rewards are huge. You and I split any profit right down the middle.'

She brought her forefinger and thumb together in front of her face. Her nose offered an emphatic bob. 'Excuse me, but if I understand you right, isn't that just the tiniest bit illegal?'

He responded with silence and a look of unquenchable boredom.

'And it sounds as if you would be taking all the risk,' she continued.

'Risk is a fact of life. I don't mind taking the risk with a partner I know and trust. I'm sure we could get to trust each other very closely; it would be vital.'

He reached out and brushed the back of her hand; there was no mistaking the glaze of distrust which flashed into her eyes.

'Before you ask, getting you into bed is not an essential part of the deal – no, don't look so damned innocent and offended. You've been flashing your tits at me from the moment you sat down so let us, as you say, cut through it all and get down to basics. Getting you on your back would be a pleasure, but this is business and in my book business comes first. I've no intention of cocking up what could be a first-class deal by letting my brains slip between my legs. You've got a body which I've no doubt you know how and when to use, but I can buy all the beauty and bum I want at very much less of a price than potentially I'm offering you. We're here to screw the competition, not each other. So . . . what's it to be? Are you interested?'

As if on cue a phone began to warble in a distant part of the room. With a grunt of exasperation he levered himself up, but as he crossed the room to answer the call there was also anticipation; his office had the strictest instruction not to bother him unless . . . He barked briefly into the phone before returning to his guest, his hands spread wide as though approaching a table laden with fine food.

'Extraordinary. My cup runs over. That was a message from Downing Street. Apparently our new Prime Minister wishes me to call on him as soon as he's back from the Palace, so I'm afraid I must rush off. Wouldn't do to keep him waiting.' His candle-wax face was contorted in what passed for a grin. She would be the focus of his attention for only a few moments longer: another place, another partner beckoned. He was already climbing into his coat. 'So make it a very special day for me. Accept.'

She stretched for her handbag on the sofa but he was there also, his huge labourer's hand completely encasing her own. They were very close and she could feel the heat from his body, smell him, sense the power beneath the bulk which was capable of crushing her instantly if he so chose. But there was no threat in his manner, his touch was surprisingly gentle. For a moment she caught herself feeling disarmed, almost aroused. Her nose twitched.

'You go sort out the nation's balance of payments. I'll think about mine.'

'Think carefully, Sally, and not too long.'

'I'll consult my horoscope. I'll be in touch.'

At that moment the seagull made another screeching attack, hurling insults as it pounded against the window, leaving it dripping with guano. He cursed.

'It's supposed to be a lucky omen,' she laughed lightly.

'Lucky?' he growled as he led her out of the door. 'Tell that to the bloody window cleaner!'

It hadn't been as he had expected. The crowds had been much thinner than in years gone by; indeed, fewer than two dozen people standing outside the Palace gates, skulking tortoise-like beneath umbrellas and plastic raincoats, could scarcely be counted as a crowd at all. Perhaps it was the approach of Christmas and the foul weather which had kept them away. Maybe the great British public simply didn't give a damn anymore who their Prime Minister was.

He sat back in the car, a man of bearing and distinction amidst the leather, his tired smile implying a casual, almost reluctant acceptance of his lot. He had a long face which led from a high and distinguished forehead to thin lips, the skin ageing but still taut beneath the chin, austere like a Roman bust with lank silver-sandy hair carefully combed away from the face. He was dressed in his habitual charcoal-grey suit with two buttons and a brightly coloured, almost foppish silk handkerchief which erupted out of the breast pocket, an affectation he had adopted to distance himself from the Westminster hordes in their banal Christmas-stocking ties and Marks & Spencer suits. Every few seconds he would bend low, stretching down behind the seat to suck at the cigarette he kept hidden below the window line, the only outward show of the tension and excitement which bubbled within. He took a deep lungful of nicotine and for a while didn't move, feeling his throat go dry as he waited for his heart to slow, pondering, only the small blue eyes moving sharply, never resting. They seemed perpetually strained, agitated, slightly damp and raw at the rims as if they had spent too long poring late into the night over official papers. The eyes attracted many women, stimulating their protective maternal instincts, while in men they aroused only anxiety. They suggested tension, an impatience, a man quick to ire and slow to forget.

The Right Honourable Francis Ewan Urquhart, MP, since six o'clock the previous evening the leader of his party and within minutes to be asked to accept the leadership of a new government, gave a perfunctory wave to the huddled group of onlookers from the rear seat of his new ministerial Jaguar as it passed into the forecourt of Buckingham Palace. His wife had wanted to lower the window in order for the assorted cameramen lurking nearby to obtain a better view of them both, but discovered that the windows on the official car were more than an inch thick and cemented in place. She had been assured by the driver that nothing less than a direct hit from a mortar with armour-piercing shells would open them.

The last few hours had seemed all but comic. After the result of the leadership ballot had been announced and with victory confirmed, he had rushed back to his house in Cambridge Street and waited with his wife. For what, they hadn't quite known. What was he supposed to do now? There had been no one to tell him. He had waited beside the phone but it stubbornly refused to ring. He'd rather expected a call of congratulation from some of his parliamentary colleagues, perhaps from the President of the United States or at the very least his sister, but already the new caution of his colleagues towards a man formerly their equal and now their master was beginning to exert itself; the President wouldn't call until he'd been confirmed as Prime Minister and his sister apparently thought his telephone would be permanently engaged for days. In desperation for someone with whom to share their joy they took to posing for photo-calls at the front door and chatting with the journalists assembled on the pavement outside.

He was not naturally gregarious, a childhood spent roaming alone with no more than a dog and a satchelful of books across the heathers of the family estates in Scotland had attuned him well to his own company, but it was never enough. He needed others, not simply to mix with but against whom to measure himself. It was what had driven him South, that and the financial despair of the Scottish moorlands. A grandfather who had died with no thought of how to avoid the venality of the Exchequer; a father whose painful sentimentality and attachment towards tradition had brought the estate's finances to their knees. He had watched his parents' fortunes and their social position wither like apple blossom in snow. Urquhart had got out while there was still something to

28

extract from the heavily mortgaged moors, ignoring his father's entreaties on family honour which in despair had turned to tearful denunciation. It had been scarcely better at Oxford. His childhood companionship with books had led to a brilliant academic career and to a readership in Economics, but he had not taken to the life. He had grown to despise the crumpled corduroy uniforms and fuzzy moralizing which so many of his colleagues seemed to dress and die in, and found himself losing patience with the dank river mists which swept off the Cherwell and the petty political posturings of the dons' dinner table. One evening the Senior Common Room had indulged in mass intellectual orgasm as they had flayed a junior Treasury Minister within an inch of his composure; for most of those present it had merely confirmed their views of the inadequacies of Westminster, for Urquhart it had reeked only of the opportunities. So he had turned his back on both the teeming moors and dreaming spires and had risen fast, while taking great care all the while to preserve his reputation as an academic. It made other men feel inferior, and in politics that was half the game.

It was only after his second photo-call, about eight thirty p.m., that the telephone jumped back to life. A call from the Palace, the Private Secretary. Would he find it convenient to come by at about nine tomorrow morning? Yes, he would find that most convenient, thank you. Then the other calls began to flow in. Parliamentary colleagues unable any longer to control their anxieties about what job he might in the morning either offer to or strip from them. Newspaper editors uncertain whether to fawn or threaten their way to that exclusive first interview they all wanted. Solicitous mandarins of the civil service anxious to leave none of the administrative details to chance. The chairman of the party's advertising agency who had been drinking and couldn't stop gushing. And Ben Landless. There had been no real conversation, simply coarse laughter down the phone line and the unmistakable sound of a champagne cork popping. Urquhart thought he might have heard at least one woman giggling in the background. Landless was celebrating, as he had every right to. He had been Urquhart's first and most forthright supporter, and between them they had manoeuvred, twisted and tormented Henry Collingridge into

29

premature retirement. Urquhart owed him, more than he could measure, while characteristically the newspaper proprietor had not been coy in identifying an appropriate yardstick.

He was still thinking about Landless as the Jaguar shot the right-hand arch at the front of the Palace and pulled into the central courtyard. The driver applied the brakes cautiously, aware not only of his regal surroundings but also of the fact that you cannot stop more than four tons of reinforced Jaguar in a hurry without making life very uncomfortable for the occupants and running the risk of triggering the automatic panic device which transmitted a priority distress alert to the Information Room at Scotland Yard. The car drew to a halt not beneath the Doric columns of the Grand Entrance used by most visitors but beside a much smaller door to the side of the courtyard, where, smiling in welcome, the Private Secretary stood. With great speed yet with no apparent hurry he had opened the door and ushered forward an equerry to spirit Elizabeth Urquhart off for coffee and polite conversation while he led Urquhart up a small but exquisitely gilded staircase to a waiting room scarcely broader than it was high. For a minute they hovered, surrounded by oils of Victorian horse-racing scenes and admiring a small yet revealingly uninhibited marble statue of Renaissance lovers until the Private Secretary, without any apparent consultation of his watch, announced that it was time. He stepped towards a pair of towering doors, knocked gently three times and swung them open, motioning Urquhart forward.

'Mr Urquhart. Welcome!'

Against the backdrop of a heavy crimson damask drape which dressed one of the full-length windows of his sitting room stood the King. He offered a nod of respect in exchange for Urquhart's deferential bow and motioned him forward. The politician paced across the room and not until he had almost reached the Monarch did the other take a small step forward and extend his hand. Behind Urquhart the doors had already closed; the two men, one ruler by hereditary right and the other by political conquest, were alone.

Urquhart remarked to himself how cold the room was, a good two or three degrees below what others would regard as comfortable, and how surprisingly limp the regal handshake. As they stood facing each other neither man seemed to know quite how to start. The King tugged at his cuffs nervously and gave a tight laugh.

'Worry not, Mr Urquhart. Remember, this is the first time for me, too.' The King, heir for half a lifetime and Monarch for less than four months, guided him towards two chairs which stood either side of a finely crafted white stone chimneypiece. Along the walls, polished marble columns soared to support a canopied ceiling covered in elaborate classical reliefs of Muses and celestial paraphernalia, while in the alcoves formed between the stone columns were hung oversized and heavily oiled portraits of royal ancestors painted by some of the greatest artists of their age. Hand-carved pieces of furniture stood around a huge Axminster, patterned with ornate red and gold flowers and stretching from one end of the vast room to the other. This was a sitting room, but only for a king or emperor, and it might not have changed in a hundred years. The sole note of informality was struck by a desk, placed in a distant corner to catch the light cast by one of the garden windows and completely covered by an eruption of papers, pamphlets and books which all but submerged the single telephone. The King had a reputation for conscientious reading; from the state of his desk it seemed a reputation well earned.

'I'm not quite sure where to start, Mr Urquhart,' the King began as they settled in the chairs. 'We are supposed to be making history but it appears there is no form for these occasions. I have nothing to give you, no rich words of advice, not even a seal of office to hand over. I don't have to invite you to kiss my hand or take any oath. All I have to do is ask you to form a Government. You will, won't you?'

The obvious earnestness of his Sovereign caused the guest to smile. Urquhart was in his early sixties, ten years older than the King, although the difference appeared less; the younger man's face was stretched and drawn beyond its years with a hairline in rapid retreat and the beginnings of a stoop. It was said that the King had replaced his complete lack of material concerns with a lifetime of tortured spiritual questioning, and the strain was evident. While Urquhart had the easy smile and small talk of the politician, the intellectual aloofness of an academic and the ability to relax of a

31

man trained to dissemble and if necessary to deceive, the King had none of this. Urquhart felt no nervousness, only the cold; indeed, he began to pity the younger man's gravity. He leaned forward.

'Yes, Your Majesty. It will be my honour to attempt to form a Government on your behalf. I can only hope that my colleagues won't have changed their minds since yesterday.'

The King missed the mild humour as he struggled with his own thoughts, a deep furrow slicing across the forehead of a face which had launched a million commemorative mugs, plates, tea trays, T-shirts, towels, ashtrays and even the occasional chamber pot, most of them made in the Far East. 'You know, I do hope it's auspicious, a new King and new Prime Minister. There's so much to be done. Here we are on the very brink of a new millennium, new horizons. Tell me, what are your plans?'

Urquhart spread his hands wide. 'I scarcely . . . there's been so little time, Sir. I shall need a week or so, to reshuffle the Government, set out some priorities . . .' He was waffling. He knew the dangers of being too prescriptive and his leadership campaign had offered years of experience rather than comprehensive solutions. He treated all dogma with a detached academic disdain and had watched with grim satisfaction while younger opponents tried to make up for their lack of seniority with detailed plans and promises, only to discover they had advanced too far and exposed vulnerable ideological flanks. Urquhart's strategy for dealing with aggressive questioning from journalists had been to offer a platitude about the national interest and to phone their editors; it had got him through the twelve tumultuous days of the leadership race, but he had doubts how long such a game plan would last. 'Above all I shall want to listen.'

Why was it that politicians uttered such appalling clichés which their audiences nevertheless seemed so blithe to accept? The Monarch was nodding his head in silent agreement, his tense body rocking gently to and fro as he sat on the edge of his chair. 'During your campaign you said that we were at a crossroads, facing the challenges of a new century while building on the best from the old. "Encouraging change while preserving continuity".'

Urquhart acknowledged the phrase.

32

'Bravo, Mr Urquhart, more power to your hand. It's an admirable summation of what I believe my own job to be, too.' He grasped his hands together to form a cathedral of bony knuckles, his frown unremitting. 'I hope I shall be able to find – that you will allow me – some way, however small, of helping you in your task.' There was an edge of apprehension in his voice, like a man accustomed to disappointment.

'But of course, Sir, I would be only too delighted . . . did you have anything specific in mind?'

The King's fingers shifted to the knot of his unfashionably narrow tie and twisted it awkwardly. 'Mr Urquhart, the specifics are the stuff of party politics, and that's your province. It cannot be mine.'

'Sir, I would be most grateful for any thoughts you have . . .' Urquhart heard himself saying.

'Would you? Would you really?' There was a rising note of eagerness in his voice which he tried to dispel, too late, with a chuckle. 'But I must be careful. While I was merely heir to the Throne I was allowed the luxury of having my own opinions and was even granted the occasional privilege of expressing them, but Kings cannot let themselves be dragged into partisan debate. My advisers lecture me daily on the point.'

'Sir,' Urquhart interjected, 'we are alone. I would welcome any advice.'

'No, not for the moment. You have much to do and I must not delay you.' He rose to indicate that the audience was at an end, but he made no move towards the door, steepling his fingers to the point of his bony, uneven nose and remaining deep in thought, like a man at prayer. 'Perhaps – if you will allow me? – there is just one point. I've been reading the papers.' He waved towards the chaos of his desk. 'The old Department of Industry buildings on Victoria Street which are to be demolished. The current buildings are hideous, such a bad advertisement for the twentieth century, they deserve to go. I'd love to drive the bulldozer myself. But the site is one of the most important in Westminster, near the parliament buildings and cheek by jowl with the Abbey itself, one of our greatest ecclesiastical monuments. A rare opportunity for us to grasp, don't you think, to create something worthy of our era, something we can pass on to future generations with pride? I do so hope that you, your Government, will ensure the site is developed . . . how shall I put it?' The clipped boarding school tones searched for an appropriately diplomatic phrase. 'Sympathetically.' He nodded in self-approval and seemed emboldened by Urquhart's intent stare. 'Encouraging change while preserving continuity, as one wise fellow put it? I know the Environment Secretary is considering several different proposals and, frankly, some of them are so outlandish they would disgrace a penal colony. Can't we for once in our parsimonious lives make a choice in keeping with the existing character of Westminster Abbey, create something which will respect the achievements of our forefathers, not insult them by allowing some misguided modernist to construct a stainless-steel monolith which crams people on the inside and has its mechanical entrails displayed without?' Passion had begun to overtake the diffidence and a flush had risen to colour his cheeks.

Urquhart smiled in reassurance, an expression which came as easily as oxygen. 'Sir, I can assure you that the Government' – he wanted to say 'my Government' but the words still seemed to dry behind his dentures – 'will have environmental concerns at the forefront of their considerations.' More platitudes, but what else was he supposed to say?

'Oh, I do hope so. Perhaps I should apologize for raising the matter, but I understand the Environment Secretary is to make a final decision at any time.'

For a moment Urquhart felt like reminding the King that it was a quasi-judicial matter, that many months and more millions had been poured into an official planning inquiry which now awaited the Solomon-like deliberation of the relevant Minister. Urquhart might have suggested that, to some, the King's intervention would look no better than jury-nobbling. But he didn't. 'I'll look into it. You have my word, Sir.'

The King's pale blue eyes had a permanent downward cast which made him appear always sincere and frequently mournful as though burdened by some sense of guilt, yet now they sparkled with unmistakable enthusiasm. He reached out for the other man's hand. 'Mr Urquhart, I believe we are going to get along famously.'

Seemingly unbidden, the King's Private Secretary was once more at the open doors and with a bow of respect Urquhart made his way towards them. He had all but crossed the threshold when he heard the words thrown after him. 'Thank you once again, Prime Minister!'

Prime Minister. There it was, for the first time. He'd done it. My Government. *My* Government. It had all seemed so improbable, but there had been so many improbable Prime Ministers. Pitt, a mere youth of twenty-four. Disraeli, a Jew. Lloyd George, an outrageous adulterer who sold peerages for hard cash. Churchill, son of a syphilitic. Macmillan, a cuckold who honoured his wife's lover with a peerage. The Earl of Home, the Tory Party's noble ruin. And Margaret Thatcher, housewife. Lord Home was a thoroughgoing gentleman whereas she was unrepentantly ruthless, yet she had won every election she fought while he led his Government to instant defeat. It took ruthlessness and even a little sin to understand power and its uses. He had learnt the lesson. Never repent. For most the art of politics was all about survival, but that alone had never been enough for him. What was the use of engaging in the battle of ideas and egos if all one was left with was survival? Political success required sacrifices, preferably of others, and he had sacrificed enough in his time. Friends, colleagues, those closest to him. Pushed, prodded, thrown from the rooftops and beneath the wheels of public opinion. And he had never repented. Leadership brought with it the awesome and inescapable responsibilities of life and death, and he knew he was worthy of such decisions.

'So . . . what did he say?' They were in the car on the way to Downing Street before his wife roused him from his reverie.

'What? Oh, not a lot. Wished me well. Talked about the great opportunities ahead. Went on about a building site near Westminster Abbey. Wants me to ensure it's built in mock Tudor or some such nonsense.'

'Will you humour him?'

'Elizabeth, if sincerity could build temples then the whole of England would be covered in his follies, but this is no longer the Dark Ages. The King's job is to give garden parties and to save us the bother of electing someone else president, not to go round interfering in the business of government.'

Elizabeth snorted her agreement as she fumbled impatiently through her bag in search of lipstick. She was a Colquhoun by birth, a family which could trace its descent in direct line from the ancient kings of Scotland. They had long since lost the feudal estates and heirlooms to the confiscations of early cross-border raiding parties and the latter-day ravages of taxmen and inflation, but she had never lost her sense of social positioning or her belief that most modern aristocracy were interlopers – including 'the current Royal Family', as she would frequently put it. Royalty was merely an accident of birth, and of marriage and of death and the occasional execution or bloody murder; it could just as easily have been a Colquhoun as a Windsor, and all the more pure stock for that. At times she became distinctly tedious on the subject, and Urquhart decided to head her off.

'Of course I shall humour him. Better a King with a conscience than not, I suspect, and the last thing I need is sour grapes growing all over the Palace. Anyway, there are other battles to be fought and I want him and his popularity firmly behind me. I shall need it.' His tone was serious and his eyes set upon a future of perceived challenges. 'But at the end of the day, Elizabeth, *I* am the Prime Minister and he is the King. He does what I tell him to, not the other way around. The job's ceremonial, that's all it is and that's all it's got to be. He's the Monarch, not a bloody architect.'

They were driving past the Banqueting Hall in Whitehall, slowing down as they approached the barriers at the head of Downing Street, and Urquhart was relieved to see there were rather more people here to wave and cheer him on for the benefit of the cameras than at the Palace. He thought he recognized a couple of young faces, perhaps party headquarters had turned out their rent-a-crowd. His wife idly slicked down a stray lock of his hair while his mind turned to the reshuffle and the remarks he would make on the doorstep, which would be televised around the world.

'So what are you going to do?' Elizabeth pressed.

'It really doesn't matter,' Urquhart muttered out of the corner of his mouth as he smiled for the cameras which were thrusting their lenses towards him as the car turned into Downing Street. 'As a new King the man is inexperienced, and as constitutional Monarch he is impotent. He has all the menace and bite of a rubber duck. But fortunately on this matter I happen to agree with him. Away with modernism!' He waved as a policeman came forward to open the heavy car door. 'So it really can't be of any consequence . . .'

'Put the papers down, David. For God's sake take your nose out of them for just a minute of our day together.' The voice was tense, more nervous than aggressive.

The grey eyes remained impassive, not moving from the sheaf of documents upon which they had been fixed ever since he had sat down at the breakfast table. The only facial reaction was an irascible twitch of the neatly trimmed moustache. 'I'm off in ten minutes, Fiona, I simply have to finish them. Today of all days.'

'There's something else we have to finish. So put the bloody papers down!'

With reluctance David Mycroft raised his eyes in time to see his wife's hand shaking so vigorously that the coffee splashed over the edge of her cup. 'What on earth's the matter?'

'You. And me. That's the matter.' She was struggling to control herself. 'There's nothing left to our marriage and I want out.'

The King's press aide and principal public spokesman switched automatically into diplomatic gear. 'Look, let's not have a row, not now, I'm in a hurry and . . .'

'Don't you realize, we never have rows. That's the problem!' The cup smashed down into the saucer, overturning and spreading a menacing brown stain across the tablecloth. For the first time he lowered his sheaf of papers, every movement careful and deliberate, as was every aspect of his life.

'Perhaps I could get some time off. Not today, but . . . We could go away together. I know it's been a long time since we had any real chance to talk . . .'

'It's not lack of time, David! We could have all the time in the world and it would make no difference. It's you, and me. The reason we don't have any rows is because we have nothing to argue about. Nothing at all. There's no passion, nothing. All we have is a shell.

I used to dream that once the children were off our hands it might all change.' She shook her head. 'But I'm tired of deluding myself. It will never change. You will never change. And I don't suppose I will.' There was pain and she was dabbing her eyes, yet held her control. This was no flash of temper.

'Are you . . . feeling all right, Fiona? You know, women at your time of life . . .'

She smarted at his patronizing idiocy. 'Women in their forties, David, have their needs, their feelings. But how would you know? When did you last look at me as a woman? When did you last look at any woman?' She returned the insult, meaning it to hurt. She knew that to break through she was going to have to batter down the walls he had built around himself. He had always been so closed, private, a man of diminutive stature who had sought to cope with his perceived physical inadequacies by being utterly formal and punctilious in everything he did. Never a hair on his small and rather boyish head out of place, even the streaks of grey beginning to appear around his dark temples looking elegant rather than ageing. He always ate breakfast with his jacket on and buttoned.

'Look, can't this wait? You know I have to be at the Palace any—'

'The bloody Palace again. It's your home, your life, your lover. The only emotion you ever show nowadays is about your ridiculous job and your wretched King.'

'Fiona! That's uncalled-for. Leave him out of this.' The moustache with its hint of red bristled in indignation.

'How can I? You serve him, not me. His needs come before mine. He's helped ruin our marriage far more effectively than any mistress, so don't expect me to bow and fawn like the rest.'

He glanced anxiously at his watch. 'Look, for goodness sake can we talk about this tonight? Perhaps I can get back early.'

She was dabbing at the coffee stain with her napkin, trying to delay meeting his gaze. Her voice was calmer, resolved. 'No, David. Tonight I shall be with somebody else.'

'There's someone else?' There was a catch in his throat, he had clearly never considered the possibility. 'Since when?'

She looked up from the mess on the table with eyes which were now defiant and steady, no longer trying to evade. This had been coming for so long, she couldn't hide from it anymore. 'Since two years after we got married, David, there has been someone else. A succession of "someone elses". You never had it in you to satisfy me – I never blamed you for that, really I didn't, it was just the luck of the draw. What I bitterly resent is that you never even tried. I was never that important to you, not as a woman. I have never been more than a housekeeper, a laundress, your twenty-four-hour skivvy, an object to parade around the dinner circuit. Someone to give you respectability at Court. Even the children were only for show.'

'Not true.' But there was no real passion in his protest, any more than there had been passion in their marriage. She had always known they were sexually incompatible; he seemed all too willing to pour his physical drive into his job while at first she had contented herself with the social cachet his work at the Palace brought them. But not for long. In truth she couldn't even be sure who the father of her second child was, while if he had doubts on the matter he didn't seem to care. He had 'done his duty', as he once put it, and that had been an end of it. Even now as she poured scorn on him as a cuckold she couldn't get him to respond. There should be self-righteous rage somewhere, surely, wasn't that what his blessed code of chivalry called for? But he seemed so empty, hollow inside. Their marriage had been nothing but a rat's maze within which both led unrelated lives, meeting only as if by accident before passing on their separate ways. Now she was leaping for the exit.

'Fiona, can't we—'

'No, David. We can't.'

The telephone had started ringing in its insistent, irresistible manner, summoning him to his duty, a task to which he had dedicated his life and to which he was now asked to surrender his marriage. We've had some great times, haven't we, he wanted to argue, but he could only remember times which were good rather than great and those were long, long ago. She had always come a distant second, not consciously but now, in their new mood of truth, undeniably. He looked at Fiona through watery eyes which expressed sorrow and begged forgiveness; there was no spite. But there was fear. Marriage had been like a great sheet anchor in strong emotional seas, preventing him from being tossed about by tempestuous winds and blown in directions which were reckless and lacking in restraint. Wedlock. It had worked precisely because it had been form without substance, like the repetitive chanting of psalms that had been forced on him during his miserable school years at Ampleforth. Marriage had been a burden but, for him, a necessary one, a distraction, a diversion. Self-denial, but also self-protection. And now the anchor chains were being cut.

Fiona sat motionless across a table littered with toast and fragments of eggshell and bone china, the household clutter and crumbs which represented the total sum of their life together. The telephone still demanded him. Without a further word he rose to answer it.

'Come in, Tim, and close the door.'

Urquhart was sitting in the Cabinet Room, alone except for the new arrival, occupying the only chair around the coffin-shaped table which had arms. Before him was a simple leather folder and a telephone. The rest of the table stood bare.

'Not exactly luxurious, is it? But I'm beginning to like it.' Urquhart chuckled.

Tim Stamper looked around, surprised to discover no one else present. He was – or had been until half an hour ago when Urquhart had exchanged the commission of Chief Whip for that of Prime Minister – the other man's loyal deputy. The role of Chief Whip is mysterious, that of his deputy invisible, but together they had combined into a force of incalculable influence, since the Whips Office is the base from where discipline within the parliamentary party is maintained through a judicious mixture of team spirit, arm twisting and outright thuggery. Stamper had ideal qualities for the job – a lean, pinched face with protruding nose and dark eyes of exceptional brightness which served to give him the appearance of a ferret, and a capacity for rummaging about in the dark corners of his colleagues' private lives to uncover their personal and political weaknesses. It was a job of vulnerabilities, guarding one's own while exploiting others'. He had long been Urquhart's protégé; fifteen years younger, a former estate agent from Essex, it was an attraction of opposites. Urquhart was sophisticated, elegant, academic, highly polished; Stamper was none of these and wore off-the-peg suits from British Home Stores. Yet what they shared was perhaps more important – ambition, an arrogance that for one was intellectual and for the other instinctive, and an understanding of power. The combination had proved stunningly effective in plotting Urquhart's path to the premiership. Stamper's turn would come, that had been the implicit promise to the younger man. Now he was here to collect.

'Prime Minister.' He offered a theatrical bow of respect. 'Prime Minister,' Stamper repeated, practising a different intonation as if trying to sell him the freehold. He had a familiar, almost camp manner which hid the steel beneath, and the two colleagues began to laugh in a fashion which managed to be both mocking and conspiratorial, like two burglars after a successful night out. Stamper was careful to ensure he stopped laughing first; it wouldn't do to outmock a Prime Minister. They had shared so much over recent months but he was aware that Prime Ministers have a tendency to hold back from their colleagues, even their fellow conspirators, and Urquhart didn't continue laughing for long.

'Tim, I wanted to see you entirely *à deux*.'

'Probably means I'm due to get a bollocking. What've I done, anyway?' His tone was light, yet Urquhart noticed the anxious downward cast at the corner of Stamper's mouth and discovered he was enjoying the feeling of mastery implied by his colleague's discomfort.

'Sit down, Tim. Opposite me.'

Stamper took the chair and looked across at his old friend. The sight confirmed just how much their relationship had changed. Urquhart sat before a large oil portrait of Robert Walpole, the first modern and arguably greatest Prime Minister who had watched for two centuries over the deliberations in this room of the mighty and mendacious, the woeful and miserably weak. Urquhart was his successor, elevated by his peers, anointed by his Monarch and now installed. The telephone beside him could summon statesmen to their fate or command the country to war. It was a power shared with no other man in the realm; indeed, he was no longer just a man but, for better or worse, was now the stuff of history. Whether in that history he would rate a footnote or an entire chapter only time would tell.

Urquhart sensed the swirling emotions of the other man. 'Different, isn't it, Tim? And we shall never be able to turn back the clock. It didn't hit me until a moment ago, not while I was at the Palace, not with the media at the front door here, not even when I walked inside. It all seemed like a great theatre piece and I'd simply been assigned one of the roles. Yet as I stepped across the threshold every worker in Downing Street was assembled in the hallway, from the highest civil servant in the land to the cleaners and telephonists, perhaps two hundred of them. They greeted me with such enthusiasm that I almost expected bouquets to be thrown. The exhilaration of applause,' he sighed. 'It was beginning to go to my head, until I remembered that scarcely an hour beforehand they'd gone through the same routine with my predecessor as he drove off to oblivion. That lot'll probably applaud at their own funerals.' He moistened his thin lips, as was his habit when reflecting. 'Then they brought me here, to the Cabinet Room, and left me on my own. It was completely silent, as though I'd fallen into a time capsule. Everything in order, meticulous, except for the Prime Minister's chair which had been drawn back. For me! It was only when I touched it, ran my finger across its back, realized no one was going to shout at me if I sat down, that finally it dawned on me. It isn't just another chair or another job, but the only one of its kind. You know I'm not by nature a humble man yet, dammit, for a moment it got to me.' There was a moment of prolonged silence, before his palm smacked down on the table. 'But don't worry. I've recovered!'

Urquhart laughed that conspiratorial laugh once more, while Stamper could only manage a tight smile as he waited for the reminiscing to stop and for his fate to be pronounced.

'To business, Tim. There's much to be done and I shall want you, as always, right by my side.'

Stamper's smile broadened.

'You're going to be my Party Chairman.'

The smile rapidly disappeared. Stamper couldn't hide his confusion and disappointment.

'Don't worry, we'll find you some ministerial sinecure to get you a seat around the Cabinet table – Chancellor of the Duchy of Lancaster or some such nonsense. But for the moment I want your mittens firmly on the Party machine.'

Stamper's jaw was working furiously, trying to marshal his arguments. 'But it's been scarcely six months since the last election, and a long haul before the next one. Three, maybe four years. Counting paper clips and sorting out squabbles amongst local constituency chairmen is scarcely my strong suit, Francis. You should know that after what we've been through together.' It was an appeal to their old friendship.

'Think it through, Tim. We've a parliamentary majority of twenty-two and a party that's been torn apart by the recent leadership battle. And we are just about to get a beating from a swine of a recession. We're no better than even in the opinion polls and our majority won't last three or four years. We'll be shot to pieces at every by-election we face and we've only to lose fewer than a dozen seats before this Government is dead. Unless, that is, you can guarantee me no by-elections, that you've found some magic means of ensuring none of our esteemed colleagues will be caught canvassing in a brothel, misappropriating church funds or simply succumbing to senility and excessive old age?'

'Doesn't sound like a lot of fun for a Party Chairman, either.'

'Tim, the next couple of years are going to be hell, and we probably don't have a sufficient majority to survive long enough for us to get through the recession. If it's painful for the Party Chairman it'll be bloody agony for the Prime Minister.'

Stamper was silent, unconvinced, unsure what to say. His excitement and dreams of a few moments before had suddenly frayed.

'Our futures can be measured almost in moments,' Urquhart continued. 'We'll get a small boost in popularity because of my honeymoon period while people give me the benefit of their doubt. That will last no longer than March.'

'You're very precise about that.'

'Indeed I am. For in March there has to be a Budget. It'll be a bastard. We let everything rip in the markets to get us through the last election campaign and the day of judgement for that little lot is just around the corner. We borrowed off Peter to buy off Paul, now we have to go back to pick the pockets of them both. They're not going to care for it.' He paused, blinking rapidly as he ordered his thoughts. 'That's not all. We'll take a beating from Brunei.'

'What?'

'The Sultan of that tiny oil-infested state is a great Anglophile and one of the world's most substantial holders of sterling. A loyal friend. Unfortunately not only does he know what a mess we're in but he's also got his own problems. So he's going to unload some of his sterling – at least three billion worth sloshing around the markets like orphans in search of a home. That'll crucify the currency and stretch the recession on for probably another year. For old time's sake he says he'll sell only as and when we suggest. So long as it's before the next Budget.'

Stamper found difficulty in swallowing, his mouth had run dry.

Urquhart began to laugh but without the slightest hint of humour. 'And there's more, Tim, there's more! To top it all the Attorney General's office has quietly let it be known that the trial of Sir Jasper Harrod will begin immediately after Easter. Which is March the twenty-fourth, to save you looking it up. What do you know of Sir Jasper?'

'Only what most people know, I guess. Self-made mega-millionaire, chairman of the country's biggest computer-leasing operation. Does a lot of work with Government departments and local authorities, and has got himself accused of paying substantial backhanders all over the place to keep hold of his contracts. Big into charities, I seem to remember, which is why he got his "K".'

'He got his knighthood, Tim, because he was one of the party's biggest contributors. Loyally and discreetly over many years.'

'So what's the problem?'

'Having come to our aid whenever we asked for it, he now expects us to come equally loyally to his. To pull a few strings with the Director of Public Prosecutions. Which of course we can't, but he refuses to understand that.'

'There's more, I know there's more . . .'

'And he insists that if the case comes to trial he will have to reveal his substantial party donations.'

'So?'

'Which were paid all in cash. Delivered in suitcases.'

'Oh, shit.'

'Enough of it to give us all acute haemorrhoids. He not only gave to the central Party but supported the constituency election campaigns of almost every member of the Cabinet.'

'Don't tell me. All spent on things which weren't reported as election expenses.'

'In my case everything was recorded religiously and will bear full public scrutiny. In other cases . . .' He arched an eyebrow. 'I'm told the Trade Secretary, later this afternoon to reinforce our glorious backbenches, used the money to pay off a troublesome mistress who was threatening to release certain compromising letters. It was made over to her, and Harrod still has the cancelled cheque.'

Stamper pushed his chair back from the table until it was balancing on its rear legs, as if trying to distance himself from such absurdity. 'Christ, Francis, we've got all this crap about to hit us at a hundred miles an hour and you want me to be Party Chairman? If it's all the same to you, I'd rather seek asylum in Libya. By Easter, you say? It'll take more than a bloody resurrection to save anybody caught in the middle of that lot.'

His waved his arms forlornly, drained of energy and resistance, but Urquhart was straining forward in great earnest, tension stiffening his body.

'By Easter. Precisely. Which means we have to move before then, Tim. Use the honeymoon period, beat up the Opposition, get in ahead of the recession and get a majority which will last until all the flak has been left well behind us.'

Stamper's voice was breathless. 'An election, you mean?'

'By the middle of March. Which gives us exactly fourteen weeks, only ten weeks before I have to announce it, and in that time I want you as Party Chairman getting the election machine as tight as it can be. There are plans to be made, money to be raised, opponents to be embarrassed. And all without anyone having the slightest idea what we're about to spring on them.'

Stamper's chair rocked back with a clatter as he endeavoured to recover his wits. 'Bloody Party Chairman.'

'Don't worry. It's only for fourteen weeks. If all goes well you can have the pick of any Government department you want. And if not . . . Well, neither of us will have to worry about a political job ever again.'

'This is truly appalling.' Elizabeth Urquhart screwed up her nose with considerable violence as she surveyed the room. It had been several days since the Collingridges removed the last of their personal effects from the small apartment above 10 Downing Street reserved for the use of Prime Ministers, and the sitting room now had the ambience of a three star hotel. It lacked any individual character, that had already been transported in the packing cases, and what was left was in good order but carried the aesthetic touch of a British Rail waiting room. 'Simply revolting. It won't do,' she repeated, gazing at the wallpaper, where she half expected to find the faded impressions of a row of flying china ducks. She was momentarily distracted as she passed by a long wall mirror, surreptitiously checking the conspicuous red tint her hairdresser had applied earlier in the week as she had waited for the final leadership ballot. A celebratory highlight, the stylist had called it, but no one could any longer mistake it for a natural hue and it had left her constantly fiddling with the colour balance on the remote control, wondering whether it was time to change the television or her hair salon.

'What extraordinary people they must have been,' she muttered, brushing some imagined speck of dust from the front of her Chanel suit while her husband's House of Commons secretary, who was accompanying her on the tour of inspection, buried herself in her notebook. She thought she rather liked the Collingridges; she was more definite in her views of Elizabeth Urquhart, whose cold eyes gave her a predatory look and whose constant diets to fend off the advance of cellulite around her expensively clad body seemed to leave her in a state of unremitting impatience, at least with other women, particularly those younger than herself.

46

'Find out how we get rid of all this and see what the budget is for refurbishment,' Mrs Urquhart snapped as she led the way briskly down the short corridor leading to the dark entrails of the apartment, fingertips tapping in rebuke the flesh beneath her chin as she walked. She gave a squawk of alarm as she passed a door on her left, behind which she discovered a tiny galley kitchen with a stainless-steel sink, red and black plastic floor tiles and no microwave. Her gloom was complete by the time she had inspected the claustrophobic dining room with the atmosphere of a locked coffin and a view directly onto a grubby attic and roof. She was back in the sitting room, seated in one of the armchairs covered in printed roses the size of elephants' feet and shaking her head in disappointment, when there came a knock from the entrance hall.

'Come in!' she commanded forlornly, remembering that the front door didn't even have a lock on it – for security reasons she had been told, but more for the convenience of civil servants as they came to and fro bearing papers and dispatches, she suspected. 'And they call this home,' she wailed, burying her head theatrically in her hands.

She brightened as she looked up to examine her visitor. He was in his late thirties, lean with razor-cropped hair.

'Mrs Urquhart. I'm Inspector Robert Insall, Special Branch,' he announced in a thick London accent. 'I've been in charge of your husband's protection detail during the leadership election and now they've been mug enough to make me responsible for security here in Downing Street.' He had a grin and natural charm to which Elizabeth Urquhart warmed, and a build she couldn't help but admire.

'I'm sure we shall be in safe hands, Inspector.'

'We'll do our best. But things are going to be a bit different for you, now you're here,' he continued. 'There are a few things I need to explain, if you've got a moment.'

'Come and cover up some of this hideous furniture, Inspector, and tell me all about it . . .'

*   *   *

47

Landless waved as the crowd applauded. The onlookers had no idea who sat behind the darkened glass of the Silver Spur, but it was an historic day and they wanted a share in it. The heavy metal gates guarding the entrance to Downing Street drew back in respect and the duty policemen offered a smart salute. Landless felt good, even better when he saw the pavement opposite his destination crowded with cameras and reporters.

'Is he going to offer you a job, Ben?' a chorus of voices sang out as he prised himself from the back seat of the car.

'Already got a job,' he growled, showing off his well-known proprietorial glare and enjoying every minute of it. He buttoned up the jacket flapping at his sides.

'A peerage, perhaps? Seat in the House of Lords?'

'Baron Ben of Bethnal Green?' His fleshy face sagged in disapproval. 'Sounds more like a music hall act than an honour.'

There was much laughter, and Landless turned to walk through the glossy black door into the entrance hall but he was beaten to the step by a courier bearing a huge assortment of flowers. Inside, the hallway was covered with a profusion of bouquets and baskets, all still unwrapped, with more arriving by the minute. London's florists, at least temporarily, could forget the recession. Landless was directed along the deep red carpet leading straight from the front door to the Cabinet Room on the other side of the narrow building, and he caught himself hurrying. He slowed his step, relishing the sensation. He couldn't remember when he had last felt so excited. He was shown directly into the Cabinet Room by a solicitous and spotty civil servant who closed the door quietly behind him.

'Ben, welcome. Come in.' Urquhart waved a hand in greeting but didn't rise. The hand indicated a chair on the other side of the table.

'Great day, Francis. Great day for us all.' Landless nodded towards Stamper, who was leaning against a radiator, hovering like a Praetorian Guard, and Landless found himself resenting the other man's presence. All his previous dealings with Urquhart had been one-on-one; after all, they hadn't invited an audience as they'd laid their plans to exhaust and overwhelm the elected head of government. On those earlier occasions Urquhart had always been the supplicant, Landless the power, yet as he looked across the table he couldn't help but notice that things had changed, their roles reversed. Suddenly ill at ease, he stretched out a hand to offer Urquhart congratulation, but it was a clumsy gesture. Urquhart had to put down his pen, draw back his large chair, rise and stretch, only to discover that the table was too wide and all they could do was to brush fingers.

'Well done, Francis,' Landless muttered sheepishly, and sat down. 'It means a lot to me, your inviting me here on your first morning as Prime Minister. Particularly the way you did. I thought I'd have to sneak in round the back by the dustbins, but I have to tell you I felt great as I passed all those cameras and TV lights. I appreciate the public sign of confidence, Francis.'

Urquhart spread his hands wide, a gesture meant to replace the words he couldn't quite find, while Stamper jumped in.

'*Prime Minister,*' he began, with emphasis. It was meant as a rebuke at the newspaperman's overfamiliarity, but it slid off the Landless hide without making a dent. 'My apologies, but the new Chancellor will be here in five minutes.'

'Forgive me, Ben. Already I'm discovering that a Prime Minister is not a master, only a slave. Of timetables, mostly. To business, if you don't mind.'

'That's how I like it.' Landless shuffled forward on his chair in expectation.

'You control the *Telegraph* group and have made a takeover bid for United Newspapers, and it falls to the Government to decide whether such a takeover would be in the public interest.' Urquhart was staring at his blotter as if reading from a script, rather like a judge delivering sentence. Landless didn't care for this sudden formality, so unlike their previous conversations on the matter.

Urquhart's hands were spread wide again as he sought for elusive words. Finally, he clenched his fists. 'Sorry, Ben. You can't have it.'

The three men turned to effigies as the words circled the room and settled like birds of prey.

'What the 'ell do you mean I can't bloody have it?' The pronunciation was straight off the streets, the veneer had slipped.

'The Government does not believe it would be in the national interest.'

'Crap, Francis. We agreed.'

'The Prime Minister was careful throughout the entire leadership campaign to offer no commitments on the takeover, his public record on that is clear,' Stamper interposed. Landless ignored him, his attention rigidly on Urquhart.

'We had a deal! *You* know it. *I* know it.'

'As I said, Ben, a Prime Minister is not always his own master. The arguments in favour of turning the bid down are irresistible. You already own more than thirty per cent of the national press; United would give you close on forty.'

'My thirty per cent supported you every step of the way, as will my forty. That was the deal.'

'Which still leaves just over sixty who would never forgive or forget. You see, Ben, the figures simply don't add up. Not in the national interest. Not for a new Government that believes in competition, in serving the consumer rather than the big corporations.'

'Bullshit. We had a deal!' His huge fists crashed down on the bare table.

'Ben, it's impossible. You must know that. I can't in my first act as Prime Minister let you carve up the British newspaper industry. It's not good business. It's not good politics. Frankly it would make pretty awful headlines on every other front page.'

'But carving me up will make bloody marvellous headlines, is that it?' Landless's head was thrust forward like a charging bull, his jowls shaking with anger. 'So that's why you asked me in by the front door, you bastard. They saw me coming in, and they'll see me going out. Feet first. You've set up a public execution in front of the world's cameras. Fat capitalist as sacrificial lamb. I warn you, Frankie. I'll fight you every step of the way, everything I've got.'

'Which only leaves seventy per cent of the newspapers plus every TV and radio programme applauding a publicly spirited Prime Minister,' Stamper interjected superciliously, examining his finger nails.

'Not afraid to turn away his closest friends if the national interest demands. Great stuff.'

Landless was getting it from both sides, both barrels. His crimson face darkened still further, his whole body shook with frustration. He could find no words with which to haggle or persuade, he could neither barter nor browbeat, and he was left with nothing but the physical argument of pounding the table with clenched fists. 'You miserable little sh—'

Suddenly the door opened and in walked Elizabeth Urquhart in full flow. 'Francis, it's impossible, completely impossible. The apartment's appalling, the decorations are quite disgusting and they tell me there's not enough money left in the budget . . .' She trailed off as she noted Landless's fists trembling six inches above the table.

'You see, Ben, a Prime Minister is not master even in his own house.'

'Spare me the sermon.'

'Ben, think it through. Put this one behind you. There will be other deals, other interests you will want to pursue, in which I can help. It would be useful to have a friend in Downing Street.'

'That's what I thought when I backed you for Prime Minister. My mistake.' Landless was once again in control of himself, his hands steady, his gaze glacial and fixed upon Urquhart, only the quivering of his jowls revealing the tension within.

'I'm sorry if I've interrupted,' Elizabeth said awkwardly.

'Mr Landless was just about to leave, I think,' Stamper cut in from his guard post beside the radiator.

'I am sorry,' Elizabeth repeated.

'Don't worry,' replied Landless, eyes still on her husband. 'I can't stay. I just learned of a funeral I have to attend.'

'Ben, seriously, if there's anything I can do . . .'

Landless offered no reply. He rose and buttoned his jacket purposefully, straightening his tie and drawing back his broad shoulders before striding out to face the cameras.

*　　*　　*

51

'I won't hear of it, David.'

It was ludicrous. Mycroft was in turmoil; there were so many unformed doubts, half-fears which he could not or dared not realize, which he needed to talk through with the King, for both their sakes. Yet he was reduced to snatching a few words along with mouthfuls of chlorinated water as they ploughed through the waves of the Palace swimming pool. The King's only concession to the interruption in his daily exercise schedule was to switch from the crawl to the breaststroke, enabling Mycroft more easily to match his pace. It was his rigid discipline that enabled the King to maintain his excellent physical shape, and kept all those who served him struggling to keep up.

The King was a fierce defender of the forms of marriage – it came with the job, he would say – and Mycroft had felt it necessary to make the offer. 'It's for the best, Sir,' he persisted. 'I can't afford to let you become embroiled in my personal difficulties. I need some time to sort myself out. Better for all of us if I resign.'

'I disagree.' The King spat out a mouthful of water, finally resolving to finish the conversation on dry land, and headed for the marbled poolside. 'We've been friends since university and I'm not going to throw away the last thirty years simply because some reptilian gossip columnist might hear of your private problems. I'm surprised you should think I would consider it.' He ducked his shiny head one last time beneath the water as he reached for the steps. 'You're part of the management board of this firm, and that's how it's going to stay.'

Mycroft shook his head like a dog, trying to clear his vision. It wasn't just the marriage, of course, it was all the other pressures he felt crowding in on him which made him feel so apprehensive and wretched. If he couldn't be completely honest even with himself, how could he expect the King to understand? But he had to try.

'Suddenly everything looks different. The house. The street. My friends. Even I look different, to myself. It's as if my marriage was a lens which gave the world a particular perspective over all these years, and now that it's gone nothing seems quite the same. It's a little frightening . . .'

'I'm sorry, truly, about Fiona. After all, I'm godfather to your eldest, I'm involved.' The King reached for his towel. 'But, dammit, women have their own extraordinary ways and I can't profess to understand them. What I do know, David, is that it would make no sense for you to try to get through your problems on your own, to cut yourself off not only from your marriage but also from what you have here.' He placed a hand on Mycroft's dripping shoulder. The contact was very close, his voice concerned. 'You understand me, David, you always have. I am known by the whole world yet understood by so few. You do, you understand. I need you. I will not allow you to resign.'

Mycroft stared into his friend's angular face. He found himself thinking the King's leanness made him look drawn and older than his years, particularly with his hair grown so thin. It was as if a furnace inside was burning the King up too quickly. Perhaps he cared too much.

Care too much – was it possible? Fiona had tossed Mycroft back into the pool and he was struggling in the deep waters, unable to touch bottom. It dawned on him that he had never touched bottom, not once in his life. Far from caring too much, he realized he had never really cared at all and the sudden understanding made him panic, want to escape before he drowned. His emotional life had been shapeless, without substance or roots. Except here at the Palace, which now provided his only support. The man he had once tossed fully clothed through the ice of the college fountain and who had come up spitting bindweed and clutching a lavatory seat was saying, in the only way a lifetime of self-control allowed, that he cared. Suddenly it mattered, very much.

'Thank you, Sir.'

'I don't know a single marriage, Royal, common or just plain vulgar, which hasn't been through the wringer; it's so easy to think you're on your own, to forget that practically everyone you know has jumped through the same hoops.'

Mycroft remembered just how many nights of their marriage he and Fiona had spent apart, and imagined what she had been up to on every one of those nights. There really had been a lot of hoops. He didn't care, not even about that. So what did he care about?

'I need you, David. I've waited all my life to be where I am today. Don't you remember the endless nights at university when we would sit either side of a bottle of college port and discuss what we would do when we had the opportunity? *We*, David, you and me. Now the opportunity has arrived, we can't throw it away.' He paused while a liveried footman deposited a silver tray with two mugs of herbal tea on the poolside table. 'If it's really over with Fiona, try to put it behind you. Look ahead, with me. I can't start on the most important period of my life by losing one of my oldest and most trusted friends. There's so much to do, for us both.' He began towelling himself vigorously as though determined to start that very minute. 'Don't make any decisions now. Stick with it for a couple of months and, if you still feel you need a break, we'll sort it out. But trust me, stay with me. All will be fine, I promise.'

Mycroft was unconvinced. He wanted to run, but he had nowhere and no one he wanted to run to. And the thought of what he might find if he ran too far overwhelmed him. After so many years he was free, and he didn't know if he could handle freedom. He stood, water dripping from the end of his nose and through his moustache, weighing his doubts against the Sovereign's certainty. He could find no sense of direction, only his sense of duty.

'So, what do you feel, old friend?'

'Bloody cold, Sir.' He managed a weak smile. 'Let's go and have a shower.'

'Circulate, Francis. And smile. This is supposed to be a celebration, remember.'

Urquhart acknowledged his wife's instruction and began forcing his way slowly through the crowded room. He hated these occasions. It was supposed to be a party to thank those who had helped him into Downing Street, but inevitably Elizabeth had intervened and turned it into another of her evenings for rubbing shoulders with anyone from the pages of the social columns she wanted to meet. 'The voters love a little glamour,' she argued, and like any self-respecting Colquhoun she had always wanted to preside over her own Court. So instead of a small gathering of

54

colleagues he had been thrust into a maelstrom of actresses, opera stars, editors, businessmen and assorted socialites, and he knew his small talk couldn't last the evening.

The guests had clattered through the dark December night into the narrow confines of Downing Street, where they found a large Christmas tree outside the door of Number Ten, placed at Elizabeth Urquhart's instructions to give TV-viewers the impression that this was simply another family eagerly waiting to celebrate Christmas. Inside Number Ten the glitterati had crossed the threshold, unaware they had already been scanned by hidden devices for weapons and explosives. They handed over their cloaks and over-coats in exchange for a smile and a cloakroom ticket, and waited patiently in line on the stairs which led to the Green Room where the Urquharts were receiving their guests. As they wound their way slowly up the stairs and past its walls covered in portraits of previous Prime Ministers, they tried not to stare too hard at the other guests or their surroundings. Staring implied you hadn't done this a hundred times before. Most had little to do with politics, some were not even supporters of the Government, but the enthusi-asm with which they were greeted by Elizabeth Urquhart left them all impressed. The atmosphere was sucking them in, making them honorary members of the team. If power were a conspiracy, they wanted to be part of it too.

For ten minutes Urquhart struggled with the confusion of guests, his eyes never resting, darting rapidly from one fixed point to another as if always on guard, or on the attack, forced to listen to the complaints of businessmen and the half-baked social prescrip-tions of chat-show hosts. At last he reached gratefully for the arm of Tim Stamper and dragged him into a corner.

'Something on your mind, Francis?'

'I was just reflecting on how relieved Henry must be not to have to put up with all this any longer. Is it really worth it?'

'Ambition should be made of more solid stuff.'

'If you must quote Shakespeare, for God's sake get it right. And I'd prefer it if you chose some other play than *Julius Caesar*. You'll remember they'd had him butchered well before the interval.'

'I am suitably reproached. In future in your presence I shall quote only from *Macbeth*.'

Urquhart smiled grimly at the cold humour, wishing he could spend the rest of the evening crossing swords with Stamper and plotting the next election. In less than a week the polls had already placed them three points ahead as the voters responded to the fresh faces, the renewed sense of urgency throughout Whitehall, the public dispatch of a few of the less acceptable faces of Government. 'They like the colour of the honeymoon bed linen,' Stamper had reported. 'Fresh, crisp, with just enough blood to show you're doing your job.' He had a style all his own, did Stamper.

Across the chatter of the crowded room they could hear Elizabeth Urquhart laughing. She was immersed in conversation with an Italian tenor, one of the more competent and certainly the most fashionable opera star to have arrived in London in recent years. She was persuading him through a mixture of flattery and feminine charm to give a rendition later in the evening. Elizabeth was nearing fifty yet she was well preserved and carefully presented, and already the Italian was acquiescing. She rushed off to enquire whether there was a piano in Downing Street.

'Ah, Dickie,' Urquhart chanted, reaching out for the arm of a short, undersized man with a disproportionately large head and serious eyes who had thrust purposefully through the crowd towards him. Dickie was the new Secretary of State for the Environment, the youngest member of the new Cabinet, a marathon runner, an enthusiast and an intervener, and he had been deeply impressed by Urquhart's admonition that he was to be the defender of the Government's green credentials. His appointment had already been greeted with acclaim from all but the most militant pressure groups, yet at this moment he was looking none too happy. There were beads of moisture on his brow; something was bothering him.

'Was hoping to have a word with you, Dickie,' said Urquhart before the other had a chance to unburden himself. 'What about this development site in Victoria Street? Had a chance to look into it yet? Are you going to cover it in concrete, or what?'

'Good heavens, no, Prime Minister. I've studied all the options carefully, and I really think it would be best if we dispense with the more extravagant options and go for something traditional. Not one of these steel and glass air-conditioning units.'

'Will it provide the most modern office environment?' Stamper intervened.

'It'll fit into the Westminster environment,' Dickie continued a little uneasily.

'Scarcely the same thing,' the Party Chairman responded.

'We'd get a howl of protest from the heritage groups if we tried to turn Westminster into downtown Chicago,' Dickie offered defensively.

'I see. Planning by pressure group.' Stamper gave a cynical smile.

The Environment Secretary looked flustered at the unexpected assault but Urquhart came quickly to his rescue. 'Don't worry about Stamper, Dickie. Only a week at party headquarters and already he can't come into contact with a pressure group without raising his kneecap in greeting.' He smiled, this was considerably greater fun than being preached at by the two large female charity workers who were hovering behind Dickie, waiting to pounce. He drew Dickie closer for protection. 'So what else was on your mind?'

'It's this mystery virus along the North Sea coast which has been killing off the seals. The scientific bods thought it had disappeared, but I've just had a report that seal carcasses are being washed up all around Norfolk. The virus is back. By morning there will be camera crews and newshounds crawling over the beaches with photos of dying seals splashed across the news.'

Urquhart grimaced. 'Newshounds!' He hadn't heard that term used in years. Dickie was an exceptionally serious and unamusing man, exactly the right choice for dealing with environmentalists. They could bore each other for months with their mutual earnestness. As long as he kept them quiet until after March . . . 'Here's what you do, Dickie. By the time they reach the beaches in the morning, I want you there, too. Showing the Government's concern, being on hand to deal with the questions of the . . . newshounds.' From the corner of his eye he could see Stamper smirking. 'I want your face on the midday news tomorrow. Alongside all those dead seals.' Stamper covered his mouth with a handkerchief to stifle the laugh, but Dickie was nodding earnestly.

'Do I have your permission to announce a Government inquiry, if I feel it necessary?'

'You do. Indeed you do, my dear Dickie. Give them whatever you like, as long as it's not money.'

'Then if I am to be there by daybreak, I'd better make tracks immediately. Will you excuse me, Prime Minister?'

As the Environment Secretary hustled self-importantly towards the door, Stamper could control himself no longer. His shoulders shook with mirth.

'Don't mock,' reproached Urquhart with an arched eyebrow. 'Seals are a serious matter. They eat all the damned salmon, you know.'

Both men burst into laughter, just as the two charity workers decided to draw breath and swoop. Urquhart spied their heaving bosoms and turned quickly away to find himself looking at a young woman, attractive and most elegantly presented with large, challenging eyes. She seemed a far more interesting contest than the elderly matrons. He extended a hand.

'Good evening. I'm Francis Urquhart.'

'Sally Quine.' She was cool, less gushing than most guests.

'I'm delighted you could come. And your husband . . . ?'

'Beneath a ton of concrete, I earnestly hope.'

Now he could detect the slightly nasal accent and he glanced discreetly but admiringly at the cut of her long Regency jacket. It was red with large cuffs, the only decoration provided by the small but ornate metal buttons which made the effect both striking and professional. The raven hair shimmered gloriously in the light of the chandeliers.

'It's a pleasure to meet you, Mrs . . . ? Miss Quine.' He was picking up her strong body language, her independence, and couldn't fail to notice the taut expression around her mouth; something was bothering her.

'I hope you are enjoying yourself.'

'To be frank, not a lot. I get very irritated when men try to grope and pick me up simply because I happen to be an unattached woman.'

58

So that's what was bothering her. 'I see. Which man?'

'Prime Minister, I'm a businesswoman. I don't get very far by being a blabbermouth.'

'Well, let me guess. He sounds as if he's here without a wife. Self-important. Probably political if he feels sufficiently at ease to chance his hand in this place. Something of a charmer, perhaps?'

'The creep had so little charm he didn't even have the decency to say please. I think that's what riled me as much as anything. He expected me to fall into his arms without even the basic courtesy of asking nicely. And I thought you English were gentlemen.'

'So . . . Without a wife here. Self-important. Political. Lacking in manners.' Urquhart glanced around the room, still trying to avoid the stares of the matrons who were growing increasingly irritated. 'That gentleman in the loud three-piece pinstripe, perhaps?' He indicated a fat man in early middle age who was mopping his brow with a spotted handkerchief as he perspired in the rapidly rising warmth of the crowded room.

She laughed in surprise and acknowledgement. 'You know him?'

'I ought to. He's my new Minister of Housing.'

'You seem to know your men well, Mr Urquhart.'

'It's my main political asset.'

'Then I hope you understand your women just as well, and much better than that oaf of a Housing Minister . . . In the political rather than the biblical sense,' she added as an afterthought, offering a slightly impertinent smile.

'I'm not sure I follow.'

'Women. You know, fifty-two per cent of the electorate? Those strange creatures who are good enough to share your beds but not your clubs and who think your Government is about as supportive and up-to-the-mark as broken knicker elastic?'

In an Englishwoman her abruptness would have been viewed as bad manners, but it was normal to afford Americans somewhat greater licence. They talked, ate, dressed differently, were even different in bed so Urquhart had been told, although he had no first-hand experience. Perhaps he should ask the Housing Minister. 'It's surely not that bad . . .'

'For the last two months your Party has been pulling itself apart while it chose a new leader. Not one of the candidates was a woman. And according to women voters, none of the issues you discussed were of much relevance to them, either. Particularly to younger women. You treat them as if they were blind copies of their husbands. They don't like it and you're losing out. Badly.'

Urquhart realized he was relinquishing control of this conversation; she was working him over far more effectively than anything he could have expected from the charity representatives, who had now drifted off in bitter disappointment. He tried to remember the last time he had torn apart an opinion poll and examined its entrails, but couldn't. He'd cut his political teeth in an era when instinct and ideas rather than psephologists and their computers had ruled the political scene, and his instincts had served him very well. So far. Yet this woman was making him feel dated and out of touch. And he could see a piano being wheeled into a far corner of the huge reception room.

'Miss Quine, I'd like very much to hear more of your views, but I fear I'm about to be called to other duties.' His wife was already leading the tenor by the hand towards the piano, and Urquhart knew that at any moment she would be searching for him to offer a suitable introduction. 'Would you be free at some other time, perhaps? It seems I know a great deal less about women than I thought.'

'I appear to be in demand by Government Ministers this evening,' she mused. Her jacket had fallen open to reveal an elegantly cut but simple dress beneath, secured by an oversized belt buckle, which for the first time afforded him a glimpse of her figure. She saw he had noticed, and had appreciated. 'I hope at least you will be able to say please.'

'I'm sure I will,' he smiled, as his wife beckoned him forward.

missed companionship. Even bickering with his wife about the brand of toothpaste had been better than silence, nothing. He needed some human contact, a touch, and he would feel no guilt, not after Fiona's performance. A chance to get back at her in some way, to be something other than a witless cuckold. He looked once again at the girl and even as he thought of revenge he found himself overcome with revulsion. The thought of her nakedness, her nipples, her body hair, the scratchy bits under her armpits, the very smell of her suddenly made him feel nauseous. He panicked, at the embarrassment of being propositioned – what if someone saw? – but more in surprise at the strength of his own feelings. He found her physically repellent – was it simply because she was the same sex as Fiona? He found a five-pound note in his hand, thrust it at her and spat, 'Go away! God sake . . . go away!' He then panicked more, realizing that someone might have seen him give the tart money, turned and ran. She followed, calling after him, anxious not to forgo the chance of any trick, particularly one who gave away free fivers. He'd run seventy yards before he realized he was still making a fool of himself out on the street and saw a door for a drinking club. He dashed in, lungs and stomach heaving.

He ignored the sardonic look of the man who took his coat and went straight to the bar, ordering himself a large whisky. It took a while before he had recovered his breath and his composure sufficiently to look around and run the risk of catching someone's eye. The club itself was nothing more than a revamped pub with black walls, lots of mirrors and plentiful disco lights. There was a raised dance floor at one end, but neither the lights nor juke box were working. It was still early, there was scarcely a handful of customers who gazed distractedly at one of the plentiful television monitors on which an old Marlon Brando film was playing, the sound turned off so as not to clash with the piped Christmas music the staff had turned on for their own entertainment. There were large photos of Brando on the walls, in motorcycle leathers from one of his early films, along with posters of Presley, Jack Nicholson, and a couple of other younger film stars he didn't recognize. It was odd, different, a total contrast to the gentlemen's clubs of Pall Mall to which Mycroft was accustomed. There were no seats; this was a watering hole designed for standing and moving, not for spending all evening mooning over a half pint. He rather liked it.

'You entered in something of a hurry.' A man, in his thirties and well presented, a Brummie by his accent, was standing next to him. 'Mind if I join you?'

Mycroft shrugged. He was still dazed from his encounter and lacked the self-confidence to be rude and turn away a friendly voice. The stranger was casually but very neatly dressed, his stone-washed jeans immaculately pressed, as was his white shirt, sleeves rolled up narrow and high and with great care. He was obviously fit, the muscles showed prominently.

'You looked as if you were running from something.'

The whisky was making Mycroft feel warmer, he needed to ease up a little. He laughed. 'A woman actually. Tried to pick me up!'

They were both laughing, and Mycroft noted the stranger inspecting him carefully. He didn't object; the eyes were warm, concerned, interested. And interesting. A golden shade of brown.

'It's usually the other way round. Women running from me,' he continued.

'Makes you sound like something of a stud.'

'No, that's not what I meant . . .' Mycroft bit his lip, suddenly feeling the pain and the humiliation of being alone at Christmas. 'My wife walked out on me. After twenty-three years.'

'I'm sorry.'

'Why should you be? You don't know her, or me . . .' Once more the confusion flooded over him. 'My apologies. Churlish of me.'

'Don't worry. Shout if it helps. I don't mind.'

'Thanks. I might just do that.' He extended a hand. 'David.'

'Kenny. Just remember, David, that you're not on your own. Believe me, there are thousands of people just like you. Feeling alone at Christmas, when there's no need. One door closes, another opens. Think of it as a new beginning.'

'Somebody else I know said something like that.'

'Which must make it right.' He had a broad, easy smile which had a lot of life to it, and was drinking straight from a bottle of exotic Mexican beer with a lime slice stuffed in the neck. Mycroft looked at his whisky, and wondered whether he should try something new, but decided he was probably too old to change his habits. He tried to remember how long it had been since he had tried anything or met anyone new, outside of work.

'What do you do, Kenny?'

'Cabin crew. Fly-the-fag BA. And you?'

'Civil servant.'

'Sounds horribly dull. Then my job sounds horribly glamorous, but it's not. You get bored fending off movie queens in first class. You travel a lot?'

Mycroft was just about to answer when the piped strains of 'Jingle Bells' was replaced by the heavy thumping of the juke box. The evening was warming up. He had to bend close to hear what Kenny was saying and to be heard. Kenny had a freshly scrubbed smell with the slightest trace of aftershave. He was bawling into Mycroft's ear to make himself heard, suggesting they might find a place to eat, out of the din.

Mycroft was trembling once again. It wasn't just the prospect of going back out alone onto the cold streets again, perhaps finding the tart waiting to accost him, or returning home to an empty house. It wasn't just the fact that this was the first time for years someone had been interested in him as a person, rather than as someone who was close to the King. It wasn't even that he felt warmed by Kenny's easy smile and already felt better than he had done all week. It was the fact that, however much he tried to hide from it or explain it away, he wanted to get to know Kenny very much better. Very much better indeed.

The two men were walking around the lake, one dressed warmly in hacking jacket and gumboots while the other shivered inside his cashmere overcoat and struggled to prevent his hand-stitched leather shoes slipping in the damp grass. Near at hand a domestic tractor was ploughing up a substantial section of plush lawn marked off inside guide ropes while, beyond, a pair of workmen manoeuvred saplings and young trees into holes which further disfigured the once gracious lawn, already scarred by the tyre marks of earth-moving equipment. The effect was to spread dark winter mud everywhere, and even the enthusiasm of the King couldn't persuade Urquhart that the gardens of Buckingham Palace would ever recover their former glories.

The King had suggested the walk. At the start of their first weekly audience to discuss matters of state, the King had clasped Urquhart with both hands and thanked him fervently for the decision on the Westminster Abbey site, announced that morning, which had been hailed as a triumph by heritage groups as vehemently as it had been attacked by the luminaries of the architects' profession. But as Urquhart had concluded at Cabinet Committee, how many votes had the architects? The King inclined to the view that his intervention had probably been helpful, perhaps even crucial, and Urquhart chose not to disillusion him. Prime Ministers were constantly surrounded by the complaints of the disappointed and it made a refreshing change to be greeted with genuine, unaffected enthusiasm.

The King was ebullient and, in the characteristically Spartan fashion that often made him oblivious to the discomfort of others, had insisted on showing Urquhart the work which had begun to transform the Palace gardens. 'So many acres of barren, closely cropped lawn, Mr Urquhart, with not a nesting-place in sight. I want this to be made a sanctuary right in the heart of the city, to recreate the natural habitat of London before we smothered it in concrete.'

Urquhart was picking his way carefully around the freshly ploughed turf, trying unsuccessfully to avoid the cloying earth and divots while the King enthused about the muddy tract. 'Here, this is where I want the wild-flower garden. I'll sow it myself. You can't imagine what a sense of fulfilment it gives me, dragging around a bucket of earth or manhandling a tree.'

Urquhart decided it would be ill-mannered to mention that the last recorded instance of someone with such an upbringing manhandling a tree had been the King's distant ancestor, George III, who in a fit of clinical madness had descended from his coach in Windsor Great Park and knighted an oak. He also lost the American colonies, and had eventually been locked away.

'I want to bring more wildlife into the garden; there's so much that can be done, so simply. Choosing the right mix of trees,

65

allowing some areas of grass to grow to their natural height so they can provide cover. Look, I'm putting up these nesting boxes.' He indicated a workman halfway up a ladder, fixing wooden boxes to the high brick wall which ran all the way around the gardens.

The King was walking, head down and fingers steepled, in the prayer posture he so often adopted when engrossed in thought. 'This could be done in every park and large garden in London, you know. It would transform the wildlife of our city, of cities all round the country. We've wasted so many opportunities in the past . . .' He turned towards Urquhart. 'I want to put an idea to you. I would like to make our weekly meetings an opportunity to discuss what the Government might do to promote such matters. And how I might help.'

'I see,' Urquhart mused, the creeping cold sending his left leg into spasm while a pair of ducks splashed their way into flight from the lake. Wonderful targets, he thought. 'That's a kind offer, of course, Sir. But I wouldn't want the Environment Secretary to feel in any way that we were undermining his authority. I have to keep a happy team around me . . .'

'You are absolutely right, I do agree. That's why I took the pre-caution of chatting about this with the Environment Secretary myself. I didn't want to put any proposal to you which might be an embarrassment. He said he would be delighted, offered to brief me himself.'

Bloody Dickie. He'd no sense of humour, that was clear, now it appeared as if he had no other sense either.

'Today this is just a muddy field,' the King continued. 'But in the years to come this could be a new way of life for us all. Don't you see?'

Urquhart couldn't. He could see only piles of mud spread around like newly turned graves. Damp was seeping through the welts of his shoes and he was beginning to feel miserably uncomfortable. 'You must take care, Sir. Environmental matters are becomingly increasingly the stuff of party politics. It's important that you remain above such sordid matters.'

The King laughed. 'Fear not, Prime Minister. If I were meant to become involved in party politics the Constitution would have allowed me a vote! No, such things are not for me; in public I shall stick strictly to matters of the broadest principle. Simply to encourage, to remind people that there is a better way ahead.'

Urquhart was growing increasingly irritable. His socks were sodden, and the thought of the public being told from on high that there was a better way ahead than the one presently being pursued, no matter how delicately phrased, smacked of grist to the Opposition's mill and filled him with unease, but he said nothing in the hope that his silence would bring an end to the conversation. He wanted a warm bath and a stiff whisky, not more regal thoughts on how to do his job.

'In fact, I thought I might pursue the point in a speech I have to make in ten days' time to the charitable foundations . . .'

'The environment?' The irritation and impatience were beginning to show in Urquhart's tone, but the King appeared not to have noticed.

'No, no, Mr Urquhart. An address intended to bring people together, to remind them how much we have achieved, and can continue to achieve, as a nation. Broad principles, no specifics.'

Urquhart felt relieved. An appeal to motherhood.

'The charitable foundations are making such prodigious efforts, when there are so many forces trying to divide us,' the King continued. 'Successful from the less well-off. Prosperous South from the Celtic fringe. Suburbs from the inner cities. No harm in encouraging families secure in their own homes this Christmas to spare a thought for those forced to sleep rough in the streets. In the rush, so many seem to have been left behind, and at this time of year it's appropriate to reach out to the less fortunate, don't you think? To remind us all that we must work towards being one nation.'

'You're intending to say that?'

'Something on those lines.'

'Impossible!'

It was a mistake, a rash outburst brought on by frustration and the growing cold. Since there was no book of rules, no written Constitution to order their conduct, it was vital to maintain the fiction of agreement, of discussing but never disputing, no matter how great their differences, for in a house of cards which lean one upon the other each card has its place. A King must not be seen to disagree with a Prime Minister, nor a Prime Minister with a King. Yet it had happened. One impatient word had undermined the authority of one and threatened both.

The King's complexion coloured rapidly; he was not used to being contradicted. The scar on his left cheekbone inflicted in a fall from a horse showed suddenly prominent and purple while his eyes carried an undisguised look of annoyance. Urquhart sought refuge in justification.

'You can't talk of one nation as if it didn't exist. That implies there are two nations, two classes, a divide which runs between us, top dogs and the downtrodden. The term reeks of unfairness and injustice. It's not on! Sir.'

'Prime Minister, you exaggerate. I'm simply drawing attention to the principle – exactly the same principle as your Government has just endorsed in my Christmas address to the Commonwealth. North and South, First World and Third, the need to secure advancement for the poor, to bring the different parts of the world community closer together.'

'That's different.'

'How?'

'Because . . .'

'Because they're black? Live in distant corners of the world? Don't have votes, Prime Minister?'

'You underestimate the power of your words. It's not what the words mean, it's how others will interpret them.' He waved his arms in exasperation and sought to pummel life back into his frozen limbs. 'Your words would be used to attack the Government in every marginal constituency in the country.'

'To read criticism of the Government into a few generalized Christmas-time sentiments would be ridiculous. Christmas isn't just for those with bank accounts. Every church in the country will be ringing to the stories of Good King Wenceslas. Would you have him banned as politically contentious? Anyway, marginal seats, indeed . . . We've only just had an election. It's not as if we have to worry about another just yet.'

Urquhart knew it was time to back down. He couldn't reveal his election plans – Palace officials were notoriously gossipy – and he had no taste for a personal dispute with the Monarch. He sensed that danger lay therein. 'Forgive me, Sir, perhaps the cold has made me a little too sensitive. Just let me say there are potential dangers with any subject as emotive and complex as this. Perhaps I could suggest you allow us to see a draft of the speech so that we can check the detail for you? Make sure the statistics are accurate, that the language is unlikely to be misinterpreted? I believe it is the custom.'

'Check my speech? Censorship, Mr Urquhart?'

'Heavens, no. I'm sure you would find our advice entirely helpful. We would take a positive attitude, I can guarantee.' His politician's smile was back, trying to thaw the atmosphere, but he knew it would take more than flattery. The King was a man of rigid principles; he'd worked hard for many years developing them, and he wasn't going to see them smothered by a smile and a politician's promise.

'Let me put it another way,' Urquhart continued, his leg once more going into spasm. 'Very soon, within the next few weeks, the House of Commons must vote on the new Civil List. You know how in recent years the amount of money provided for the Royal Family has become increasingly a subject of dispute. It would help neither you nor me if you were engaged in a matter of political controversy at a time when the House wanted to review your finances in a cool, constructive manner.'

'You're trying to buy my silence!' the King snapped. Neither man was renowned for his patience, and they were goading each other on.

'If you want a semantic debate then I put it to you that the whole concept of a constitutional monarchy and the Civil List is precisely that – we buy your silence and active cooperation. That's part of the job. But really . . .' The Prime Ministerial exasperation was undisguised. 'All I'm offering is a sensible means for us both to avoid a potential problem. You know it makes sense.'

The King turned away to gaze across the bedraggled lawns. His hands were behind his back, his fingers toying irritably with the signet ring on his little finger. 'What has happened to us, Mr Urquhart? Just a few moments ago we were talking of a bright new future, now we haggle over money and the meaning of words.' He looked back towards Urquhart, who could see the anguish in his eyes. 'I am a man of strong passion, and sometimes my passion runs ahead of what I know is sensible.' It was as close to an apology as Urquhart was going to get. 'Of course you shall see the speech, as Governments have always seen the Monarch's speeches. And of course I shall accept any suggestion you feel you must make. I suppose I have no choice. I would simply ask that you allow me to play some role, however small and discreet, in pushing forward those ideals I hold so deeply. Within the conventions. I hope that is not too much to ask.'

'Sir, I would hope that in many years to come you and I, as Monarch and Prime Minister, will be able to look back on today's misunderstanding and laugh.'

'Spoken like a true politician.'

Urquhart was uncertain whether the words implied compliment or rebuke. 'We have our principles, too.'

'And so do I. You may silence me, Prime Minister, that is your right. But you will not get me to deny my principles.'

'Every man, even a monarch, is allowed his principles.'

The King smiled thinly. 'Sounds like an interesting new constitutional concept. I look forward to discussing it with you further.' The audience was over.

Urquhart sat in the back of his armoured Jaguar, trying vainly to scrape mud from his shoes. He remembered that George III, finished with the oak tree, had also made a general of his horse. His mind filled with visions of a countryside turned over once again to the yoke and plough and city streets smothered in decaying horse manure, By Royal Appointment. His feet were frozen, he thought he was developing a cold, his Environment Secretary was a complete dolt and it was scarcely nine weeks before he wanted to call an election. He could take no chances, there was no time for cockups. There could be no suggestion of a Two Nation debate with the Government inevitably on the receiving end. It was impossible; he couldn't take the risk. The King would have to be stopped.

*　　*　　*

70

The taxi picked her up from home seven minutes late, which made her furious. She decided it would be for the last time; they'd been late three times this week. Sally Quine didn't want to be mistaken for other women, the kind who arrive for client meetings habitually late, flash a leg in excuse and laugh a lot. She didn't mind showing off a leg but she hated having to offer excuses and always ensured she arrived anywhere five minutes before the rest so she would be fully prepared and in charge of proceedings. The early bird always hijacks the agenda. She would fire the taxi firm first thing in the morning.

She closed the door to her home behind her. It was a terraced house in a highly fashionable part of Islington with small rooms and reasonable overheads. It represented all that she'd been able to squeeze out of the wreckage she had left behind in Boston, but in the banks' view it was good collateral for the loans on her business and at the moment that was more important than running the sort of gin palace and entertainment lounge preferred by most of her larger competitors. It had two bedrooms, one of which had come set up as a nursery. It had been the first room to be ripped apart; she couldn't bear the sight of any more bears bouncing across the wallpaper and the memories they brought with them. The room was now covered in impersonal filing cabinets and shelves carrying thick piles of computer print-out rather than talcum powder and tubs of vaseline. She didn't think of her baby too often, she couldn't afford to. It hadn't been her fault, no one's fault really, but that hadn't dammed the flood of guilt. She had sat and watched the tiny hand clutching her little finger, the only part of her body small enough for him to cling to, his eyes closed, struggling for each breath, all but submerged beneath the impersonal tubes and anonymous surgical paraphernalia. She had sat and sat and watched, and watched, as the struggle was gradually lost and the strength and spirit of the tiny bundle had faded away, to nothing. Not her fault, everyone had said so. Everyone, that is, except that slimehound of a husband.

'Downing Street, you say,' commented the cab driver, ignoring a barbed rejoinder about his timing. 'You work there, do you?' He seemed relieved to discover she was simply another ordinary sufferer and began a steady monologue composed of complaints and observations about their political masters. It was not that he was ill-disposed towards the Government, which seemed one stage removed from his daily life since he took all his fares in cash and therefore paid practically no income tax. 'It's just the streets are looking grim, luv. A week before Christmas and it's not really happening. Shops half-empty, fewer people needing cabs and those what do're skimping on the tips. Dunno what your pals in Downing Street are saying, but tell 'em from me the tough times are right around the corner. Old Francis Urquhart better pull his socks up or he won't be long in following whatsisname . . . er, Collingridge.'

Less than a month out of office and already the memory was beginning to slip inexorably from the mind.

She ignored his chatter as they meandered through the dark, drizzly streets of Covent Garden, past the restored monument of Seven Dials which marked what had been some of the worst slums of Dickensian London with its typhoid and footpads, and which now presided over the heart of London's theatreland. They passed a theatre that stood dark and empty; the show had closed, in what should have been the busiest time of year. Straws in the wind, she thought, remembering Landless's warning, or maybe great armfuls of hay.

The taxi dropped her off at the top of Downing Street and in spite of his blunt hints she refused to sign for a tip. The policeman at the wrought-iron gate consulted the personal radio tucked away beneath his rain cape, there was a crackle in response and he let her through. A hundred yards away loomed the black door, which swung open even before she had put her foot on the step. She signed a visitors book in the entrance hall, which was deserted except for a couple of policemen. There was none of the bustle and activity she had expected and none of the crowds of the evening she had met Urquhart. It seemed as if Christmas had arrived early.

Within three minutes she had passed through as many sets of hands, each civil servant contriving to appear more important than the last, as she was led up stairs, through corridors, past display cases full of porcelain until she was shown into an inner office and the door closed behind her. They were on their own.

'Miss Quine. So good of you to come.' Francis Urquhart stubbed out a cigarette and held out his hand, guiding her towards the comfortable leather chairs placed in the corner of his first-floor study. The room was dark, book-lined and very masculine, with no overhead light and the sole illumination coming from a desk lamp and two side lights. It was reminiscent of the timeless, smoky atmosphere of the gentlemen's club on Pall Mall she had visited one ladies' night.

As he offered her a drink she studied him carefully. The prominent temples, the tired but defiant eyes which never seemed to rest. He was thirty years older than she. Why had he brought her here? What sort of research was he truly interested in? As he busied himself with two glasses of whisky she noted he had soft hands, perfectly formed, with slender fingers and nails which were carefully manicured. So unlike those of her former husband. She couldn't imagine those hands clenched and balled, thrusting into her face or pounding her belly into miscarriage, the final act of their matrimonial madness. Damn all men!

Her memories bothered her as she took the proffered crystal tumbler and sipped the whisky. She spat in distaste. 'Do you have any ice and soda?'

'It's a single malt,' he protested.

'And I'm a single girl. My mother always told me never to take it neat.'

He seemed amused by her outspokenness. 'Of course. But let me ask you to persevere, just for a little. It really is a very special whisky distilled near my birthplace in Perthshire, and would be ruined by anything other than a little water. Try a few sips to acquire the taste and, if not, I'll drown you in as many club sodas and ice cubes as I can find.'

She sipped again, it was a little less fiery. She nodded. 'That's something I've learned this evening.'

'One of the many benefits of getting older is that I have learned a lot about men and whisky. About women, however, it seems I am still quite ignorant. According to you.'

'I've brought some figures . . .' She stretched down for her bag.

'Before we look at that, I have another topic.' He settled back in his chair, a reflective mood on his face as he held his glass in both hands, like a don quizzing one of his charges. 'Tell me, how much respect do you have for the Royal Family?'

Her nose wrinkled as she savoured the unexpected question. 'Professionally, I'm completely uncommitted. I'm not paid to respect anything, only to analyse it. And personally . . . ?' She shrugged her shoulders. 'I'm American, from Paul Revere country. Used to be when we saw one of the King's men, we shot him. Now it's just another kind of show business. Does that upset you?'

He ducked the question. 'The King is keen to make a speech about One Nation, about pulling together the divisions in the country. A popular theme, do you think?'

'Of course. It's a sentiment expected of a nation's leaders.'

'A powerful theme, too, then?'

'That depends. If you're running for Archbishop of Canterbury then it's bound to help. The nation's moral conscience and all that.' She paused, waiting for some sign that she was moving in the right direction. All she got was the arched eyebrow of a professor in his lair; she would have to fly this one entirely on instinct. 'But politics, that's a different matter. It's expected of politicians, but rather like background music is expected in a lift. What matters to the voters is not the music but whether the lift they're travelling in is going up or down – or more accurately, whether they *perceive* the lift to be going up or down.'

'Tell me about perceptions.' He studied her with more than academic interest. He liked what he heard, and what he saw. As she talked and particularly when she became animated, the point of her nose bobbed up and down as if she were conducting an orchestra of thoughts. He found it fascinating, almost hypnotic.

'If you were brought up on a street where no one could afford shoes, yet now you've got a sackful of shoes but are the only family in the street without a car and a continental holiday, you feel as if you've got poorer. You look back on your childhood as the good old days, the fun of running to school in bare feet, while you resent not being able to drive to work like all the rest.'

'And the Government gets the blame.'

'Certainly. But what matters politically is how many others in

74

the street feel the same way. Once they're locked behind their front doors, or in a polling booth come to that, their conscience about their neighbour down the street matters much less than whether their own car is the latest model. You can't feed a family or fill up a gas tank on moral conscience.'

'I've never tried,' he mused. 'So what about the other divisions? Celtic fringe versus prosperous South. Home owners versus homeless.'

'Bluntly, you're down to less than twenty per cent support in Scotland anyway, you don't have many seats there left to lose. And as for the homeless, it's difficult to get onto the electoral register with an address like Box Three, Row D, Cardboard City. They're not a logical priority.'

'Some would say that's a little cynical.'

'If you want moral judgements, call a priest. I analyse, I don't judge. There are divisions in every society. You can't be all things to all men and it's a waste of time trying.' The nose wobbled aggressively. 'What's important is to be something to the majority, to make them believe that they, at least, are on the right side of the divide.'

'So, right now, and over the next few weeks, which side will the majority perceive themselves to be?'

She pondered, remembering her conversations with Landless and the taxi driver, the closed theatre. 'You're gaining a small lead in the polls, but it's finely balanced. Volatile. They don't really know you yet. The debate could go either way.'

He was staring at her directly across the rim of his glass. 'Forget debate. Let's talk about open warfare. Could your opinion polls tell who would win such a war?'

She leaned forward in her chair, as if to get closer to him in order to share a confidence. 'Opinion polls are like a cloudy crystal ball. They can help you look into the future, but it depends what questions you ask. And on how good a gypsy you are.'

His eyes fired with appreciation.

'I couldn't tell you who would win such a war. But I could help wage it. Opinion polls are weapons, mighty powerful weapons at times. Ask the right question at the right time, get the right answer, leak it to the press . . . If you plan a campaign with expertise, you can have your opponent pronounced dead before he realizes there's a war on.'

'Tell me, O Gypsy, why is it that I don't hear this from other opinion pollsters?'

'First, because most pollsters are concerned with what people are thinking right now, at this moment in time. What we are talking about is moving opinion from where it is now to where you want it to be in the future. That's called political leadership, and it's a rare quality.'

He knew he was being flattered, and liked it. 'And the second reason?'

She took a sip from her glass, recrossed her legs and took off her glasses, shaking her dark hair as she did so. 'Because I'm better than the rest.'

He smiled in return. He liked dealing with her, both as a professional and as a woman. Downing Street could be a lonely place. He had a Cabinet full of supposedly expert Ministers whose duty it was to take most of the decisions, leaving him only to pull the strings and carry the can if the rest of them got it horribly wrong. Few Government papers came to him unless he asked for them. He was protected from the outside world by a highly professional staff, a posse of security men, mortar-proof windows and huge iron gates. And Elizabeth was always off taking those damned evening classes . . . He needed someone to confide in, to gather his ideas and sort them into coherent order, who had self-confidence, who didn't owe their job to him, who looked good. Who believed she was the best.

'And I suspect you are.'

Their eyes enjoyed the moment.

'So you think there will be war, Francis? Over One Nation? With the Opposition?'

He rested back in his chair, staring into a distance, struggling to discern the future. This was no longer the energetic exchange of academic ideas, nor the intellectual masturbation of cynical old men around a Senior Common Room dining table. The horrid stench of reality clung to his nostrils. When he answered his words were slow, carefully considered. 'Not just with the Opposition. Maybe even with the King – if I let him make his speech.' He was pleased to see no trace of alarm in her eyes, only intense interest.

'War with the King . . . ?'

'No, no . . . Not if I can avoid it. I want to avoid any confrontation with the Palace, truly I do. I have enough people to fight without taking on the Royal Family and every blue-rinsed loyalist in the country. But . . .' He paused. 'Let us suppose. If it did come to that. I should need plenty of gypsy craft, Sally.'

Her lips were puckered, her words equally deliberate. 'If that's what you want, remember – you only have to say please. And anything else I can help you with.'

The gyrations of the end of her nose had become almost animalistic and, for Urquhart, exquisitely sensuous. They remained looking at each other in silence for a long moment, careful not to say a word in case either of them should destroy the magic of innuendo which both were relishing. He had only ever once – no, twice – combined tutorials with sex. He would have been drummed out had he been discovered, yet the risk was what had made it some of the best sex of his life, not only rising above the lithe bodies of his students but in the same act rising above the banality and pathetic pettiness of the university establishment. He was different, better, he had always known it, and no more clearly than on the huge overstuffed Chesterfield in his college rooms overlooking the Parks.

The sex had also helped him rise above the memory of his considerably older brother, Alistair, who had died defending some scrappy bit of France during the Second World War. Thereafter, Urquhart had lived in his dead brother's shadow. He had not only to fulfil his own substantial potential but, in the eyes of his mourning mother, to fulfil that of the lost first-born, whom time and grief had imbued with almost mythical powers. When Francis passed exams, his mother reminded him that Alistair had been Captain of the school. Where Francis became one of the fastest-travelling dons of his age, in his mother's eyes Alistair would already have arrived. As a small boy he would climb into his mother's bed, for comfort and warmth, but all he found were silent tears trickling down her cheeks. He could remember only the feeling of rejection, of being somehow inadequate. In later life he could never completely expel

77

from his mind his mother's look of misery and incomprehension, which seemed to haunt any bedroom he entered. While a teenager he had never taken a girl to bed, it only served to remind him that for his mother he had always been second-born and second-best. There had been girls, of course, but never in bed – on floors, in tents, standing up against the walls of a deserted country house. And, eventually, on Chesterfields, during tutorials. Like this one.

'Thank you,' he said softly, breaking the moment and his lurid reminiscence by swirling the whisky around in his glass and downing it in a gulp. 'But I must deal with this speech.' He took a sheaf of papers from a coffee table and waved them at her. 'Head him off at the pass, or whatever it is you say.'

'Drafting speeches isn't exactly my line, Francis.'

'But it is mine. And I shall treat it with the greatest respect. Like a surgeon. It will remain a fine and upstanding text, full of high sentiment and ringing phrases. It simply won't have any balls left when I send it back . . .'

December: The Third Week

The Detective Constable squirmed in his seat as he tried to regain some of the feeling he had lost in his lower limbs. He'd been stuck in the car for four hours, the drizzle prevented him from taking a walk around the car, and his mouth felt like a mouse nest from sucking at the cigarettes. He'd give the weed up. Again. Tomorrow, he vowed, just as he always did. *Mañana.* He reached for a fresh thermos of coffee and poured a cup for himself and the driver beside him.

They sat gazing at the small house in the exotically named Adam and Eve Mews. It stood behind one of London's most fashionable shopping thoroughfares, but the mews was well protected from the capital's bustle and stood quiet, secluded and, for onlookers, unremittingly dull.

'Christ, I should think her Italian's perfect by now,' the driver muttered mindlessly. They had exchanged similar sentiments on all five trips to the mews over the last fortnight, and the Special Branch DC and driver found their conversation going round in circles.

The DC broke wind in response. The tide of coffee was getting to him and he desperately wanted to take a leak. His basic training had provided instruction in how to take an unobtrusive leak beside the car while pretending to make running repairs so that he never left his vehicle and its radio, but he would get soaked in the steady drizzle. Anyway, last time he'd tried it the driver had driven off, leaving him kneeling in full flow in the middle of the bloody street. Funny bastard.

He had been enthusiastic when they offered him a job as a Protection Officer in Downing Street. They hadn't told him it would be for Elizabeth Urquhart and her endless round of shopping, entertaining, socializing. And Italian lessons. He lit another cigarette and cracked the window to allow in some fresh air, coughing as it hit his lungs. 'Naw,' he offered in reply. 'I reckon we've got weeks of this. I bet her teacher's one of the really slow, methodical types.'

They sat gazing at the mews house with the leafless ivy clinging to its walls, the dustbin in its neat little alcove and in the front window a miniature Christmas tree, complete with lights and decorations, £44.95 from Harrods. Inside, behind the drawn curtains, Elizabeth Urquhart was lying on a bed, naked and sweating, taking yet another slow, methodical lesson from her Italian opera star with the beautiful tenor voice.

It was still dark when Mycroft woke, stirred by the clatter of milk bottles being deposited on doorsteps. Outside a new day was beginning, dragging him back to some semblance of reality. He was a reluctant captive. Kenny was still asleep, one toy bear from his immense collection propped precariously beside his pillow, the rest tumbled to the floor beside the Kleenex, victims of a long night's loving. Every corner of Mycroft's body ached, and still cried out for more. And somehow he would ensure he would get it, before he returned to the real world waiting beyond Kenny's front door. The last few days had been like a new life for him, getting to know Kenny, getting to know himself, becoming lost in the mysteries and rites of a world he scarcely knew. There had been times at Eton and university, of course, during those days of the hash-smoking free-for-all do-everything-screw-anything sixties, but that had proved to be a limited voyage of self-discovery which had been all too self-indulgent and lacking in direction ever to be complete. He had never fallen in love, never had the chance, his affairs had been all too brief and hedonistic. With time he might have got to know himself better, but then had come the call from the Palace, a summons which did not allow for exhaustive and, at that time, illegal sexual experimentation. And so for more than twenty years he had pretended. Pretended he didn't look at men as anything other than colleagues. Pretended that he was happy with Fiona. Pretended that he wasn't who he knew he was. It had been a necessary sacrifice but now, for the first time in his life, he had begun to be completely honest with himself, to be his own person. At last his feet had touched bottom. He was in at the deep end, not knowing whether he had been pushed by Fiona or had jumped, but it didn't matter. He was there. He knew he might drown in the depths, but it was better than drowning in corrupt respectability.

He wished Fiona could see him now and hoped she would be hurt, disgusted even; it was like shitting all over their marriage and everything she stood for. But she probably wouldn't give a damn. He'd found more passion in the last few days than he had experienced during the entire course of his marriage, enough to last him a lifetime perhaps, though he hoped there would be more. Much more.

The real world was waiting for him outside and he knew he would have to return to it soon. Leave this Kenny-Come-Lately, perhaps for good. He had no illusions about his new lover, with a teddy in every port 'and a franky and a miguel too', he had bragged. Once the adrenaline of initiation had worn off Mycroft doubted whether he would have the physical stamina to keep hold of a man twenty years his junior with a velvet skin and a tongue which was both inexhaustible and utterly uninhibited, but it would be fun trying. Before he returned to the real world . . .

Could an incorrigible air steward with the inhibitions of a Calcuttan street dog coexist beside the duties and obligations of his other world? He wanted it to be, but he knew others would not let him, not if they knew, not if they found him here amidst the clutter of teddy bears, underpants and dirty towels. They would say he was failing the King. But if he ran away now, he would be failing himself, and wouldn't that be far worse?

He was still confused but happy, more elated than he could remember, and he would remain that way so long as he stayed beneath this duvet and didn't venture outside that front door. Kenny was stirring now, his long-haul tan stretching all the way from the stubble on his chin to the trunk line just above his white buttocks. Damn it, let Kenny decide. He leaned over, ran his lips across Kenny's neck just where the vertebrae protruded, and started working his way down.

*   *   *

As he waited, Benjamin Landless gazed at the barrel-vaulted ceiling, illuminated by six great chandeliers, where Italianate plaster cherubs with pouting cheeks chased each other through an abundance of clouds, gilded stars and spectacular plasterwork squiggles. He hadn't been to a carol service in more than thirty years and he'd never before been inside St Martin-in-the-Fields but, as he always mused, life is full of new experiences. Or at least new victims.

She had a reputation for being late for everything except meals, and this evening was no exception. The drive was less than three miles, complete with police motorcycle escort, from Kensington Palace to the fine Hanoverian church overlooking Trafalgar Square, but presumably she would make some asinine excuse like getting stuck in the traffic. Or perhaps as a Royal Princess she no longer bothered making excuses.

Landless did not know Her Royal Highness Princess Charlotte well. They had only met twice before, at public receptions, and he wanted to meet her more informally. He was not a man who accepted delay or excuses, particularly from the chinless and indigent son of minor nobility he paid twenty grand a year for 'consulting services' – which meant fixing private lunches or soirées with whomever he wanted to meet. Even Landless had to compromise this time, however; the Princess's Christmas schedule was so hectic as she prepared for seasonal festivities and the Austrian piste that sharing a private box at a carol service was as good as he was going to get, and even that had cost him a hefty donation to the Princess's favourite children's charity. Still, charitable donations came from a private trust set up by his accountants to mitigate his tax position and he had found that a few carefully targeted donations could bring him, if not acceptability, then at least access and invitations. And they were worth paying for, particularly for a boy from Bethnal Green.

At last she was there; the organist struck up the strains of Handel's 'Messiah' and the clergy, choristers and acolytes processed down the aisle. As they peeled off to occupy their allotted positions, in the Royal Box above their heads Landless nodded respectfully while she smiled from beneath the broad brim of a matador's hat, and the service began. Their seating was, indeed, private, at gallery level and beneath a finely carved eighteenth-century canopy affording them a view of the choir but keeping her at some distance from most of the congregation, who in any event were largely Christmas tourists or refugees from the cold streets. She leaned across to whisper as the choir struck up their interpretation of 'O Come O Come Emmanuel'.

'I'm dying for a pee. Had to rush here straight from lunch.'

Landless had no need to consult his watch to know that it was already past five thirty. Some lunch. He could smell stale wine on her breath. The Princess was renowned for her bluntness: putting people at their ease, as her defenders argued; displaying her basic coarseness and congenital lack of authentic style, according to her rather greater number of detractors. She had married into the Royal Family, the daughter of an undistinguished family who counted more actuaries than aristocrats amongst their number, a fact of which the less respectful members of the press never ceased to remind their readers. Still, she had done her job, allowing her name to be used by endless charities, opening new hospital wings, cutting the ribbons, feeding the gossip columns and providing the nation with a daughter and two sons, the elder of whom would inherit the throne if some dozen of his more senior royal relatives all suddenly succumbed. 'A disaster waiting for a disaster,' as the *Daily Mail* had once ungraciously described her after a dinner during which she had been overheard suggesting that her son would make an excellent monarch.

She looked at Landless quizzically. There were small, fragile creases underneath and at the corners of her slate-green eyes which became more prominent when she frowned, and the flesh at the bottom of her neck was beginning to lose its elasticity, as happened with women of her age, but she still retained much of the good looks and appeal for which the Prince had married her all those years ago, ignoring the advice of his closest friends.

'You've not come here to write some scandalous nonsense about me, have you?' she demanded roughly.

'There are enough journalists in the gutter taking advantage of your family without my joining in.'

She nodded in agreement, the brim of her hat bobbing up and down in front of her face. 'Occupational hazard. But what can one do about it? You can't lock an entire family away, even a Royal one, not in this day and age. We've got to be allowed to participate like other people.'

It was her endless refrain of complaint and justification: Let us be an ordinary family. Yet her desire to be ordinary had never stopped her embracing the paparazzi, dragging all the First Women of Fleet Street backstage behind the royal footlights to write gushing tributes, being seen eating at London's most fashionable restaurants and sedulously ensuring she received more column inches than most other members of the Royal Family, including her husband. With each passing year her desire not to fade from the spotlight had grown more apparent. It was part of being a modern Monarchy, she had contended, not getting oneself cut off, being able to join in. It was an argument borrowed from the King before he ascended the throne, but it was one she had never understood. He had been seeking to find a concrete but constitutional role for the heir, while she saw it in terms of being able to find some form of personal fulfilment and excitement to take the place of a family life which had largely ceased to exist.

They nodded deferentially through a prayer before picking up the conversation during the reading of the lesson from Isaiah – 'For a boy has been born for us, a son given to us, to bear the symbol of dominion on his shoulder; and he shall be called . . .'

'That's what I wanted to talk to you about, the gutter press.'

She leaned closer and he tried to shift his bulk around in the narrow chair, but it was an unequal struggle.

'There's a story going round which I'm afraid could do you harm.'

'Not counting the empty liquor bottles in my dustbin again?'

'A story that you're getting designer clothes worth thousands of pounds from leading fashion houses and somehow forgetting to pay for them.'

'That old rubbish! Been floating around for years. Look, I'm the best advertisement those designers have. Why else would they still keep sending me clothes. They get so much free publicity it's me who ought to be charging them.'

'As they offered gifts most rare, At Thy cradle rude and bare,' the choir rang out.

'That's only part of it, Ma'am. The story goes that you are then taking these clothes which have been . . . donated, shall we say, and selling them for cash to your friends.'

There was a moment of guilty silence before she responded, deeply irritated. 'What do they know? It's nonsense. Can't possibly have any evidence. Who, tell me who. Who's supposed to have these bloody clothes?'

'Amanda Braithwaite. Your former flatmate, Serena Chiselhurst. Lady Olga Wickham-Furness. The Honourable Mrs Pamela Orpington. To name but four. The last lady received an exclusive Oldfield evening dress and an Yves St Laurent suit, complete with accessories. You received one thousand pounds. According to the report.'

'There's no evidence for these allegations,' the Princess snapped in a strangulated whisper. 'Those girls would never—'

'They don't need to. Those clothes are bought to wear, to show off. The evidence is all in a series of photographs of you and these other ladies taken over the last few months, quite properly, in public places.' He paused. 'And there's a cheque stub.'

She considered in silence for a moment, finding reassurance lacking as the choir sang sentiments of bleak midwinter and frosty winds.

'Won't look too good, will it. There'll be a bloody stink.' She sounded deflated, the self-confidence waning. She studied her gloves intently for a moment, distractedly smoothing out the creases. 'I'm expected to be in five different places a day, never wearing the same outfit twice. I work damned hard to make other people happy, to bring a little Royal pleasure into their lives. I help to raise millions, literally millions, every year for charity. For others. Yet I am expected to do it all on the pittance I get from the Civil List. It's impossible.' Her voice had become a whisper as she took in the inevitability of what Landless had said. 'Oh, stuff it all,' she sighed.

'Don't worry, Ma'am. I think I'm in a position to acquire these photographs and ensure they never see the light of day.'

She looked up from the gloves, relief and gratitude swelling in her eyes. Not for a moment did she realize that Landless already had the photographs, that they had been taken on his explicit instructions after a tip-off from one of the women's disgruntled Spanish au pair who had overheard a telephone conversation and stolen the cheque stub.

'But that's not really the point, is it,' Landless continued. 'We need to find some way of ensuring you don't run into this sort of trouble ever again. I know what it's like to be the victim of constant press sneering. I feel we're in this together. I'm British, born and bred and proud of it, and I've no time for those foreign creeps who own half our national press yet who don't understand or care a fig about what makes this country great.'

Her shoulders stiffened under the impact of his bombastic flattery as the vicar began an appeal for help to the homeless built heavily around images of insensitive innkeepers and quotations from the annual report of a housing action charity.

'I'd like to offer you a consultancy with one of my companies. Entirely confidential, only you and me to know about it. I provide you with a suitable retainer, and in return you give me a few days of your time. Open one or two of our new offices. Meet some of my important foreign business contacts over lunch. Perhaps host an occasional dinner at the Palace. And I'd love to do something like that on the Royal Yacht, if that's possible. But you tell me.'

'How much?'

'A dozen times a year, perhaps.'

'No. How much money?'

'A hundred thousand. Plus a guarantee of favourable coverage and exclusive interviews in my newspapers.'

'What's in it for you?'

'The chance to get to know you. Meet the King. Get some great PR support for me and my business. Get the sort of exclusive Royal coverage which sells newspapers. Do you need more?'

'No, Mr Landless. I don't particularly care for my job, it's brought me no great personal happiness, but if I do something I like to do it properly. Without making too much of the matter, I need more money than the Civil List makes available. In the circumstances, so long as it remains an entirely private arrangement and requires nothing which will demean the Family, I'd be delighted to accept. And thank you.'

There was more, of course. Had she known Landless better she would have known there was always more. A Royal connection would have its uses, filling the gap left by his withered line to Downing Street, a tool to impress those who still thought majesty mattered. But this was a particularly versatile connection. He knew the Princess was usually indiscreet, occasionally unwise, frequently uninhibited – and unfaithful. She was despair waiting to be exposed at the heart of the Royal Family and when at last the despair became too large to contain, as eventually he was sure it would, his news-papers would be at the front of the jackal pack, armed with their exclusive insights, as they tore her to pieces.

The room had a hushed, almost reverential atmosphere. It was a place of contemplation, of escape from the outside world with its persistent telephones and interruptions, a haven where busi-nessmen could repair after a heavy lunch to collect their thoughts. At least, that was what they told their secretaries, unless, of course, their secretaries were waiting in one of the simple bedrooms upstairs. The Turkish Bath of the Royal Automobile Club on Pall Mall is one of those many London institutions which never adver-tise their blessings. It is not a case of English modesty, simply that if the institution is good enough its reputation will circulate suf-ficiently without causing an influx of what is called 'the wrong type of people'. It is impossible to define what is the wrong type of people, but gentlemen's clubs have generations of experience in spotting it as soon as it walks through the door, and assisting it straight back out. Such people do not normally include politicians or newspaper editors.

The politician, Tim Stamper, and the editor, Bryan Brynford-Jones, sat in a corner of the steam room. It was still morning and the after-lunch crush had not yet developed; in any event, the denseness of the steamy atmosphere made it impossible to see further than five feet. It clouded the dim wall lights like a London fog and muffled any sound. They would be neither seen, nor over-heard. A good place to share confidences. The two men leaned forward on their wooden bench, working up a sweat, the perspiration dripping off their noses and trickling down their bodies. Stamper had draped a small crimson towel across himself while BBJ, as he liked to be known, sat completely naked. He was as overweight and fleshy as Stamper was gaunt, his stomach practically covering his private parts as he leaned forward. He was extrovert, opinionated, insecure, mid-forties and very menopausal, beginning to turn that delicate corner between maturity and physical decrepitude. He was also deeply disgruntled. Stamper had just given him a flavour of the New Year's Honours list soon to be announced, and he wasn't on it. What was worse, one of his fiercest rivals amongst the national editors' club was to get a knighthood, joining two other Fleet Street 'K's.

'It's not so much I feel I deserve one, of course,' he had explained. 'But when all your competitors are in on the act it makes people point their fingers at you, as if you're second rate. I don't know what the hell I have to do to establish my credentials with this Government. After all, I've turned *The Times* into your biggest supporter amongst the quality press. You might not have scraped home at the last election had I turned on you, like some of the rest.'

'I sympathize, really I do,' the Party Chairman responded, looking less than sincere as he offered condolence while perusing a copy of the *Independent*. 'But you know these things aren't entirely in our hands.'

'Bullshit.'

'We have to be even-handed, you know . . .'

'The day a Government starts being even-handed between its friends and its enemies is the day it no longer has any friends.'

'All the recommendations have to go before the Scrutiny Committee. You know, checks and balances, to keep the system smelling sweet. We don't control their deliberations. They often recommend against . . .'

'Not that ancient crap again, Tim.' Brynford-Jones was beginning to feel increasingly indignant as his ambitions were brushed aside without Stamper even lifting his eyes from the newspaper. 'How many times do I have to explain. It was years ago. A minor offence. I only pleaded guilty to get rid of it. If I'd fought it the whole thing would have been dragged out in court and my reputation smeared much more badly.'

Stamper looked up slowly from his newspaper. 'Pleading guilty to a charge of flashing your private parts at a woman in a public place is not designed to recommend you to the good and the great of the Scrutiny Committee, Bryan.'

'For Chrissake, it wasn't a public place. I was standing at the window of my bathroom. I didn't know I could be seen from the street. The woman was lying when she said I made lewd gestures. It was all a disgusting stitch-up, Tim.'

'You pleaded guilty.'

'My lawyers told me to. My word against hers. I could've fought the case for a year and still lost with every newspaper in the country having a field day at my expense. As it was it only got a couple of column inches in some local rag. Christ, a couple of column inches is probably all that prying old bag wanted. Maybe I should have given it to her.'

Stamper was struggling to fold the pages of the *Independent*, which had become flaccid in the damp atmosphere, his apparent lack of concern infuriating Brynford-Jones further.

'I'm being victimized! I'm paying for the lies of some shrivelled old woman almost fifteen years ago. I've worked my balls off trying to make up for all that, to put it behind me. Yet it seems I can't even rely on the support of my friends. Maybe I should wake up and realize they're not my friends after all. Not the people I thought they were.'

The bitterness, and the implied threat to withdraw his editorial support, were impossible to misunderstand, but Stamper did not respond immediately, first carefully attempting to refold his newspaper, but it was pointless: the *Independent* was beginning to disintegrate amidst the clouds of steam, and Stamper finally thrust it soggily to one side.

'It's not a matter of just friends, Bryan. To override the objections of the Scrutiny Committee and be willing to put up with the resulting flak would require a very good friend. To be quite honest,

Henry Collingridge was never that sort of friend for you, he'd never stick his neck out.' He paused. 'Francis Urquhart, however, is a very different sort of dog. Much more of a terrier. And right now, with a recession around the corner, he's a strong believer in friendship.'

They paused as, through the murk, the door opened and a shadowy figure appeared, but the cloying atmosphere was evidently too much and after two deep breaths he coughed and left.

'Go on.'

'Let's not beat about the bush, Bryan. You don't have a cat in hell's chance of getting your gong unless you find a Prime Minister willing to fight in the last ditch for you. A Prime Minister isn't going to do that unless you're willing to reciprocate.' He wiped a hand over his forehead to clear his line of vision. 'Your unstinting support and cooperation all the way up to the next election. In exchange for informed briefings, exclusive insights, first shot at the best stories. And a knighthood at the end of it. It's a chance to wipe the slate clean, Bryan, and put the past behind you. No one argues with a "K".'

Brynford-Jones sat, his elbows on his knees and the folds of his belly piled one upon the other, staring straight ahead. A smile began to etch its way across his damp face like a beam of light through this murky, misting world of fallen chests and sagging scrota.

'You know what I think, Tim?'

'What?'

'I think you may have just rekindled my faith.'

*   *   *

Buckingham Palace
16 December

My dear Son,

You will soon be back with us for Christmas, but I felt I needed someone with whom to share. There are so few people to trust.

My life, and yours to come, are beset by frustration. We are expected to be examples – but of what? Apparently of servility. At times I despair.

As we discussed when last you came down from Eton, I had planned to make a speech drawing the country's attention to the growing divisions within the country. Yet the politicians have 'redrafted' some of my thoughts, so I no longer recognize them as my own. They are trying to make me a eunuch and force me to deny my own manhood.

Is the role of the King to reign mute over a nation being led to dissolution and division? There seem to me to be few clear rules, except that of caution. My anger at the Government's treatment of my speech must remain private. But I cannot be a Monarch without also retaining my self-respect as a man – as you will find when your time comes.

If we have not the freedom to defend those things in which we believe passionately, then at least we can avoid colluding in those actions we oppose and feel dangerously inappropriate. Never let them put words into your mouth. I have simply omitted large chunks of the Government's draft.

My task, and yours to come, is a heavy burden. We are meant to be figureheads, to symbolize the virtues of the nation. To do so grows increasingly difficult in a modern world which surrounds us with many temptations but so few occupations. But if our role is to mean anything, then it must at very least allow us our conscience. I would sign a bill proclaiming a republic tomorrow if it were put to me approved by Lords and Commons, but I will not speak politicians' nonsense and bless it as my own.

Everything I do, every blunder I make, every morsel of respect I gather, will in time be passed on to you. I have not always been able to be the sort of father I would want. Formality, convention, distance too often come between a King and his son – me and you, as they did between me and my own father. But I will not betray you and your inheritance, on that you have my word. In previous times they have taken our forefathers to a public place and chopped off their heads! At least they had the dignity of dying with their conscience intact.

The world seems dark to me at the moment. I eagerly await the light which your return for the seasonal holiday will bring.

With my warmest affection to you, my son.

Father.

*   *   *

Mycroft had spent the evening pacing disconsolately around his cold, empty house, searching for distraction. It had been a miserable day. Kenny had been called off at short notice for a ten-day tour to the Far East which would keep him away over the holiday. Mycroft had been with the King when Kenny called, so all he got was a message left with his secretary wishing him Happy Christmas. As Mycroft gazed at the four walls, he imagined Kenny already cavorting along some sun-kissed beach, laughing, enjoying himself, enjoying others.

The King hadn't helped, either, spitting incandescence at the Government's redraft of his speech. For some reason Mycroft blamed himself. Wasn't it his job to ensure that the King's views got across? He felt as if he had failed. It was another pang of the guilt which plagued him whenever he was away from Kenny and out from under his spell.

The house was so neat, orderly, impersonal, he even longed for the sight of some of Fiona's clutter but there wasn't even a dirty dish in the sink. He'd paced all evening, unable to settle, feeling ever more alone, drinking too much in a vain attempt to forget, drowning once again. Thoughts of Kenny only made him jealous. When he tried to distract himself by thinking of his other life, all he could feel was the force of the King's passion and his bitterness at the Prime Minister. 'If only I hadn't been so open with him, thought he might be different from the rest. It's my fault,' he had said. But Mycroft held himself to blame.

He sat at his desk, the King's emasculated draft in front of him, the photo of Fiona in the silver frame still not removed, his diary open with a ring around the date of Kenny's return, his refilled glass leaving rings of dampness on the leather top. God, but he needed someone to talk with, to remind himself there was a world out there, to break the oppressive silence around him and to distract from his feeling of guilt and failure. He felt confused and vulnerable, and the drink wasn't helping. He was still feeling confused and vulnerable when the phone rang.

'Hello, Trevor,' he greeted the *Telegraph*'s Court Correspondent. 'I was hoping someone would ring. How can I help? Good God, you've heard what . . . ?'

* * *

'I am not an 'appy man. I am not an 'appy bloody man.' The editor of the *Sun*, an undersized and wiry man from the dales of Yorkshire, began swearing quietly to himself as he read the lead item in the *Telegraph* first edition. The profanity became louder as he read down the copy until he could contain his frustration no longer. 'Sally. Get me that bastard Incest.'

'He's in hospital. Just had his appendix out,' a female voice floated through his open door.

'I don't care if he's in his bloody coffin. Dig him up and get him on the phone.'

Roderick Motherup, known as Incest throughout the newspaper world, was the paper's Royal Correspondent, the man paid to know who was doing what to whom behind the discreet facades of any of the Royal residences. Even while he lay flat on his back.

'Incest? Why the hell did we miss this story?'

'What story?' a weak voice sounded down the line.

'I pay you a whole truckful of money to spread around enough Palace servants, chauffeurs and snitches so we know what's going on. Yet you've bloody gone and missed it.'

'What story?' the voice chimed in again, more weakly.

The editor began reading the salient facts. The extracts from the King's draft speech excised by the Government. The replacement sections suggested by the Government, full of economics and optimism, which the King had refused to use. The conclusion that behind the King's recent address to the National Society of Charitable Foundations lay one hell of a row.

'So I want the story, Incest. Who's screwing who. And I want it for our next edition in forty minutes.' He was already scribbling draft headlines.

'But I haven't even seen the story,' the correspondent protested.

'Have you got a fax?'

'I'm in hospital!' came the plaintive protest.

'I'll bike it round. In the meantime get on the phone and get back to me with something in ten.'

'Are you sure it's true?'

'I don't care if the damned thing's true. It's a fantastic ball-breaking story and I want it on our front page in forty minutes!'

In editorial offices all around London similar words of motivation were being relayed to harassed Royal-watchers. There was the sniff of a downturn in the air, advertising revenues were beginning to fall, and that meant nervous proprietors who would more happily sacrifice their editors than their bottom lines. Fleet Street needed a good circulation-boosting story. This would put many tens of thousands on tomorrow's sales figures, and had the promise of being a story which would run and run.

A long time ago, at a point lost in the mists of time, an incident took place during a war fought in Canada between the British and the French. At least, it was probably in Canada, although it could have taken place at almost any point on the globe where the two fiercely imperialist nations challenged each other, if indeed it took place at all. According to the reports two armies, one British and the other French, marched up opposite sides of the same hill, discovering unexpected confrontation on the brow. Heavily packed ranks of infantrymen faced each other, readying themselves for battle, hastily preparing their muskets in a deadly race to shed first blood.

But the troops were led by officers who were also gentlemen. The English officer, seeing his counterpart but a few feet away, was quick to see the demands of courtesy and, taking off his hat with a low sweep, invited the French to shoot first.

The Frenchman could be no less gallant than his English enemy and, with a still deeper bow, offered: 'No, sir. I insist. After you.'

At which the English infantrymen fired and blew the French apart.

Prime Minister's Question Time in the House of Commons is much like that confrontation in Canada. All MPs are addressed as 'honourable' and all in trousers as 'gentlemen', even by their fiercest enemy. They are drawn up facing each other in ranks only two sword lengths apart and, in spite of the apparent purpose of asking questions and seeking information, the real intent is to leave as many of your opponents' bodies as you can manage bleeding on the floor of the Chamber. But there are two crucial differences

94

with the confrontation on the hilltop. It is the one who strikes second, the Prime Minister with the last word, who normally has the advantage. And MPs on all sides have learnt the lesson that the midst of battle is no place for being a gentleman.

The news of the dispute over the King's speech hit the newspapers on the last full day of business before the Christmas recess. There was little seasonal goodwill to be found anywhere as His Majesty's Loyal Opposition sensed its first good opportunity of testing the mettle of the new Prime Minister. At three fifteen p.m., the hour appointed for the Prime Minister to take questions, the Chamber of the House of Commons was packed. Opposition benches were strewn with copies of that morning's newspapers and their graphic front-page headlines. During the course of the previous night editors had worked hard to outbid each other, and headlines such as 'A Right Royal Rumpus' had given way to 'King's Draft Daft Says PM', eventually becoming simply 'King of Cardboard City'. It was all richly amusing and luridly speculative.

The Leader of the Opposition, Gordon McKillin, rose to put his question amidst a rustle of expectation on all sides. Like Urquhart he had been born north of the border but there the resemblance ceased. He was considerably younger, his waistline thicker, his hair darker, his politics more ideological and his accent much broader. He was not noted for his charm but had a barrister's mind, which made his words always precise, and he had spent the morning with his advisers wondering how best to circumvent the rules of the House which forbid any controversial mention of the Royal Family. How to raise the topic of the King's speech, without touching on the King?

He was smiling as he reached out to lean on the polished wooden Dispatch Box which separated him from his adversary by less than six feet. 'Will the Prime Minister tell us whether he agrees . . .' – he looked theatrically at his notes – 'it is time to recognize that more people than ever are disaffected in our society, and that the growing sense of division is a matter for grave concern?'

Everyone recognized the direct quote from the King's forbidden draft.

'Since the question is a very simple one, which even he should

95

be able to understand, a simple yes or no will suffice.' Very simple indeed. No room for wriggling away from this one.

He sat down amidst a chorus of approval from his own back-benchers and a waving of newspaper headlines. When Urquhart rose from his seat to respond he, too, wore an easy smile, but some thought they saw a distinct reddening of his ears. No wriggling. The only sensible course of action was direct avoidance, not to risk a cacophony of questions about the King's views, yet he didn't like to be seen running away from it. But what else could he do?

'As the Right Honourable Gentleman is aware, it is not the custom of this House to discuss matters relating to the Monarch, and I do not intend to make it my custom to comment on leaked documents.'

He sat down, and as he did so a roar of mock anger arose from the benches in front of him. The bastards were enjoying this one. The Opposition Leader was already back on his feet, his smile broader still.

'The Prime Minister must have thought I asked a different question. I don't recall mentioning His Majesty. It is entirely a matter between him and the Palace if the Prime Minister chooses to censor and cut to ribbons His Majesty's remarks. I wouldn't dream of raising such matters in this place.' A howl of mockery was hurled towards Urquhart from along the Opposition benches. Beneath her long judicial wig Madam Speaker shook her head in disapproval at such obvious circumvention of the rules of the House, but decided not to intervene. 'So can the Prime Minister get back to the question which was actually asked, rather than the one he wishes had been asked, and give a straight question a straight answer?'

Opposition MPs were pointing fingers at Urquhart, trying to get under his skin. 'He's chicken, running away!' exclaimed one. 'Can't face up to it,' said another. 'Happy Christmas, Francis,' mocked a third. Most simply rocked back and forth on the leather benches in delight at the Prime Minister's discomfort. Urquhart glanced at the Speaker, hoping she might slap down such conduct and with it the entire discussion, but she had suddenly found something of great interest to study on her Order Paper. Urquhart was on his own.

'The purpose of the question is clear. My answer remains the same.'

There was pandemonium now as the Opposition Leader rose for the third time. He leaned with one elbow on the Dispatch Box for many long moments without speaking, savouring the state of passion of his audience, waiting for the din to die, enjoying the sight of Urquhart impaled on his hook.

'I have no way of knowing what passed between the Prime Minister and the Palace. I know only what I read in the newspapers' – he waved a copy of the *Sun* for the benefit of the television cameras – 'and I have long ceased to believe anything I read there. But the question is simple. Such concerns about the growth of division within our society are shared by millions of ordinary people, whether or not they are held by those, shall we say, somewhat less than ordinary. But if the Prime Minister is having trouble with the question, let me rephrase it. Does he agree' – McKillin glanced down, a copy of the *Telegraph* now in his hand – 'with the sentiment that we cannot rest content while tens of thousands of our fellow citizens sleep rough on our streets, through no fault of their own? Does he accept that in a truly United Kingdom the sense of belonging of unemployed crofters in the Scottish Highlands is just as vital as that of home-owners in the southern suburbs? Would he support the view that it is a sign for concern rather than congratulation if more people drive our streets in Rolls-Royces while the disabled in their wheelchairs are left in the gutters, still unable to catch a Number 57 bus?' Everyone recognized the words which had been hijacked from the censored speech. 'And if he doesn't like those questions, I've got lots more.'

They were baiting Urquhart now. They didn't want answers, just blood, and in parliamentary terms they were getting it. Yet Urquhart knew that once he responded to any point concerning the King's speech he would lose all control of the matter, that he would be open to attack without restraint.

'I will not be drawn. Particularly by a pack of jackals.' From the Government backbenches, which had grown increasingly quiet during the exchanges, came a growl of support. This was more like the exchanges they were used to handling, and insults began to fly freely across the Chamber as Urquhart continued, shouting to make himself heard above the din. 'Before he takes his pretence of interest in the plight of the homeless and unemployed too far, perhaps the Right Honourable Gentleman should have a word with his trade union paymasters and tell them to stop pushing through inflationary pay claims which only force decent citizens out of their jobs and out of their homes.' The roar was almost deafening. 'He greets the problems of others with all the relish of a grave digger!'

It was an adept attempt at self-preservation. The insults had at last dragged attention away from the question and a tide of protest swept across the Chamber creating waves of heaving arms and invective which crashed like surf on either side. The Opposition Leader was back on his feet for a fourth attempt but Madam Speaker, conscious that perhaps she should have done more to curtail the questioning and protect the Prime Minister, decided that enough was enough and handed the floor over to Tony Marples, a prison officer elected to represent the marginal constituency of Dagenham at the last election who regarded himself as a saviour of 'the ordinary chap' and who made no secret of his ambition to get a Ministerial job. He wouldn't get one, of course, not simply because he probably wouldn't last long in the House nor because he was homosexual, but because an estranged boyfriend had recently retaliated by wrecking the MP's Westminster flat before being carted away by the police. Disaffected lovers had dragged down many finer men than Marples, and no Prime Minister was going to give him the chance to follow in their footsteps, no matter how well trodden. But in Madam Speaker's eyes his ambition made Marples just the man to lob the PM an easy ball to hit and so provide the House with an opportunity to regain its composure.

'Wouldn't the Prime Minister agree with me,' Marples began in strong Cockney tones; he hadn't prepared a question in advance, but he thought he knew how to help his beleaguered leader, 'that this Party stands second to none in its respect for the institutions of this country, and in particular in its respect, love and devotion to our wonderful Royals?' He paused for a second. Once on his feet he was suddenly uncertain how to finish. He coughed, hesitated, too long, exposing a gap like a chink in medieval armour. The Opposition lunged. Interventions were hurled at him from across the Chamber, throwing him even further off-stride until his mind jammed in second and stalled. His jaw sagged and his eyes grew wide with the terror of those who wake from a dream to find that nightmare has become reality and they are naked in a public place. 'Our wonderful Royals,' he was left repeating, ever more feebly.

It was left to an Opposition MP to deliver the final blow, putting him out of his misery with a stage whisper which carried to all parts of the House.

'Particularly our queens!'

Even many on Marples' own side failed to restrain their smug grins. Marples saw an Opposition member blow a silent kiss of mockery in his direction, his confidence drained from him for all to see, and he sank miserably back into his seat as the Opposition once more reached a state of euphoria.

Urquhart closed his eyes in despair. He had hoped he'd staunched the flow of blood; now he would need a tourniquet. He thought he would apply it to Marples' neck.

The King was standing, as was his custom, near the window of his sitting room. He was toying self-consciously with the crested signet ring on his left hand, and made no move towards Urquhart. The Prime Minister had been kept waiting outside for a period which was not actually discourteous but was noticeably longer than usual, now he was forced to pace across the full length of the room before the King extended his hand. Once again Urquhart was surprised at the limp handshake, remarkable for someone who took such pride in his physical fitness. A sign of inner weakness? Or an occupational injury? At the King's silent direction they sat in the two chairs by the fireplace.

'Your Majesty, we must put an end to this open sore.'

'I do so agree, Prime Minister.'

The informality of their earlier meetings had been replaced by an almost theatrical precision, like two chess players taking patient turns with the pieces. They sat just a few feet apart, knees together, waiting for the other to begin. Eventually Urquhart was forced to make his move.

'I must ask that this never happens again. Such material emanating from the Palace makes my task impossible. And if the leak came from a Palace servant, then he should be disciplined as an example to others for the future—'

'Confound your insolence!'

'I beg—?'

'You come here to impugn my integrity, to suggest that I or one of my staff leaked these wretched documents!'

'You don't for one moment think that *I* leaked them, not for all the damage they have done . . .'

'That, Mr Urquhart, is politics, which is your game and *not* mine. Downing Street is notorious for leaking documents when it serves their purpose. I am not in that game!'

The King's head was thrust forward, his balding temples glowing with indignation and the bony bridge of his long and much broken nose showing prominently, like a bull about to charge. The limp handshake had been deceptive. Urquhart couldn't fail to mistake the sincerity of the other man's anger, and knew he had misjudged the situation. He flushed and swallowed hard.

'I . . . apologize, Sir. I can assure you I played no part in the leaking of these documents, and I had assumed that, perhaps, a Palace servant . . . ? I misconstrued.' The knuckles of his tightly clenched hands were cracking with frustration, while the King snorted through his nose several times, banging a hand down upon his right knee as if to expend his anger and to regain control of his temper. They both sat silent for several moments, gathering their wits.

'Sir, I am at a loss as to which devil is responsible for the leak and our misunderstanding.'

'Prime Minister, I am well aware of my constitutional duties and restraints. I have made a deep study of them. Open warfare with my Prime Minister is not within my prerogative and it is not my desire. Such a course of action can only be damaging, perhaps disastrous, for us both.'

'The damage has already been inflicted for the Government.

After this afternoon's Question Time, I have no doubt that tomorrow's newspapers will be full of coverage supporting what they believe to be your view and attacking what they will describe as an insensitive and heavy-handed Government. They will say it is censorship.'

The King smiled grimly at Urquhart's recognition of the balance of popular sentiment.

'Such coverage will only do us both harm, Sir. Drive a wedge between us, expose those parts of our Constitution which are best left in the privacy of darkness. It would be a grave error.'

'On whose part?'

'On all our parts. We must do whatever we can to avoid that.' Urquhart left the statement hanging in the air while he tried to judge the other man's reaction, but all he could see was the continuing puffiness of exasperation around the eyes. 'We must try to prevent the newspapers ruining our relationship.'

'Well, what do you expect that I can do? I didn't start this public row, you know.'

Urquhart took a deep breath to blunt the edge of his tongue. 'I know, Sir. I know you didn't start it. But you can stop it.'

'Me? How?'

'You can stop it, or at least minimize the damage, here from the Palace. Your press secretary must phone round the editors' offices this evening to tell them that there is no dispute between us.'

The King nodded as he considered the proposal. 'Maintain the constitutional fiction that the King and his Government are as one, eh?'

'Precisely. And he must suggest that the press leaks have got it wrong, that the draft does not represent your views. Perhaps implying that it was prepared for you by some adviser or other?'

'Deny my words?'

'Deny that there is any difference between us.'

'Let me be clear about this. You want me to disown my own beliefs.' A pause. 'You want me to lie.'

'It's more a smoothing over the cracks. Repairing the damage . . .'

'Damage which I did not cause. I have said nothing in public to dispute your position and I shall not. My views are entirely private.'

'They are not private when they are spread all over the front pages of the newspapers!' Urquhart could not control his exasperation; winning this argument was crucial.

'That is your problem, not mine. I discussed my ideas only with a small circle of my own family, around the dinner table. No Palace servants. No journalists. Certainly no politicians.'

'Then you did discuss it.'

'In private. As I must, if my advice to my Government is to be of any use.'

'There are some types of advice the Government can do without. We are elected to run this country, after all.'

'Mr Urquhart!' The blue eyes were ablaze with indignation, his hands white as they gripped the arm of his chair. 'May I remind you that you have not been elected as Prime Minister, not by the people. You have no mandate. Until the next election you are no better than a constitutional caretaker. Meanwhile I am the Monarch with the right accorded by tradition and all the constitutional law books ever damn well written to be consulted by you and to offer advice.'

'In private.'

'There is no constitutional duty on me to lie publicly to save the Government's skin.'

'You must help with the editors.'

'Why?'

'Because . . .' Because if he didn't, Urquhart would be stranded and done to death by a dribble of by-elections. 'Because you cannot be seen to dispute matters of policy with the Government.'

'I will not repudiate my own beliefs. It would be offensive to me not only as a Monarch, but as a man. And you have no damned right to ask!'

'In your capacity as Monarch you have no right to personal beliefs, not on politically sensitive matters.'

'You deny me my rights as a man? As a father? How can you look your children in the eye—'

'On such matters you are not a man, you are a constitutional tool . . .'

'A rubber stamp for your folly? Never!'

102

'. . . who must support the duly elected Government on all matters in public.'

'Then I suggest, Mr Urquhart, that you go get yourself elected, by the people. Tell them you have no care for their future. Tell them that you are content to see the Scots drift away in discontent and despair. That you don't find it obscene for thousands of Englishmen to have no concept of home other than a cardboard box in some pestilential urban underpass. That large swathes of our inner cities are no-go areas for either police or social workers. Tell them you don't give a damn about anything except trying to line the pockets of your own supporters. Tell them all that, get yourself elected, and then you come back here and issue me with your orders. But until then, I will not lie for you!'

The King was on his feet, propelled upwards more by the energy of his uncontrollable rage than any conscious desire to finish the audience. But Urquhart knew there was no point in continuing. The King was unshakable, he would not agree to bend, not, at least, until after Urquhart had won an election in his own right as Prime Minister. And as Urquhart strode slowly out of the room, he knew the King's intransigence had torn to shreds any chance of holding that early election, and winning.

The telephone rang in the private apartments of Kensington Palace. It was past eight o'clock in the evening and Landless hadn't expected to find the Princess at home. Her husband was away in Birkenhead opening a gas terminal and he thought she would either be with him or out on the town celebrating her freedom, but she answered the phone herself.

'Good evening, Your Royal Highness. I'm delighted to find you in.'

'Benjamin, this is a pleasant surprise.' She sounded reserved, slightly distracted, as though she was holding something back. 'I'm recuperating from the rigours of a day spent with two thousand members of the Women's Institute. You can't imagine how tired one gets after shaking all those hands and listening to all that sincerity. I'm in the middle of a massage.'

103

'Then I apologize for disturbing you, but I have some good news.'

He had spent the afternoon pondering how she might react to the furore caused by the speech she had passed to him as the first fruit of their new arrangement. Her intention had been to illustrate the integrity and deep concerns of the private King; she'd less than half an idea it would be published and no idea of the storm it would cause. There might even be an inquiry. Had she now taken fright?

'I just wanted you to know that the newspapers tomorrow will be overflowing with articles in praise of the King. It's remarkable, done him a huge amount of good. And all because we handled matters the right way. You've done a fine job.'

She stretched out on the massage table in search of a glass of champagne. 'Great team, eh, Benjamin?'

'Yes, Ma'am. A great team.' She was still standing off; had he ruined it already? 'And I've been thinking, doing some recalculation. You know, now I've had the chance to meet you and see how capably you handle yourself, I think the value of your help is going to be even greater than I originally thought. Another fifty thousand pounds. How does that sound?'

'Benjamin, you serious? Sounds brillig.'

He winced at the garble of slang, the cultural product of an endless diet of gossip columns, fashion magazines and adult comics. He'd left school at fifteen and had fought his way through life burdened with all his uncut edges, his rough tongue and even rougher accent. It had given him a sense of self-esteem yet it was a brutal road, not one he had wanted for his three daughters who had found their own paths littered with the finest in educational opportunities. As he listened to the Princess he could neither understand nor abide those who, having been born with every advantage, proceeded to disgrace them. Still, he knew he had found his woman. He chuckled amiably down the phone.

After she replaced the receiver she took another sip from her glass. She wondered if she were getting herself in too deep. She had long ago learned that there was no such thing as a free lunch for any member of the Royal Firm, let alone a free fifty thousand pounds. There were strings to everything, and she suspected that Ben Landless would pull hard.

'You're tensing up, Ma'am.'

She rolled over, the towel slipping from her body as she examined her newly tightened breasts.

'Forget the shoulder muscles, Brent. Time to take care of the inner woman.'

Lieutenant Brentwood Albery-Hunt, a six foot three Guards Officer on secondment to the Palace as the Princess's personal equerry, gave a sharp salute and stood to attention as his own towel fell to the floor and the Princess cast a critical eye over him in mock inspection. He knew from past form that she was a demanding Colonel of the regiment, and that night-duty under her supervision would be arduous.

December: Christmas Week

'It can't be done, Francis.'

I don't appoint Ministers to tell me things can't be done, Urquhart raged inside. But the Chancellor of the Exchequer was insistent, and Urquhart knew he was right.

They were huddled in the corner of a reception room at party headquarters where the good and the great of the party had gathered to save money and time by celebrating Christmas and bidding farewell to a long-serving official. The pay of such officials was appalling, their working conditions usually pitiable and they were expected to show independence neither of mind nor manner. In return they expected, after the passage of many years, recognition, in the form either of an invitation to a Buckingham Palace Garden Party, a modest mention in the Honours List, or a farewell reception at which busy Ministers gathered to drink sweet German wine and nibble cocktail sausages while the retiring and frequently unrecognizable servant was fêted. But Urquhart had been pleased to attend this function, for an elderly but ebullient tea lady named Mrs Stagg. No one else was sufficiently senior to remember how long she had been there. Her tea was poisonous and her coffee indistinguishable from her tea, but her sense of fun had cut through the pomposity which so frequently befogs politicians and her bustling presence in a room usually managed to defuse even the most sombre of occasions. Urquhart had fallen for her when, as an aspiring MP more than thirty years ago, he had watched transfixed as she had spotted a button loose on Ted Heath's jacket and had insisted on stripping the bachelor party leader to his shirt sleeves while she repaired the damage on the spot. Urquhart was aware that this was her third attempt at retirement but, at the age of seventy-two, it seemed likely to be her very last and he had looked forward to the

106

escape from official business. But it was not to last.

'It simply cannot be done,' the Chancellor repeated. 'Christmas has scarcely happened in the shops and the recession is going to be here earlier than we expected. We can massage the statistics a bit, explain them away for a month or two as rogues, but we won't be able to massage away the school leavers who'll be flooding into the workforce at Easter. Most of them are going to go straight from the classroom to the dole queue, and there's sod all you or I can do about it.'

The four men standing with heads bowed in their huddle drew closer together, as if to protect a great secret. Urquhart had asked the Chancellor what he thought of the chances of putting off the impact of recession for a month or two, squeezing out a little more time. But the Treasury Minister only confirmed what he already knew.

Stamper was next to speak, very briefly. There was no use in making a feast of bad news. 'Four points, Francis.'

'In front?'

'Behind. This aggravation with the King has shot our lead to hell. Four points and moving in the wrong direction.'

Urquhart ran his tongue along thin lips. 'And what of you, Algy? What bucketful of sorrows do you bring to drench me?'

As Urquhart turned to the Party Treasurer they had to huddle still closer, for the financier was scarcely more than five feet tall and listening to him in a room full of the buzz of conversation was an effort. Unlike the Chancellor and Stamper, he'd not been told of the plans for an early election, but he was no fool. When a Treasurer is asked how a party living on an overdraft might raise ten million pounds in a hurry, he knows that mischief is afoot. His well-lunched face was flushed as he craned his neck to look at the others.

'Can't be done. So soon after an election, immediately after Christmas and just about to go into recession . . . I couldn't raise ten million pounds this year, let alone this month. Let's be realistic, why would anyone want to lend that sort of money to a party with a slim majority about to get slimmer.'

'What do you mean?' Urquhart demanded.

'Sorry, Francis,' Stamper explained. 'The message must be waiting on your desk. Freddie Bancroft died this morning.'

Urquhart contemplated the news about one of his backbenchers from the shires. It was not entirely unexpected. Bancroft had been a political corpse for many years, and it was time the rest of him caught up. 'That's a pity, what's his majority?' Urquhart had to struggle to provide any form of punctuation or pause between the two thoughts. They were all too aware of his concern, how the lurid headlines of a by-election campaign had a habit of creating a new national mood, usually at the Government's expense as their candidate was put to ritual slaughter.

'Not enough.'

'Bollocks.'

'We'll lose it. And the longer we delay the worse it will be.'

'The first by-election with me as Prime Minister. Not a great advertisement, eh? I was rather hoping I'd be riding the bandwagon, not being shoved under its wheels.'

Their deliberations were interrupted by a sallow-faced youth in much-creased suit and crooked tie, whose reluctance to invade what was clearly a very private confabulation had been overcome by the Liebfraumilch and a bet made with one of the lissom secretaries, who had wagered her bed against his bashfulness. 'Excuse me, I've just joined the party's research department. Can I have your autographs?' He thrust a piece of paper and grubby pen into their midst.

The others waited for Urquhart to move, to instruct that the youth be keelhauled for impudence and dismissed for ill-judgement. But Urquhart smiled, welcoming the interruption. 'You see, Tim, somebody wants me!' He scribbled on the paper. 'And what are your ambitions, young man?'

'I want to be Chancellor, Mr Urquhart.'

'No vacancy!' the Chancellor insisted.

'Yet . . .' the Prime Minister warned.

'Try Brunei,' Stamper added, in less frivolous tones.

There was more merriment as the piece of paper did its round, but as the banter died away and the youth retreated in the direction of a deeply blushing secretary, Urquhart found himself staring into the humourless, uncompromising eyes of Stamper. Unlike the others they both knew how important was an early election. If recession and overdraft were the brush of the noose around their necks, then the news of the by-election had come as the sound of the trapdoor-bolt beginning its final slide. There had to be a way out, or else.

'Merry Christmas, Tim?'

Stamper's words sighed with the edge of perpetual Arctic night. 'Not this year, Francis. It can't be done. You must recognize the fact. Not now, not after the King. It simply cannot be done.'

PART TWO

New Year

Buckingham Palace
31 December

My dearest Son,
Today I begin my first full year as the King, and I am filled
with foreboding.

Last night I had a dream. I was in a room, all white, in soft
focus as things sometimes are in dreams, a hospital I think. I
was standing beside a bath, white like everything else, in which
two nurses were bathing my father, old and wasted, as he was
before he died. They were treating him with such tenderness and
care, floating him in the warm water, he was at peace, and so
was I. I felt a calm, a serenity I have not felt for many months.

Then there appeared another nurse. She was carrying a bundle.
A baby. You! Wrapped in a white shawl. But even as I reached
so eagerly for you the nurse, and the two others attending my
father, were gone. I held on to you but without support my
father was no longer floating but suddenly submerged in the bath,
water washing over his face, his eyes closed. I reached for him with
one arm, but you began to fall. To help him, save him, I had to
allow you to fall. I could not save you both. I had not a moment
longer to decide, he was drowning, you were falling from my arms
. . . Then I awoke.

It is all too clear to me. The Royal Family is intended to
symbolize the continuity between the past and the future; I no longer
think this possible. A King can cling to the past, the traditions,
the decay. Or choose to reach out for the future, with all its
uncertainties, its dangers, and its hopes. We must choose.

I am at a crossroads, both as a man and as a Monarch. I know
I am well loved, but I take no pleasure in the fact. When that

popularity is claimed in part at the expense of the Prime Minister,
it can bring neither any good. Mr Urquhart is a man of great
resolution and, I believe, little scruple. He lays exclusive claim to
the future – perhaps any Prime Minister would – but he does
so with an unstinting lack of reserve. Yet if I can have no part in
building that future, either as man or Monarch, then I have
no manhood, no soul, nothing.

   I shall not seek confrontation, because in the end I will lose.
But I will not become merely a silent cipher for an unscrupulous
and unwise Government. Watch carefully how this great dispute
develops. And learn, for your own time will come.
   Your devoted,
      Father.

*   *   *

It was supposed to be a masked ball to welcome in the New Year,
but Stamper had refused to cooperate. For the first time in his
political career people had begun to recognize him, to make all
those fawning motions which suggested he was important and to
blame only themselves if they became bored talking to him. He was
damned if he were going to wrap it all up behind some ludicrous
headgear just to please his hostess. Lady Susan 'Deccy' Kassar was
the wife of the governing chairman of the BBC. He spent his year
trying to ensure that the Corporation's increasingly meagre budget
eked out sufficiently to cover his commitments, while she spent it
planning how to destroy half his salary in one go at her renowned
and monumental New Year's Eve bash. The extravagance of the
hospitality was matched by that of the guest list, compiled on computer over the course of the year to ensure none but the most
powerful and notorious were included. It was said to be insufficient
simply to be a spy master or bank robber in order to gain inclusion,
you had to be caught and very publicly identified as such, preferably
by the BBC. Stamper had been included only after a second recount.
'Deccy' – named after the décolleté for which she had been justifi-
ably famed ever since passing from her teens to the first of three
husbands – had decided the invitation was a mistake as soon as she
saw Stamper arrive in nothing more elaborate than a dinner jacket.

She had a passion for masked balls, which hid her eyes and enabled her to be on constant lookout for still more glittering victims while concentrating the guests' attention undistractedly upon her neckline. She didn't care for mutineers at her parties, particularly ones who greased their hair. Deliberately and as publicly as possible she had mistaken Stamper for a television soap star who had recently emerged from a drying-out clinic, while privately vowing not to invite him next year unless he was by then at least Home Secretary. She was soon off in search of more cooperative prey, fluttering her mask aggressively to carve a passage through the crowd.

It was shortly before midnight when Stamper spied the ample figure of Bryan Brynford-Jones holding forth from within the folds of a Laughing Cavalier's uniform, and passed in front of him.

'Tim! Great to see you!'

'Hello, BBJ. Didn't see you there.'

'This is one for the Diary. Chairman of the Party come disguised as a human being.'

'Should be worth at least a mention on the front page.'

'Not unless you leak the information, old chap. Sorry, forgot. Leaks not the favourite vocabulary in Government circles at the moment.'

The other guests enjoyed the banter, although Stamper had the distinct feeling he'd come off second best. It was not a sensation he relished. He drew the editor to one side.

'Talking of leaks, old friend, tell me. Who was the bastard who leaked the King's speech? Always wondered.'

'And wonder you shall. You know I couldn't possibly reveal journalistic sources.' Brynford-Jones chuckled mischievously, but there was a nervous corner to his smile.

'Yes, of course. But our informal inquiry ran into the sand, bound to over Christmas, never had a chance. This would be just between friends. Very close friends, remember. Who was it?'

'Never! Trade secret, you know.'

'I'm very good with trade secrets. Or had you forgotten?'

The editor looked perplexed. 'Look, Tim, I'll support you in every way I can, you know that. But sources . . . They're the crown jewels. Journalistic integrity, and all that.'

Stamper's dark eyes burned bright. The pupils were small, almost unnaturally so, which gave Brynford-Jones the impression they were carving at him.

'Just so we don't misunderstand each other, BBJ . . .' The hubbub around them had fallen to an expectant hush as a voice over the radio announced the chimes of Big Ben were about to strike. Stamper had to lower his voice to a whisper, but not so low that Brynford-Jones could be sure others would not hear. 'Integrity comes in many shapes and sizes, but not in your size and not through an open bathroom window. Don't go coy on me now.'

There was dead silence as the wheels of the great clock began to turn and engage. The editor wriggled in discomfort.

'Truth is, I can't be sure. Seriously. *Telegraph* got it first. We only followed up in the later editions.'

'But.'

Brynford-Jones' eyes darted nervously around the room, not settling. The introductory peal of the bells had begun giving him a little cover. The bastard wasn't going to let go. 'But. The story was written by their Court Correspondent, good contacts with the Palace. When we enquired in Downing Street and other Government departments, all we got were squawks of outrage and confusion.'

'And from the Palace?'

'Nothing. No denial, no outrage. No confirmation, either. I spoke to the King's press man, Mycroft, myself. Said he'd check it out and get back if he could, but he never did. He knew we'd have to print without a pretty authoritative denial.'

'So.'

'It came from the Palace. The King, or one of his merry men. Must've been. They could have stopped it. They didn't.' He was sweating, wiping his pink brow with a handkerchief he had lodged beneath the lace ruffles of his cavalier's sleeve. 'Christ, Tim. I don't know for certain.'

Big Ben struck and the room echoed with the sound of renewed revelry. Stamper leaned close, forced to shout into the other's ear. 'So you've told me nothing but gossip and your integrity's intact. See how easy it was, old friend?' Stamper squeezed the editor's arm tightly, with surprising force for one whose frame seemed so narrow and pinched.

'Peace and goodwill to all men, eh, Tim?'

'Don't be a bloody fool.'

In a bar not more than two miles from Lady Susan's party, Mycroft was also welcoming in the New Year. It would have been easy, too easy, to have moped. At this time of year, alone. Kenny away. An empty, cheerless house. But Mycroft didn't feel sorry for himself. To the contrary, he felt better, more at ease with himself, cleaner than he could remember ever feeling. His feelings had surprised him, but there could be nothing grubbier than going through the motions of sex while pretending it was love, when in truth there was no love to be shared, and he realized he had felt grubby all his married life. Yet with Kenny, Mycroft felt surprised, astonished at some of the things he had been asked to do, but totally untainted. He had wandered around Kenny's flat all afternoon, reading his postcards, playing his records, flopping about in Kenny's slippers and one of his favourite jumpers, trying to touch him in any way he could. He'd never been in love and he was far too old to be misty eyed, but he felt about Kenny as he had done for no other person. He didn't know if it was love but what the hell, at very least it was immense gratitude for Kenny's sharing, his understanding, for putting him straight. Straight! Mycroft smiled as he enjoyed his own joke.

The desire to share something of Kenny's on New Year's Eve had driven him back to the place where they had first met. This time the club was packed, with lights flashing and a DJ with moustache dyed party purple keeping up a steady patter on the disco. He had propped himself quietly in the corner, enjoying the spectacle. Three very athletic young men provided a floor show, doing something with balloons which necessitated their taking off most of their clothing, with 'more to come' as the DJ eagerly promised. Mycroft had been anxious that someone would bother him, try to pick him up – 'those queers are such tarts,' Kenny had once teased. He didn't know if he would be able to handle it, but no one tried. He was

117

clearly at ease with himself and his bottle of Mexican beer with lime twist and, anyway, Mycroft mused, he was probably ten years older than anyone else in the bar. Grandfather deserved his bit of peace.

As the evening progressed the noise level had grown and the company became more boisterous. Men were queuing to have provocative photographs taken with one of the floor-show artistes, a drag queen who was promised for the after-midnight cabaret. Almost out of sight on the far side of the room, men disappeared into the scrum of the dance floor, to reappear many minutes later glowing with heat and often with rumpled clothing. He suspected he would not care for all he might find going on beneath the pulsating lights of the disco's laser system, deciding he was content with his ignorance. There were some doors he wasn't yet ready to pass through.

Midnight approached. The crush grew. Everyone else was jostling, dancing, stealing kisses, waiting. The radio was on. Big Ben. One man was already overcome, the tears cascading down his cheeks and onto his T-shirt, but they were obviously tears of happiness. The atmosphere was warm and emotional as all around couples held hands. He imagined Kenny's. Then the hour struck, a cheer went up and the whole bar became a confusion of balloons, streamers, 'Auld Lang Syne' and passionate embraces. He smiled in contentment. Quickly the embraces became less passionate and more free-wheeling as everyone in the room seemed to be kissing each other in a game of musical lips. One or two tried it on with Mycroft but with a smile he waved them coyly away. There was another shadow beside him, bending for a kiss, a portly man in a leather waistcoat with one hand on Mycroft's shoulder and the other attached to an unhealthy looking youth with a bad case of barber's rash.

'Don't I know you?'

Mycroft froze. Who the hell could know him in here?

'Don't worry, old man. No need to look so alarmed. Name's Marples, Tony Marples. Lady Clarissa to my friends. We met at the Garden Party during the summer. You obviously don't recognize me in my party frock.'

118

It began to come back. The face. The bristles at the top of the cheek he habitually missed while shaving. The thick lips and crooked front tooth, the sweat gathered along the crease in his chin. Now he remembered. 'Aren't you . . . ?'

'MP for Dagenham. And you're Mycroft, the King's press secretary. Didn't know you were one of the girls.'

The youth with pimples looked scarcely sixteen with unpleasant yellow stains between his teeth. Mycroft felt sick.

'Don't worry, old love. I'm not from the News of the Screws or anything. If you want to lock it away, your dark and dreadful secret's safe with me. All girls together now, aren't we? Happy New Year!' A gurgle began in the back of Marples' throat which passed as a chuckle and he leaned to kiss Mycroft. As two thick wet lips extended towards him Mycroft knew he was on the verge of vomiting and gave a lunge of desperation, pushing the MP away as he made a dash for the door.

Outside it was pouring with rain and he'd left his mohair overcoat inside. He was freezing and would soon be soaked. It didn't matter. As he fought to rid himself of the taste of bile and to cleanse his lungs with fresh air, he decided the overcoat was the least of his concerns. With creatures like Marples inside, he would rather die of pneumonia than go back to collect it.

She studied his face meticulously. It had lost its brightness and energy. The eyes sagged, looked older, the high forehead was rutted, the lips dry and inelastic, the jaw set. The atmosphere was heavy with cigarette smoke.

'You arrive in this place, believing you'll remould the world to your will. And all it does is to close in around you until you feel there's no way out. Reminds you how mortal you are.'

He was no longer a Prime Minister, an elevated figure above the rest. All she saw was a man, like any other, with troubles piled high upon his shoulders.

'Mrs Urquhart not here . . . ?'

'No,' he responded, brooding, until he seemed to realize he might have given the wrong impression. He looked up at her from his glass of whisky. 'No, Sally. It's not that. It's never quite like that.'

'Then what?'

He shrugged slowly, as if his muscles ached from the unseen burden. 'Normally I'm not prone to self-doubt. But there are times when all you've planned seems to slip like sand between your fingers, the more you scrabble for it the more elusive and intangible it becomes.' He lit another cigarette, sucking the harsh smoke down hungrily. 'It has, as they say, been one of those fortnights.'

He looked at her silently for a long moment through the fresh blue haze which hung like incense in a cathedral. They were seated in the two leather armchairs of his study, it was past ten and the room was dark except for the light of two standard lamps which seemed to reach out and embrace them, forming a little world of their own and cutting them off from what lay in darkness beyond the door. She could tell he'd already had a couple of whiskies.

'I'm grateful for the distraction.'

'Distraction from what?'

'Ever the businesswoman!'

'Or gypsy. What's bothering you, Francis?'

His eyes, rims red, held her, wondering how far he should trust her, trying to burrow inside to discover what thoughts hid behind the coyness. He found not pools of feminine sentimentality but resilience, toughness. She was good, very good, at hiding the inner core. They were two of a kind. He took another deep lungful of nicotine; after all, what did he have to lose? 'I was thinking of holding an election in March. Now I'm not. I can't. It will all probably end in disaster. And God save the King.'

There was no hiding the bitterness, or the genuine anguish of his appraisal. He had expected her to be taken aback, surprised by the revelation of his plans, but she seemed to show no more emotion than if she were studying a new recipe.

'The King's not standing for election, Francis.'

'No, but the Opposition are walking in his shadow, which is proving to be exceptionally long. What are we . . . eight points behind? And all because of one, naive ribbon cutter.'

'And you can't deal with the Opposition without dealing with the King?'

He nodded.

'Then what's the problem? You were willing to have a crack at him before Christmas.'

His gaze was rueful. 'I was trying to silence him, not slaughter him. And I lost. Remember? Over a simple, silly speech. Now his words have become weapons on the field of parliamentary battle and I can't discredit them without discrediting the King.'

'You don't have to kill him, just kill off his popularity. A public figure is only as popular as his opinion-poll ratings, and they can be fixed. At least temporarily. Wouldn't that do?'

He swilled another mouthful of whisky, staring hard at her body. 'O Gypsy, there is fire in your breast. But I have already taken him on once, and lost. I couldn't afford to lose a second time.'

'If what you say about the election is true, it seems to me you can't afford not to take him on. He's only a man,' she persisted.

'You don't understand. In an hereditary system the man is everything. You are all George Washingtons, you Americans.' He was dismissive, deep into his glass.

She ignored the sarcasm. 'You mean the same George Washington who grew to be old, powerful, rich – and died in his bed?'

'A Monarch is like a great oak beneath which we all shelter . . .'

'Washington was cutting down trees when he was a boy.'

'An attack on the Monarchy would turn the electorate into a lynch mob. Bodies – my body – swinging from the highest branches.'

'Unless you lopped off the branches.'

They were engaged in a verbal duel, thrust and parry, parry and thrust, automatic responses, using the honed edges of their intellects. Only now did Urquhart pause to reflect, and as his eyes ran over her she could feel the tension begin to drain from him, the malt beginning to dissolve the shards of glass grating inside. She felt his gaze wandering up from her ankles, over her knees, admiring the waist. Then he was lingering at her breasts, oh, and how he lingered, peeling off layer after layer, and she knew the mellowness had already been replaced by a renewed tightening inside. He was changing from victim to hunter. It brought back a sense of boldness, of command, as the energy of fresh ideas began to flow

121

through his veins and wipe away the lines of despondency which had crowded in around his eyes. In their small world of the armchairs, he began to rise above his troubles and to feel once more in control. As if he were back on his Chesterfield. When, finally, his thoughts had travelled up her body and their eyes met, she was smiling, slightly mocking, reproachful but not discouraging. Her body had been massaged by his imagination, and responded. He brightened.

'To do battle with the Monarch would be . . .'

'Constitutionally improper?' She was goading.

'Bad politics. As I have already learned, to my cost. The King's speech gave him the high ground and I cannot afford to be seen once again in public dispute with him . . .' He arched an eyebrow, exquisitely. She had never known an eyebrow to express such passion. 'But perhaps you are right. If I am denied the high ground, then there is always the low ground.' Once more he was alive, tingling, she could feel the energy and renewed hope. 'An hereditary Monarchy is an institution which defies all logic. An opiate we sprinkle on the masses from time to time to reassure them, to fill them full of pride and respect, to extract their allegiance without them asking too many questions.'

'Isn't that what tradition is all about?'

'Yet once they start asking questions about an hereditary system there is little logic left to sustain it. All inbreeding and isolation, palaces and princely privilege. It is not the stuff of a modern world. Or of a debate about the underprivileged. Of course, I couldn't possibly be seen to lead such an attack. But if such an attack were to be mounted . . .'

'The King is Dead, Long Live the Prime Minister!'

'No, you go too far! You're talking revolution. If you start hacking away at the greatest tree in the forest, there's no telling how many others will be brought down with it.'

'But maybe that's not necessary,' she continued, picking up his thought. 'Perhaps simply cut it down to size. No shadow for the Opposition to hide in.'

'No branches from which to lynch me.'

'No more Royal bark?' She smiled.

'You might say that.' He nodded in appreciation.

'Not so much off with his head as . . . off with his limbs?'

'*You* might say that, Sally. But as Prime Minister I couldn't possibly comment.'

He spread his hands wide and they both began to laugh. She thought she heard the sound of an axe being gently honed.

'Did you have any specific limbs in mind?'

'There are many branches to our beloved Royal Family. Some easier to reach than others.'

'The King and his kind embarrassed, harassed, and on the defensive. A public spotlight probing the darker corners of the Palace. The shine knocked off him and his words, his motives discredited. And all backed by an opinion poll or two? The right questions, eh?'

Suddenly his face went rigid. He leaned across and placed his hand firmly above her knee. Considerably higher above her knee than was necessary. The fingers were stiff with tension and she could smell the whisky on his breath. 'By God, but it would be dangerous. We would be taking on hundreds of years of history. A tussle behind the scenes over a simple speech left me humiliated. If this were to turn into a public battle, me and the King, there would be no going back. If I were to lose, it would be the end for me. And for all who were with me.'

'But unless you have your election in March, you're dead anyway.' She placed her own hand upon his, warming it gently, massaging away the tension with her palm and the caress of her own fingers, welcoming his closeness.

'You would take such risks? For me?'

'Just say please, Francis. I told you, anything you want. Anything. Just say please.' She turned his hand over so that it was palm up, and began to stroke it with the tips of her fingers. Her nose was quivering. 'And you know how to say please, don't you?'

He brought his other hand across to still the sensuousness of her fingers. Theirs couldn't be solely a professional relationship, not if he were to tilt full at the King. There was too much at stake. He knew he would have to make her commitment deeper, more personal, tie her to him.

'There are civil servants just beyond that door. And no lock . . .'

She took off her glasses and shook her hair. It glowed like midnight in the light of the lamps. 'Life is full of risks, Francis. I find risk makes it all the better.'

'Makes life better?'

'Certain parts of it. What risks are you willing to take, Francis?'

'With the King? As few as possible. With you . . . ?'

And already she was in his arms.

Urquhart didn't care for opera, but being Prime Minister involved him in so many things he had no liking for. Attending the Slaughter House twice a week for Question Time. Being affable to visiting presidents, smiling black faces who, calling themselves colonial freedom fighters, had brought their countries to impoverishment and dictatorship, and who Urquhart could remember in their youth having been nothing but murderous thugs. Listening to the front door of the so-called private apartment in Downing Street, the door with no lock, bounce on its hinges as civil servants cascaded still more red boxes and ministerial papers down upon him. As Prime Minister, he had discovered, there was no hiding place.

Elizabeth had insisted he come to the opening night of a new opera and had been so persistent he had been forced to succumb, even though he had no ear for Janáček or forty-member choruses who seemed intent on singing from forty different scores, all at the same time. Elizabeth sat transfixed, her attention upon the tenor who was battling to drag his beloved back from the dead. Rather like the leader of the Liberal Party, Urquhart mused.

Stamper had also encouraged him to come and had secured the private box. Anyone who can afford three hundred pounds a seat for the stalls, he had said, must be worth bumping into. He'd arranged with the management to swap the publicity of Urquhart's presence for the address list of the Opera House patrons, all of whom within a week would be hit with an invitation to a Downing Street reception, a vaguely worded letter about future support for the arts, and a telephone call asking for cash.

And there was Alfredo Mondelli, a man with a face like a light bulb, round, solid, all bone and no hair, with eyes which bulged as if the bow tie of his evening dress had been secured too tightly. The Italian businessman sat with his wife alongside Stamper and the Urquharts; judging by the fidgeting which could be heard coming from his direction, he was equally filled with tedium. For several endless minutes Urquhart tried to find distraction from the music in the procession of gilded female figures who chased plaster cherubs around the domed ceiling, while beside him the creaking of Mondelli's chair grew more persistent. When finally the interval came it was a release for them all; a clearly exulted Elizabeth and Signora Mondelli rushed off to the powder room, permitting the three men to take refuge in a bottle of vintage Bollinger.

'A pity to spoil business with so much pleasure, don't you think, Signor Mondelli?'

The Italian rubbed life back into his buttocks and thighs. 'When God was giving out 'is gifts, Prime Minister, 'e was a little short on musical appreciation when it came to my turn.' His English was proficient, his pronunciation slow and distinctly Soho bistro.

'Then let us make sure we use the interval well before we get drenched in another dose of culture. Straight to it. How can I help you?'

The Italian nodded in gratitude. 'As I think Mr Stamper 'as told you, I am proud to be one of my country's leading manufacturers of environmentally friendly products. To 'alf of Europe I am Mr Green. I employ tens of thousands of people, 'ole communities depend upon my business. A big research institute in Bologna named after me . . .'

'Very commendable.' Urquhart recognized the Latin exaggeration. Mondelli ran a company which, though significant by Italian standards, was not in the same league as the far more powerful multinationals.

'But now, now it is all threatened, Your Excellency. Bureaucrats who understand nothing about business, about life. They terrorize everything I 'ave built.' Champagne washed over the side of his glass and spilt as the passion built in his voice. 'Those foolish *bambini* at the European Community and their draft regulations. You know, in two years' time they wish to change the 'ole way we dispose of chemical waste.'

'Why does that concern you?'

'Mr Akat . . .' He made it sound as if he were clearing his throat. 'These are the chemicals I spend my life taking out of my products. What you wrap your food in, wash in, dress in, the paper you write on. I make them environmentally friendly by taking the wretched . . .' – he gesticulated with his stubby fingers and screwed up his face as if performing on the stage – 'wretched chemicals out of them. What the 'ell am I supposed to do with them now? Governments, you run your nuclear power stations and you bury all your nuclear waste, but that's not good enough for businessmen. We shall no longer be allowed to bury the by-products, or simply burn them, or dispose of them deep in the ocean. Those *bastardi* in Brussels even want to stop me exporting them to store in the deserts of the Third World, no matter that the people of those countries are starving and are in desperate need for the income. Africans will starve, Italians will starve, my family will starve. It is madness!' He took a huge draught of champagne, emptying the glass.

'Forgive me, Signor Mondelli, but aren't all your competitors in the same position?'

'My competitors are mainly German. They 'ave the Deutschmarks for such 'uge investments to dispose of the chemicals 'ow the bureaucrats want. I do not. It is a conspiracy by the Germans to force the competition out of business.'

'So why come to me? Why not your own Government?'

'Oh, Mr Akat, do you not know Italian politics? My Government will not 'elp because they 'ave done a deal with the Germans over the wine lake. Italian farmers to carry on producing subsidized wine which nobody wants, in exchange for the new regulations on chemical dumping. There are three 'undred thousand Italian wine producers and only one Mondelli. You are a politician, you know 'ow such numbers add up.'

Mondelli refrained from adding that he had complicated matters notoriously by running off with a young television actress from Naples while still married to the sister of the Italian Minister of

Finance. He was now greeted in Rome with as much warmth as a coachload of English soccer fans.

'Very sad, Signor Mondelli, I feel for you. But surely this is an Italian matter.'

'It is a European matter, Signor Akat. The bureaucrats act in the name of Europe. They overstretch themselves. And you and the British are well known for being the best and most strong opponents of interfering bureaucrats in Brussels. So I ask you, for consideration. For 'elp. Stop the directive. The Environment Commissioner in Brussels. 'E is English. Your friend, eh?'

'You might say that . . .'

'A nice man – a little weak, perhaps. Too easily led astray by 'is officials. But nice.'

'You might say that, too . . .'

'I understand 'e wishes you to reappoint 'im when 'is term of office expires. 'E will listen to you.'

It was true, of course, every word.

'You might conclude that, Signor Mondelli, but I couldn't possibly comment.'

'Prime Minister, I could not describe 'ow grateful I would be.'

This was not accurate. Urquhart knew from his Party Chairman that Mondelli had described precisely how grateful he wished to be. He had suggested one hundred thousand pounds, paid to party funds. 'In recognition of a great internationalist', as he had put it. Stamper had thought himself very skilful in bringing such a prize to the party; Urquhart was about to disillusion him.

'I'm afraid I cannot help you, Signor Mondelli.'

'Ah, your British sense of 'umour.' He did not sound as if he appreciated it.

Urquhart's expression suggested he'd been weaned on pickles. 'Your personal problems are really something for the Italian authorities to sort out. You must understand that.'

'I will be ruined . . .'

'A great pity.'

'But I thought . . .' The Italian threw a beseeching look at Stamper, who shrugged his shoulders. 'I thought you could 'elp me.'

'I cannot help you, Signor Mondelli, not as an Italian citizen. Not directly.'

Mondelli was tearing at his black tie and his eyes seemed to bulge still further in consternation.

'However, in the serious circumstances perhaps I can share something with you. The British Government, too, is unenthusiastic about the Brussels proposals. In our own interest, you understand. If it were left entirely up to me, I would veto the whole scheme.' The orchestra were beginning to reassemble in the pit, and a buzz of expectation began to rise around the opera house.

'Unfortunately,' Urquhart continued, 'this is one of but a number of issues we have to negotiate with our European partners and with the Commissioners, even the British ones. There will be give and take. And we have so many distractions on the home front. Times are likely to get tough, very distracting.'

'My entire business is at stake, Prime Minister. Either the regulations go under, or I do.'

'As serious as that?'

'Yes!'

'Well, it would be a happy coincidence if my Government's interests were to coincide with your own.'

'I would be so grateful . . .'

'If I were in your position, Signor Mondelli, facing ruin . . .' – he paused to sniff the air, like a prowling wolf – 'I think I should be ten-fold grateful.'

Urquhart gave a perfunctory laugh to suggest lightheartedness, but the Italian had understood. Urquhart had led him to the edge of the cliff and made him peer over; now he offered a lifeline. Mondelli stopped to consider for a few moments, and when he spoke there was no alarm left in his voice. They were no longer talking lifeline, but business. The sum represented around two per cent of his annual profit – significant, but affordable. And his accountants might find a way to write it off against tax as an overseas investment. He nodded his head slowly.

'As you say, Signor Akat, I would indeed be grateful. Ten-fold.'

Urquhart appeared not to have heard, as if he were pursuing his own idea quite separately from the Italian. 'You know, it's about time we had another shot at putting Brussels back in its box. I think this might be just the issue to do it on. There are several British companies who would suffer . . .'

'I would like to 'elp your campaigning activities.'

'Oh, really? Talk to Stamper, he's the man. Nothing to do with me.'

'I 'ave already told 'im that I think you are a great internationalist.'

'Most kind. It really has been a splendid evening.'

'Yes. But I am not a great lover of opera, Prime Minister.' He was massaging his thighs again. 'You would excuse me if I did not stay for the second 'alf?'

'But Stamper here has paid for the tickets . . .'

''E 'as paid for the tickets, but I believe I 'ave paid for my freedom.' The bow tie hung limply down his chest.

'Then goodnight to you, Signor Mondelli. It has been a pleasure.'

Stamper offered words of rueful admiration as the bulk of the Italian benefactor disappeared through the door, then Elizabeth Urquhart was with them once more, wafting perfume and muttering something about attending a reception for the cast after the opera was finished. Urquhart heard scarcely a word. His fighting fund had been opened and the wind had started blowing in his direction yet again. But even as he felt the satisfaction wash over him, he dared not forget that winds in politics rarely blow fair for long. He mustn't let this one blow out of control, if he did it would form a whirlwind of destruction, probably his own. But if they blew strong enough, and long enough, perhaps it was possible after all. By March. As the cymbals clashed to announce the commencement of the second act, he sat back in his seat and gazed at the ceiling. The cherub bottoms reminded him of someone, an undergraduate, on a Chesterfield. He couldn't recall her name.

The Leader of the Opposition was an earnest man, the son of a crofting family from the Western Isles of Scotland. He was not noted for his sense of humour, the peat moors of the Western Isles being

129

too dour to encourage frivolity, but even his rivals acknowledged his dedication and hard work. Government Ministers privately acknowledged he made an excellent Leader of the Opposition, while in public providing every assistance to ensure he continued in this well-fitting job. At times it appeared as if the inevitable pressure on him came more from within his own ranks than from his political opponents; there had been several press stories in recent days suggesting that, following the narrow election defeat of the previous year and the arrival of a fresh face in Downing Street, his party was getting restless and his position coming under threat. The stories were vague and thin, tending to feed off each other as much as on hard views, but *The Times* seemed to have a particularly strong handle on it and had quoted one 'senior party source' as suggesting that 'the party leadership is not a retirement job for losers'. It was more a rumble than a revolution, the polls still pointed to the Opposition having a four-point lead, yet political parties always find difficulty in containing the swirling personal ambitions of its also-rans and, as one editorial had put it, there was no smoke without someone lighting a few matches. So Gordon McKillin had welcomed the opportunity to clear the air on a popular current affairs programme which pitted politician against three leading journalists.

For most of the forty minutes the programme had been uneventful, a little dull even, certainly unsuccessful from the point of view of the producer, whose own job security depended on the regular spillage of someone else's blood. McKillin had parried every thrust with skill and patience – none of the supposed opponents had been identified, he suggested, the real issue was not his leadership but the looming recession which threatened millions of jobs. It was the Prime Minister's job under threat, not his. The story of his troubles had been whipped up by the press, he argued, casting a baleful eye in the direction of Bryan Brynford-Jones, whose journal had published the first and most dramatic report. 'Are you able to name a single one of your sources for this story?' he challenged. The editor, unaccustomed to being in the firing line, quickly moved the discussion on.

Scarcely two minutes remained before the wrap and, much to

the producer's despair, the discussion had become stranded in the marshy fields of the Opposition's environmental credentials. It was Brynford-Jones' turn once again. McKillin smiled generously, as a farmer might eye a prize hog on market day. He was enjoying it.

'Mr McKillin, let me turn in the short time we have left to a more personal question.' Brynford-Jones was toying with some form of brochure. 'You are an elder of the Wee Free Church of Scotland, are you not?'

The politician nodded sagely.

'Now the Church has just published a pamphlet – I have it here – which is entitled "Towards the Twenty First Century: A Moral Guide for Youth". It's fairly wide-ranging and contains, in my view, some excellent prescriptions. But there is one section which intrigued me. On page . . . fourteen, it reaffirms its attitude to homosexuality, which it describes as "a pernicious sin". Do you, Mr McKillin, believe homosexuality is a pernicious sin?'

The politician swallowed. 'I'm not sure this is the right time to get into this sort of complex and difficult discussion. This is, after all, a programme on politics rather than the Church—'

'But it's a relevant question, nonetheless,' Brynford-Jones interrupted. 'A simple one, too. Do you hold homosexuality to be a sin?'

A small bead of sweat had begun to gather in the politician's sideburn, only just perceptible to the professional eye of the producer, who began to brighten.

'I find it difficult to imagine how to respond to such a broad-ranging question as that on a programme like this—'

'Let me help you, then. Imagine your dreams have been fulfilled and you are Prime Minister, at the Dispatch Box, and I'm the Leader of the Opposition. I'm asking you a direct question. Do you believe homosexuality to be evil, a sin? I think the accepted parliamentary phrase goes: "Since the question is a very simple one, which even he should be able to understand, a simple yes or no will suffice".'

All those present and several million viewers recognized the phrase, McKillin's own, which he had used so frequently in taunting Urquhart at Question Time. It was his own hook. The bead of sweat was beginning to trickle.

131

'Let me rephrase it, if you like,' the editor encouraged. 'Do you believe your kirk's moral guidance is wrong?'

McKillin struggled for his words. How could he explain, in an atmosphere like this, that it had been his kirk's guidance which since his earliest days had fuelled the desire to help others and to mount his own crusade, giving him a clear personal creed on which he had based his political beliefs and guiding him through the moral cesspits around Westminster, that as an elder he had to accept his kirk's teachings with an open heart and without question or compromise. He understood sin and others' weaknesses and could accept them, but his faith would not permit him to deny them.

'I am an elder of the Kirk, Mr Brynford-Jones. Of course I accept my church's teachings, as an individual soul. But as a politician such matters can be more complicated—'

'Let me be clear, *absolutely* clear. You accept your church's edict on this matter?'

'As an individual, I must. But allow me to—'

It was too late. The end credits were already rolling and the signature music beginning to flood the studio. Several million viewers had to struggle to discern Brynford-Jones' sign-off. 'Thank you, Mr McKillin. I'm afraid that's all we have time for. It's been a fascinating forty minutes.' He smiled. 'We are grateful to you.'

Kenny and Mycroft had watched the evening news in silence. It had contained a factual report of McKillin's interview, and also of the volcanic response. The Opposition Leader's office was said to be in the process of issuing a statement of clarification, but it was inevitably too late. Leaders of rival church groups had already opined, gay campaigners had assailed, his own Front Bench transport spokesman had stated boldly that on this issue his leader was utterly, miserably and inexcusably wrong. 'Is there a leadership crisis?' he had been asked. 'There is now,' had been his response.

There was no need for the newspapers to keep their sources anonymous any longer, the protesters were tripping over themselves in the rush to denounce bigotry, medieval morality and cant. Even those who agreed with McKillin had been of no help, a leading anti-gay campaigner being dragged from obscurity to demand in venomous tones that McKillin sack all homosexual MPs in his party or be branded a hypocrite.

Kenny switched off the television. Mycroft sat silently for some time, slumped amongst bean bags piled in front of the screen, while Kenny quietly prepared two mugs of hot coffee, laced with brandy out of miniatures smuggled back from one of his trips. He had seen it all before, the outrage, the alarm, the invective, the inevitable suspicion it brought. He could also see how upset was Mycroft. The older man had seen none of this before, not from this angle.

'God, I'm confused,' Mycroft eventually muttered, biting his lip. He was still staring at the blank screen, unwilling to look directly into Kenny's eyes. 'All this fuss, this talk about rights. I just can't help remembering that odious man Marples dragging along the young boy. Didn't the boy have rights, too?'

'All queers tarred with the same brush, eh?'

'I sometimes ask myself what the hell I'm doing. What does it all mean for my job, for me. You know, I still can't identify, join the club, not when I see men like Marples and some of those militants jumping up and down on the screen.'

'I'm gay, David. A queer. A faggot. A fairy queen. Nancy boy. Poof. Call it what you like, that's what I am. You saying you can't identify with me?'

'I'm . . . not very good at this, am I? All my life I've been brought up to conform, to believe that such things are . . . Christ, Kenny, half of me agrees with McKillin. Being a queer is wrong! Yet, and yet . . .' He raised troubled eyes to look directly at his partner. 'I've had more happiness in the last few weeks than I ever thought possible.'

'That's gay, David.'

'Then I suppose I must be, Kenny. I must be. Gay. Because I think I love you.'

'Then forget about all that crap.' Kenny waved angrily in the direction of the television. 'Let the rest of the world go mount their own soap boxes and get splinters in their dicks, we don't have to join them in slagging off everybody else. Love's meant to be inside, private, not open bloody warfare on every street corner.' He looked earnestly at Mycroft. 'I don't want to lose you, David. Don't go getting guilty on me.'

'If McKillin is right, we may never get to heaven.'

'If heaven's full of people who are so utterly stinking miserable, who can't even accept what they are or what they feel, then I don't think I want to join. So why don't we just stick with what we've got here, you and me, and be happy.'

'For how long, Kenny?'

'For as long as we've got, old love.'

'For as long as they leave us alone, you mean.'

'Some people come to the edge of the cliff and they look over, then run away in fear. They never realize it's possible to fly, to soar away, to be free. They spend their lives crawling along cliff tops without ever finding the courage. Don't spend your life crawling, David.'

Mycroft gave a weak smile. 'I never knew you were poetic.'

'Until now I never knew I cared so much for you.'

Slowly, Mycroft lifted his coffee mug in salutation. 'A toast, Kenny. To jumping off cliff tops?'

Slowly and with agonizing care, the rifle sight lined up on its target exactly twenty-five yards away, the head of Gordon McKillin, embossed upon one of his old campaign posters. Slowly, steadily, the finger squeezed, and there was a sharp retort as the .22-calibre bullet sped on its way. A perfect hole appeared exactly where the Opposition Leader's mouth had been, before the badly peppered target disintegrated and fluttered like orphaned pieces of tissue to the floor.

'Don't make campaign posters like they used to.'

'Nor Leaders of the Opposition.'

Urquhart and Stamper enjoyed their joke. Directly beneath the dining room of the House of Lords in a low, wood-lined cellar strewn with the piping, conduits and other architectural entrails of the Palace of Westminster, the two men lay side by side in the narrow rifle range where parliamentarians retreat to vent their murderous instincts on paper targets rather than each other. It was where Churchill had practised his gunnery in preparation for the expected German invasion, vowing to fight it personally and to the last from behind the sandbags at the top of Downing Street. And it was where Urquhart practised for Question Time, freed from the inhibitions of Madam Speaker's censorious stare.

'A stroke of luck yours, coming up with that church pamphlet,' Stamper acknowledged somewhat grudgingly, adjusting the leather wrist sling which supported the heavy bolt-action target rifle. He was a much less experienced shot than Urquhart, and had never beaten him.

'The Colquhouns are a rather exotic tribe, members of which descend upon Elizabeth from time to time bearing all sorts of strange gifts. One of them thought I would be interested in the morality of youth, strange man. It wasn't luck, Tim. Simply good breeding.'

The former estate agent glowered. 'You want to shoot any more?' he enquired, placing another bullet in the chamber.

'Tim, I want a veritable war.' Urquhart raised the rifle to his well-padded shoulder once more, peering fixedly down the telescopic sight. 'I've decided. It's on again.'

'Another of your campus jokes.'

Urquhart obliterated a further paper portrait before turning to Stamper. His smile was withering.

'McKillin's in trouble. He went out on a limb, and it broke. So sad.'

'We're not ready, Francis. It's too soon,' Stamper objected, deeply unconvinced.

'The Opposition will be even less well prepared. Parties facing an election are like tourists being pursued by a man-eating lion. You don't have to outrun the lion – you can't. All you have to do is make sure you run faster than the other bastard.'

'The country might be buried under a foot of snow at this time of year.'

'Great! We've got more vehicles with four-wheel drive than they have.'

'But we're still four points behind in the polls,' the Party Chairman protested.

'Then there's no time to lose. Six weeks, Tim. Let's get a grip on them. A major policy announcement every week. A high profile foreign trip, the new PM taking Moscow or Washington by storm. Let's have a row in Europe, demand some money back. I want dinner with every friendly editor in Fleet Street, on his own, while you tickle the political correspondents. And, if we can get away with it, a cut in interest rates. Castrate a few criminals. Get a bandwagon rolling. We've got McKillin on the floor, let's be sure to kick hell out of him while he's down. No prisoners, Tim. Not for the next six weeks.'

'Let's hope His Majesty decides to cooperate this time.' Stamper couldn't hide his scepticism.

'You're right. I've been thinking we should take a new approach to the Palace. Build a few bridges. Put your ear to the ground, find out what the gossip is. What's going on in the dark places.'

Stamper cocked an ear, as if he heard the sound of prey lumbering through the forest.

'And we need foot soldiers, Tim. Loyal, dedicated. Not too bright. Men who would be happy to charge across those bridges, should the need arise.'

'That does sound like war.'

'Better win it, old boy. Or they'll be putting us up there as targets. And I'm not talking about paper images, either.'

January: The Second Week

The gravel of the long drive leading from the gate lodge to the front of the old manor house rattled against the bodywork of the car as it drew up alongside the other vehicles. The polished dark-blue Rolls-Royce seemed out of place alongside the battered Land-Rovers and muddy estate cars, and Landless already knew he would not fit in. He didn't mind, he was used to it. The manor house was the ancestral home of Mickey, Viscount Quillington, and commanded magnificent views over the rolling countryside of Oxfordshire, although a grey January afternoon was not the best of settings. The fabric of the building charted the chaotic progress of an ancient aristocratic family and was mostly William and Mary or Victorian with a hint of Tudor in the wing nearest the tiny chapel, but of the twentieth century there was little sign.

The damp seemed to follow him into the rough and tumble of the large entrance hall filled with tangled hunting dogs, mucky Wellington boots and a variety of anoraks and outer garments all struggling to dry. The floor tiles were badly chipped and there was not a hint of central-heating anywhere. It was the type of house which in many other parts had been rescued from decay by an expanding Japanese hotel group or golf-course consortium, but not here, not yet. He was glad he had declined the invitation to stay the night.

The Quillingtons traced their line back to the time when one of their ancestors had travelled to Ireland with Cromwell, collected his estates for bloody services rendered, and returned to England at the time of the Restoration to make a second fortune. It was a fine history, on which the current generation of Quillingtons, impoverished by time, misfortune and inadequate tax planning, reflected with awe. The estates had gradually been whittled away, the ties with Ireland finally broken, many of the paintings sold, the best pieces of furniture and silver auctioned, the large staff pared. This was old money, and it was growing increasingly short.

Meeting the other guests proved something of a trial for the businessman. They were all old friends, some dating from nursery days and displaying the type of public-school clannishness boys from Bethnal Green find impossible to penetrate. His clothes hadn't helped. 'Country casual' he'd been told. He had turned up in a check two-piece with waistcoat and brown shoes; they were all wearing jeans. Not until Princess Charlotte greeted him warmly did he begin to feel less defensive.

The weekend had been built around the Princess. Arranged by Quillington's younger brother, David, it was an opportunity for her to relax amongst old friends away from the petty intrigues of London's socialites and gossip columnists. Here they were almost all scions of old families, some older than the Windsors, and to them she was a friend with a job to do, still the 'Beany' of childhood squabbles in the swimming pool and fancy-dress parties organized by po-faced nannies. She had insisted on a private bedroom well away from other guests and David had seen to all the arrangements, tidying the two detectives and chauffeur of the Royal Protection Group well away at the back of the house. The Princess had the Chinese Room, not so much a suite but more a single vast room on the first floor of the East Wing, with David occupying the only other bedroom on the floor. Her privacy was ensured.

There was a certain sadness in surveying the house with its ancient wiring, frayed edges, dank corners and one wing almost completely closed down, yet it had character and a great sense of history, and the dining room was magnificent. Fifty feet long, oak-panelled, lit by two fern-like chandeliers whose lights shone deep into a burnished table constructed from the timbers of an old Man o' War and crafted by prisoners from Napoleon's navy. The silver was old and monogrammed, the crystal assorted, the effect timeless. Old money, even in short supply, certainly knew how to eat. Quillington presided at the head of the table, on his right the Princess and on his left Landless, with others further down, and they listened politely to the publisher's stories of City life as their ancestors might have listened to explorer's tales of the South Sea islands.

After dinner they took their port and cognac into the Old Library, where the ceiling was high and the winter air clung tenaciously to the far corners, where leather-clad books were piled along endless shelves and smoke-darkened oil paintings covered the one free wall. Landless thought he could see marks on the wall where paintings had been removed, presumably for auction, with the remainder spread around a little more thinly. The furniture seemed as old as any part of the house. One of the two large sofas crowding around the roaring log fire was covered in a car rug to hide the ravages of age, while the other stood battered and naked, its dark-green fabric torn by the insistent scratching of dogs, with its stuffing of horse hair dribbling out like candle wax from underneath one of the cushions. Within the embrace of the Library, dinner guests became almost family and the conversation grew more relaxed and uninhibited.

'Shame about today,' Quillington muttered, kicking the fire with the heel of his leather boot. The fire spat back, sending a shower of sparks up the broad chimney. He was a tall, streaky figure much used to wandering around in tightly tailored jeans, high boots and a broad kangaroo-skin fedora, which looked eccentric if not vaguely ridiculous on a fifty-year-old. Eccentricity was a useful cover for encroaching impoverishment. 'Damned hunt-saboteurs, buzz like flies around horse shit. There they are, on my land, and the police refuse to arrest them or even move them on. Not unless they actually attack someone. God knows what this country is coming to when you can't even prevent layabouts like that rampaging all over your own land. Home a man's damned castle, 'n'all that.'

It had not been a successful day's hunting. The animal-rights protesters had waved their banners and spread their pepper and aniseed, unsettling the horses, confusing the hounds and outraging the huntsmen. It had been a soggy morning overflowing with drizzle, not good for picking up trails, and they had lumbered through the heavy clay of the countryside to find nothing more enthralling than the carcass of a dead cat.

'You can't throw them off your own land?' enquired Landless.

'Not bloody likely. Trespass isn't criminal, police'll do damn-all about it. You can ask them politely to move on, they tell you to piss off. You so much as lay a finger on them and you find yourself in court on assault charges. For protecting your own bloody property.'

'Chalked up one of the yobs, I did,' the Princess intervened gaily. 'Saw him hovering close behind my horse so I backed the beast up. Scared all hell out of him when he saw sixteen hands shunting straight towards him. He jumped back, stumbled, and fell straight into a pile of fresh crap!'

'Bravo, Beany. Filled his pants, I hope,' David Quillington interjected. 'You hunt, Mr Landless?'

'Only in the City.'

'You should try it sometime. See the countryside at its best.'

Landless doubted that. He had arrived in time to find the stragglers returning from the hunt, faces red and blotched, covered in mud and thoroughly soaked. Mix in the sight of a fox being torn apart, its entrails smeared over the ground and squelched beneath horses' hooves, and he thought he could well do without such pleasures. Anyway, boys born and brought up in concrete tower-blocks surrounded by broken street lamps and derelict cars tend to have a naive empathy for the countryside and the things that live in it. He hadn't seen any of England's green and pleasant pastures until a school day-trip when he was thirteen and, in truth, he held an undemanding admiration for the fox.

'Foxes are vermin,' the younger Quillington continued. 'Attack chickens, ducks, new-born lambs, even sick calves. Scrounge off city rubbish dumps and spread disease. It's too easy to knock the landowners but, I tell you, without their work in protecting the countryside, keeping it clear of pests like foxes, rebuilding the walls and hedgerows, planting woodlands for fox and pheasant cover – all at their own expense – those protesters would have a lot less countryside to protest about.'

Landless noticed that the younger Quillington, seated on the sofa next to the Princess, was moderate both in his language and his drinking. That could not be said of his brother, leaning against the Adam fireplace, glass in hand. 'Under threat. Everything under

140

threat, you know. They trample over your land, shouting, screaming like Dervishes, waving their banners and blowing their bloody horns, trying to pull the hounds onto busy roads and railway lines. Even when they manage to get themselves arrested some damned fool magistrate takes pity on them. And me, because I've got land, because my family have worked it for generations, devoted themselves to the local community, done their bit for the country in the House of Lords, because I've tried so hard and got no bloody money left and nothing but bills and bank letters to read, I'm supposed to be a parasite!'

'There's no sense of proportion anymore,' the Princess agreed. 'Take my family. Used to be held in respect. Nowadays journalists are more interested in what goes on in the bedroom than the State Room.'

Landless noticed the exchange of looks between the Princess and the younger Quillington. It was not their first. They had begun the evening sitting well apart at opposite ends of the sofa, but they seemed to have drawn ever closer, like magnets.

'Absolutely, Beany. They know you can't defend yourself so they lay into you without pity,' Mickey continued from his position by the fire. 'We've all worked damned hard for what little we have. Yet they get at the fox-hunting, they attack the landowners, they undermine the hereditary principle, and the next thing you know we're a sodding republic. It's about time we started sticking up for ourselves, stopped taking it on the chin and turning the other cheek.'

Charlotte had finished her glass and was holding it out towards the younger Quillington for a refill. 'But, Mickey, I can't, none of my lot can. The Family's supposed to be the silent service.' She turned to Landless. 'What do you think, Benjamin?'

'I'm a businessman, not a politician,' he protested coyly, but checked himself. She had offered him a chance to break into their tight circle of concerns, there was no point in turning it down. 'Very well, take a lesson from the politician's book. If a Minister wants something said but finds it injudicious to say it himself, he gets somebody else to do the talking. A fellow MP, a business leader, a newspaper editor even. You have friends,

141

influential friends. Like Lord Quillington here, with a voice and seat in the House of Lords.'

'Slave labour, rowing the Government's galley, that's all they reckon we are,' Quillington sniffed.

'And so you shall remain if you don't speak up for yourselves,' Landless warned.

'Sounds like mutiny,' his brother said from the drinks table, 'taking on the Government.'

'So what? You've got nothing to lose. Better than staying silent simply in order to be abused. Remember what they tried with the King's speech? You're in the same firing line.'

'Never did have any time for that Urquhart,' Quillington muttered into his brandy balloon.

'The press wouldn't report it anyway,' his brother commented, handing a full glass back to the Princess. When he sat down, Landless noticed he had drawn even closer to her. Their hands were side by side on the car rug.

'Some press would,' Landless interjected.

'Benjamin, of course, *you're* a darling,' Charlotte said soothingly, 'but all the rest of them are interested in is a photograph of me with my dress blown up around my ears so they can gossip about where I buy my knickers.'

It was not an entirely accurate picture, mused Landless. The press were mostly interested in where she left her underwear, not where she bought it.

'Shouldn't give honours to press men,' Mickey continued. 'Particularly peerages. Clouds their objectivity. Makes them too damned self-important.'

Landless didn't feel insulted; rather, he felt as if slowly they were beginning to offer him acceptance, setting aside the fact that he was born to a different world.

'You know, perhaps you're right,' Quillington continued. 'Hell, about the only right they allow us nowadays is to get on our hind legs in the Lords, and it's about time we started using it properly. You know, making the Lords and the hereditary principle the first line of defence for you and yours, Beany.'

'If you've anything you want to say, I'll make sure it gets an outing,' Landless offered. 'Just like we did with the Christmas speech.'

'I think we've hit on a damned fine idea, Beany,' Quillington said. Already he was beginning to expropriate the idea for his own. 'Anything you want said, I'll say it for you. If the King can't make a public speech, then I'll make it for him. Into the public record on the floor of the Lords. We mustn't let them gag us.' He nodded in self-approval. 'Sorry you can't stay the night, Landless,' he continued. 'Plenty of other ideas I'd like to try on you.' The conversion was complete. 'Some other time, eh?'

Landless understood the hint and glanced at his watch. 'Time I was going,' he offered, and rose to his feet to make his rounds of farewell.

He would be glad to get out into the fresh air. He didn't belong here, not with these people: no matter how polite they were and no matter how successful he became, he would never belong. They wouldn't allow it. He might have purchased a ticket to the dinner table, but he could never buy his way into the club. He didn't mind, he didn't care to join. This was yesterday, not tomorrow. Anyway, he'd look ridiculous on a horse. But he had no regrets. As he glanced behind him from the door, he could see his host standing by his fireplace, dreaming of chivalrous battles yet to come on the floor of the House of Lords. And he could see the Princess and the younger Quillington, already anticipating the disappearance of the outsider, holding hands on the sofa. There were stories here aplenty, with patience. It had been worth it.

The House of Commons attendant entered the gentlemen's lavatory in search of his quarry. He had an urgent message for Tom Worthington, a Labour MP from what used to be a mining constituency in Derbyshire before they closed the mines, who prided himself on his working-class origins in spite of the fact that it had been more than twenty years since anything other than ink and ketchup had stained his hands. The lavatory was inescapably Victorian with fine antique tiles and porcelain, sullied only by an electric hot-air drier at which Jeremy Colthorpe, an ageing and notoriously pompous Member from the pretentious shires, was drying his hands.

'By chance seen Mr Worthington, sir?' the attendant enquired.

'Can only handle one shit at a time in here, my man,' Colthorpe responded through his nose. 'Try one of the bars. In some corner under a table, most likely.'

The attendant scurried off as Colthorpe was joined at the wash basins by the only other man in the room, Tim Stamper.

'Timothy, dear boy. Enjoying party headquarters? Making an excellent job of it, if you don't mind my saying.'

Stamper turned from the basin and lowered his head in appreciation, but there was no warmth. Colthorpe was known for his airs, purporting to be a leader of local society, yet he'd married into every penny, which only made him still more condescending towards former estate agents. Classlessness was a concept Colthorpe would never support, having spent most of his life trying to escape from its clutches.

'Glad for a chance to speak with you actually, old chap,' Colthorpe was saying, his smile more a simper as he searched keenly in the corners of the mirror for reassurance that he and Stamper were alone in the echoing room. 'Confidentially, man to man,' he continued, trying to glance surreptitiously beneath the doors of the cubicles.

'What's on your mind, Jeremy?' Stamper responded, mindful that during all of his years in the House Colthorpe had never done more than pass the time of day with him.

'Lady wife. Getting on a bit, seventy next year. And not in the best of health. Brave gal, but finding it more than ever difficult to help in the constituency – it's damned large, forty-three villages, don't you know, takes some getting round, I can tell you.' He moved over towards Stamper at the basins and started washing his hands for the second time, trying to evince confidentiality but clearly ill at ease. 'Owe it to her to take off some of the pressure, spend a little more time together. No way of telling how long she may have.' He paused while he worked up a considerable lather as if he were always meticulous about hygiene and to emphasize the depth of his concern for his wife. Both effects were wasted on

144

Stamper who, when Deputy Chief Whip, had seen Colthorpe's private file, which included reference to the regular payments he made to a single mother who used to tend bar in his local pub.

'To be frank, I'm thinking of giving up my seat at the next election. For her sake, of course. But it'd be a damnable pity to see all that experience I've gained over the years go to waste. Would love to find some way of . . . still being able to contribute, don't you know. To go on doing my bit for the country. And the party, of course.'

'What did you have in mind, Jeremy?' Stamper already knew precisely where the conversation was headed.

'Open to suggestion. But obviously the Lords would seem a sensible option. Not for me, so much, but for the little lady. Mean a lot to her after all these years. Particularly when . . . you know, she might not have very long to enjoy it.'

Colthorpe was still splashing water around to make a pretence at casualness and had succeeded in drenching the front of his trousers. He realized he was beginning to make a fool of himself and turned the taps off with a savage twist, turning directly towards Stamper, hands by his side, water dripping from his soaked cuffs. 'Would I have your support, Tim? The backing of the party machine?'

Stamper turned away and headed for the electric hand dryer, its harsh noise forcing Colthorpe to follow him across the room, and them both to raise their voices.

'There will be quite a few colleagues retiring at the next election, Jeremy. I expect a number of them will want a seat in the Lords.'

'Wouldn't press my own case, but for the wife. I'd work hard at the job, wouldn't skive off like so many of the others.'

'Ultimately, of course, it's up to Francis. He'll have a tough job deciding between the various claims.'

'I voted for Francis . . .' – that was a lie – 'I'd be loyal.'

'Would you?' Stamper threw over his shoulder. 'Francis does value loyalty above everything.'

'Absolutely. Anything the two of you want, rely on me!'

The hand drier suddenly ceased its raucous huffing and in a moment the atmosphere had grown hushed, almost confessional.

Stamper turned to stare at Colthorpe from only a few inches away.

'Can we really rely on you, Jeremy? Loyalty first?'

Colthorpe was nodding.

'Even as far as the King is concerned?'

'The King . . . ?' Confusion crept in.

'Yes, Jeremy, the King. You've already seen how he's rocked the boat. And Francis fears it's going to get worse. The Palace needs reminding, very firmly, who's in charge.'

'But I'm not sure . . .'

'Loyalty, Jeremy. That's what will make the difference between those who get what they want out of this Government, and those who don't. It's an unpleasant business, this thing with the Palace, but somebody has to stand up and defend the important constitutional principles at stake. Francis can't, you see, not formally and publicly as Prime Minister. That would create a constitutional crisis, which he absolutely does not want. The only way to avoid that may be to get someone other than a Minister, someone with great seniority and authority – someone like you, Jeremy – to remind the Palace and the public what's at stake. It's the least Francis has a right to expect from his loyal supporters.'

'Yes, but . . . Get into the House of Lords by attacking the King?'

'Not attacking. Reminding him of the highest constitutional principles.'

'But it's the King who creates new peers—'

'Solely and exclusively on the advice of the Prime Minister. The King cannot refuse his recommendations.'

'It's a little like *Alice In Wonderland*—'

'So's a lot of what the Palace has been saying.'

'I'd like to think about it a little.'

'You need to think about loyalty?' Stamper's tone was harsh, accusatory. His lip curled in contempt and there was fire in the sepulchral eyes. Without a further word the Party Chairman turned on his heel and made his way towards the door. His hand was already on the shiny brass door knob, and Colthorpe realized his ambitions were ruined if the door closed on this conversation.

'I'll do it!' he squealed. 'Tim, I know where my loyalties lie. I'll do it.' He was breathing heavily with the tension and confusion, trying to regain his self-control, wiping his hands on his trousers. 'You can rely on me, old chap.'

Stamper held his stare, spreading his lips in the coldest of smiles. Then he closed the door behind him.

The lunch had started excellently. Both Mickey Quillington and his first cousin, Lord Chesholm of Kinsale, appreciated a good claret and the cellar of the House of Lords dining room had a large number from which to choose. They had chosen to drink Leoville-Barton but were unable to decide between the '82 and '85 vintage. So they had ordered a bottle of both and slipped gently into mid-afternoon in the warm embrace of the elegant mahogany panelling and attentive staff. Chesholm was a good twenty years older than Quillington and substantially more wealthy, and the impecunious younger peer had hoped to use the lunch for the launch of an appeal to family solidarity which would involve his relative in leasing several hundred of Quillington's Oxfordshire acres at a generous rate, but sadly his tactics had gone awry. The claret proved too much for the elderly peer to manage and he couldn't concentrate, repeatedly exclaiming that he didn't live in Oxfordshire. The bill, although heavily subsidized, still reflected the exceptional nature of the wine and Quillington felt bruised. Maybe the old bugger would regain his wits by teatime.

They were attending the House to voice objection to a Bill which sought a total ban on fox-hunting, and the debate was well underway by the time they took their places on the deep-red morocco benches in the Gothic chamber. Within minutes Chesholm was asleep while Quillington slouched with his knees tucked beneath his chin as he listened with growing resentment to a former polytechnic lecturer, recently elevated to the life-peerage for his diligence in the study of trade union matters, expounding his belief in the decay and corruption of those who still believed they owned the countryside as if by divine right. Debates in the Lords are conducted in far less pompous and vitriolic style than in the Lower Chamber, as befits its aristocratic and almost familial atmosphere,

147

but the lack of outright rudeness did not prevent the peer from putting across his point of view forcefully and effectively. From around the Chamber, uncharacteristically packed for the occasion by hereditary peers and noble backwoodsmen from distant rural parts, came a growl of wounded pride, like a stuck boar at bay. Such displays of emotion are not commonplace in the Upper Chamber, but such a concentration of hereditary peers was also unusual outside the circumstance of state funeral or Royal wedding. It may not have been the Lords at their norm, nor even at their best, but it was certainly their Lordships at their most decorous.

Quillington cleared his throat; the debate was threatening to spoil the warm glow left by the claret. The poly-peer had broadened his attack from fox-hunting itself to those who hunted, and Quillington took great exception. He was not the type of person who rode roughshod over others' rights; he'd never forced any farm labourer out of a tied cottage, and any damage inadvertently caused while hunting was always paid for. Blast the man, the Quillingtons had been dedicated custodians. It had cost them their fortune and his father's health and had left his mother with little but years of tearful widowhood. Yet here was an oaf who had spent all his working life in some overheated lecture room living off an inflation-proofed salary, accusing him of being no better than a scrounger. It was too much, really too bloody much. This sort of wheedling and insolent insinuation had gone on for too long, harking back to a style of class warfare which was fifty years out of date.

''Bout time we put them in their place, don't you think, Chesy?' Almost before he realized it, Quillington was on his feet.

'This debate is only nominally about fox-hunting, that is merely the excuse. Behind it lies an insidious attack on the traditions and values which have not only held our countryside together, not only held this House together, but have held the whole of society together. There are wreckers in the land, some maybe even amongst our number here' – he deliberately avoided looking at the previous speaker, so that everyone would know precisely whom he meant – 'who in the name of democracy would force their own narrow, militant opinions upon the rest, the silent majority which is the true and glorious backbone of Britain.'

148

He licked his lips, there was a flush in his cheeks, a mixture of Leoville-Barton and real emotion that succeeded in engulfing the unease he customarily felt in public, which on more than one occasion had left him tongue-tied and floundering at the opening of the annual village fête. 'They want revolution, no less. They would abandon our traditions, abolish this Chamber, stamp on our rights.' Quillington waved a finger at the canopied Throne which dominated one end of the hall and stood empty and forlorn. 'They even seek to reduce to silence and insignificance our own Royal Family.'

Several of Their Lordships raised a collective eyebrow. The rules about discussion of the Royal Family were very restrictive, particularly in a debate on blood sports. 'To the point, my Lord,' one growled in warning.

'But, noble Lords, this *is* the point,' protested Quillington. 'We are not here to rubber-stamp what comes from the Lower House. We are here to offer counsel, advice, warning. And we do so, just as the Monarch does, because we represent the true long-term interests of this country. We represent the values which have made our nation great over previous centuries and which will continue to guide her well into the next century. We are not here to be swayed by every passing fashion and fad. We do not suffer from the corruption of having to get ourselves elected, of having to pretend that we are all things to all men, of making promises we know we cannot keep. We are here to represent what is immutable and constant in society.'

Mutters of 'Hear, hear' could be heard from the crowded benches around Quillington. The Lord Chancellor drummed his fingers as he concentrated in bewigged and ermined splendour from his seat on the Woolsack; the speech was most unusual, but really rather a splendid entertainment.

'It may seem a long way from the plottings of hunt-saboteurs to assaults on Buckingham Palace, but what we have seen of both recently should encourage us to stand firm in our beliefs, not to run for the cover of undergrowth like terrified vermin.' His long, thin arms were extended theatrically away from his body, as if trying to haul in their sympathy. He needn't have bothered, peers were beginning to nod and tap their knees to indicate support.

149

'Both this House and the Royal Family are here to defend those timeless aspects of the national interest, unfettered by the selfishness of The Other Place. There is no need for this House to kowtow to the muscle and money of commercial interests!' The poly-peer was sitting upright, ready to try and intervene. He was sure Quillington was about to go too far. 'Not for us the temptations of bribing the public with their own money, we are here to defend the public against shortsightedness and falsehood. And at no time is that duty more pressing upon us than when we have a new Cabinet and a Prime Minister who have not even been elected by the people. Let him go to the country promising to castrate the Monarch and abolish the House of Lords if he dare, but until he has won that right and power at an election, let us not allow him to do quietly and privately what he has not yet been able to do publicly.'

The poly-peer had had enough. He was not quite sure what transgression Quillington was making, but the emotional temperature in the Chamber had soared, shouts of support for Quillington were coming from all sides, and the poly-peer suddenly felt the Chamber close in around him like a courtroom dock. 'Order! The noble Lord must restrain himself,' he interjected.

'Why . . . ?' 'No, let him go on . . .' 'Allow him to finish . . .' On all sides Quillington was being offered advice and encouragement, while the poly-peer sprang to his feet, shouting across the Chamber and wagging his finger in vain. Quillington had won, and knew it.

'I have finished, my Lords. Do not forget your duty, nor your allegiance to the King, nor the sacrifices which you and your forefathers accepted in order to make this nation great. Use this wretched Bill to remind others that you have not forgotten, and let the lion roar once more!'

He sat down as peers took their Order Papers and rapped them sharply on the leather benches in front of them to show their approbation.

As Order Papers beat down either side of his head, the elderly Chesholm woke with a start. 'What? What was that? Did I miss something, Mickey?'

*   *   *

'On a Point of Order, Madam Speaker.'

'Point of Order, Mr Jeremy Colthorpe.'

Madam Speaker's shrill voice cut through the din of the House of Commons as MPs milled around preparing to vote after an Opposition debate on sub-standard housing, which had just wound its way through three turbid hours. Normally Madam Speaker was caustic about points of order raised during divisions and, indeed, the ancient rules of the House made such interruptions problematic by requiring the MP to have his head covered – in order better to be seen amidst the confusion, so said the rule book; to deflect idle time-wasters, according to common sense. But Colthorpe was a Member of long standing and not a renowned trouble-maker; he stood defiantly if somewhat absurdly attired in a collapsible opera hat kept in the Chamber for the purpose. Points of order often had an element of comedy to them, and the bustle in the Chamber subsided as MPs strained to hear what was upsetting the old man.

'Madam Speaker, on rare occasions a question of such importance and urgency arises that it is of overriding importance to the business of the House, and you decide it is necessary for the appropriate Minister to be summoned before us to answer for it. I believe this matter is just that.' It was more than that. News of Quillington's speech had drifted through the tea rooms and bars of the House of Commons even as Colthorpe was still chiding himself for making such a nonsense of his exchange with Stamper; he didn't have much practice in grovelling to estate agents, he told himself, and he knew he'd made a hash of it. He had listened to reports of the peer's words like a drowning man greets the sound of an approaching rescue ship, and had bustled off to find Stamper, terrified that someone else would find him first. Within forty minutes he was back in the Chamber, and on his feet.

'Earlier this afternoon, in Another Place, a noble Lord accused this House of political corruption, of seeking to deprive both their Lordships and His Majesty the King of their constitutional rights, and claiming that His Majesty had been improperly silenced. Such a challenge to the actions of this House and to the office of the Prime Minister is such as to—'

151

'Hold on a minute!' Madam Speaker enjoined Colthorpe to silence in a broad Lancashire accent. 'I've heard nothing about this. Most improper. You know it's against the rules of this House to discuss personal matters relating to the King.'

'This is not a personal matter but a constitutional matter of the highest importance, Madam Speaker. The rights of this House are enshrined in custom and established over the course of many years. When they are challenged, they must be defended.'

'Nevertheless, I want to see what was said before I allow this one to run.' The Speaker waved Colthorpe down but he was not to be deflected.

'We tarry and delay at our peril, Madam Speaker. This is just another example of the interfering, interventionist tendencies of the mod-Monarchy—'

'That's enough!' She was on her feet now, staring furiously over half-moon glasses, demanding Colthorpe subside.

'But Madam Speaker, we must be allowed to respond to attacks made on us, no matter from what source those attacks emanate. The debate in Another Place, ostensibly about fox-hunting, has been turned into a direct assault on this Chamber. Now, Madam Speaker, I don't wish to impugn the integrity of anyone wishing to make such attacks . . .'

She liked the sound of that, and hesitated.

'It is possible, I suppose,' Colthorpe continued, 'to care passionately for the welfare of the nation from the back of a horse while out pursuing foxes.' There was an amused growl of support from the benches around. 'It may even be possible to identify with the plight of the homeless from within the luxury of a palace – indeed, several palaces. It may even be possible, I could not deny it, that being driven around the country in chauffeured limousines and private trains with forty carriages affords a unique insight into the problems of those confined to wheelchairs . . .'

'Forty coaches?' a voice queried. 'What on earth does he need with forty coaches?'

Madam Speaker was on her feet again, lifting onto her toes, trying to give herself added height and authority and angrily pointing her glasses in his direction, but Colthorpe, voice rising in turn, ignored her.

'It may also be possible for those who live entirely off the backs of taxpayers and who pay no tax at all to accuse those who do of greed and selfishness. It is possible, Madam Speaker, but isn't it more likely that this is just another load of the organic fertilizer which gets spread all over the Palace Gardens?'

The Speaker's cries of 'Order! Order!' were lost amidst the instant hubbub. 'If the Honourable Gentleman doesn't resume his seat immediately I shall be forced to name him,' she mouthed, threatening Colthorpe with the procedure that would eject him from Parliament for the rest of the week's business. But already it was too late. As Colthorpe looked towards the press gallery he could see scribes furiously tearing at their notebooks. There would be a posse of them waiting as he left the Chamber. His point had already been made; he would be named in every morning newspaper. 'Order! O-o-o-order!' cried the Speaker. With what he hoped was a bow of great dignity, which caused the opera hat to tumble from his head and roll across the floor, Colthorpe resumed his seat.

Landless was having his hair trimmed when the call came through, and he didn't care for being disturbed at such moments. His secretary thought his reluctance arose from embarrassment because his hairdresser, who visited the businessman once a fortnight at his office, was what she called 'delicate', but Landless didn't mind. Quentin was the only barber he'd ever found who could manage to keep his rope-like hair under control without larding it in hair cream and, besides, the Landless reputation with women was sufficiently beyond dispute to survive contact with an affected queen. In truth the hairdresser was a disgraceful gossip who had a fund of stories about his other fashionable clients, all of whom seemed to regard him as a father-confessor for their sex lives. Landless never ceased to be intrigued by what others would admit to or fantasize about under the influence of nothing more potent than shampoo and an expert scalp massage. He kept his own mouth shut, and

153

listened. He was engrossed in a fascinating report of what other parts of his body the country's leading romantic soap star shaved, and in what designs, when the whine of the telephone dragged him away.

It was his editor-in-chief, seeking guidance, covering his ass as usual. But Landless didn't object, not on this occasion. This was his story, after all.

'How are the others going to play it?' he growled.

'No one's quite sure. This story's so out of the ordinary.' The issue involved King, Prime Minister, Lords and Commons – the Archbishop wasn't in there yet, but doubtless the *Sun* or *Mirror* would find some connection. Yet it had been raised by two such nonentities – few had heard of Colthorpe, none of Quillington. It was a sensitive issue, perhaps an item on the parliamentary page?

'Any guidance from Downing Street?'

'They're cautious. Clean hands, so they insist. Serious issues which they understand must be reported and all that, but suggest Quillington's a fool and Colthorpe went over the top. They don't want a repeat of what happened before Christmas.'

'But they didn't request we spike it, either?'

'No.'

'Colthorpe tried to shift the argument away from a divided nation to hard cash. Clever – too clever for him on his own. They're flying kites. Trying it out with Colthorpe to see if it gets a fair wind.'

'So what do we do?'

It was not so much that he had promised Quillington, it was more instinct – the instinct of a man who had been used to street-fighting all his life, used to recognizing the difference between shadows that provided cover and those that hid the enemy. He trusted his instincts, and they told him that amongst these shadows there lurked the figure of Francis Urquhart. If Landless threw a little light around, who knows what he might flush out. Anyway, he had a lot of money invested in the Royal Family and there was no dividend in it unless the Royal Family was news. Good, bad, indifferent news, he didn't mind – so long as it was news.

'Splash it. Page One lead.'

'You think it's that big?'

'We make it that big.'

There was agitated breathing on the end of the phone as the editor tried to catch up and comprehend his proprietor's flow of logic. 'Peers Attack Urquhart?' he suggested, practising a few headlines. 'PM Unelected and Unelectable, Say King's Allies?'

'No, you bloody idiot. Six weeks ago we were telling the world what a fine, noble creature he was. From Roger Rabbit to Rasputin in one bound is more than even our readers will swallow. You make it balanced, fair, authoritative. Just make it big.'

'You want to catch the others standing on this one.' It was an assumption, not a question: this was going to be a front page like none of the competition.

'No, not on this one,' Landless responded thoughtfully. 'Spread word around the news room.'

'But that'll mean it will be all through Fleet Street in under an hour.' They both knew there were journalists in the news room taking backhanders for alerting their rivals to what was going on, just as they paid for whispers in the other direction. 'They'll all follow. Think we're up to something, know something they don't. No one will want to be caught out, it'll be used on every front page . . . ?'

'Precisely. This one is going to be a runner, because we're going to make it run. Freely, fairly, in the national interest. Until the time comes for us to climb down off the fence, by which time the noise we make will give our Mr Urquhart nightmares for months. That's when we make sure he's not only unelected, but unelectable.'

He dropped the phone back into its cradle and turned to Quentin, who was propping himself up against a far wall of the huge marble-covered private bathroom, seemingly engrossed in pursuit of a stray eyelash.

'Quentin, do you remember King Edward the Second?'

'You mean the one they did for with the red-hot poker?' He puckered his lips in distaste at the legend of sordid butchery.

'If I hear a word of this conversation breathed outside these walls, you're going to become Quentin the First. And I personally am going to administer the poker. Get it?'

Quentin tried hard, very hard, to imagine the newspaper man

155

was joking. He smiled encouragingly, but all he received in return was a sustained glare which left no room for doubt. Quentin remembered that Landless had never joked. He went back to cutting the hair, and said not another word.

She had taken the first editions up herself. She'd bumped into the messenger on the stairs.

'Nice to see you again, Miss.'

'Again' – Sally thought she detected undue inflexion on the word. Perhaps it was her imagination – or her guilt? No, not guilt. She had long ago decided not to run her life by codes and rules which others so blithely ignored. She owed no one, and there was no sense in being the only impoverished virgin in the cemetery.

He laid the newspapers side by side on the floor, and stood over them for a considerable time, lost in thought.

'It's started, Sally,' he said at last. She noted an edge of apprehension. 'Soon we shall be beyond the point of no return.'

'To victory.'

'Or to hell.'

'Come on, Francis, it's what you wanted. People beginning to ask questions.'

'Don't misunderstand. I'm not despondent, only a little cautious. I'm an Englishman, after all, and he is my King. And it appears we are not alone in asking questions. Who is this Quillington, this unknown peer with a mission?'

'Don't you know? He's the brother of the man who is, as it is said, close enough to Princess Charlotte to catch her colds. Always in the gossip columns.'

'You read gossip columns?' He was surprised; it was one of Elizabeth's least attractive breakfast traits. He eyed Sally closely, wondering if he would ever get the chance to eat breakfast with her.

'Many of my clients live in them. Pretend to be upset when they appear, are mortified when they don't.'

'So Quillington's a King's man, is he? And the King's men are already answering the call to battle.' He was still standing over the papers.

156

'Talking of clients, Francis, you said you'd introduce me to some new contacts, but I've not met anyone apart from the occasional messenger and tea lady. For some reason we seem to spend all our time alone.'

'We're never truly alone. It's impossible in this place.'

She came behind him and slid her hands around his chest, burying her face in the crisp, clean cotton of his shirt. She could smell him, the male smell, its muskiness mixed with the pine starch and the faint tang of cologne, and she could feel the body heat already rising. She knew it was the danger he enjoyed, which made him feel he was conquering not only her but, through her, the entire world. The fact that at any moment a messenger or civil servant might blunder in only heightened his sense of awareness and drive; while he was having her he felt invincible. The time would come when he would feel like that all the time, would dispense with caution and recognize no rules other than his own, and even as he reached the height of his powers he would begin the downward slide to defeat. It happened to them all. They begin to convince themselves that each new challenge is no longer new but is simply a repeat of old battles already fought and won. Their minds begin to close, they lose touch and flexibility, are no longer attuned to the dangers they confront. Vision becomes stale repetition. Not Urquhart, not yet, but sometime. She didn't mind being used, so long as she could use him, too, and so long as she remembered that this, like all things, couldn't last forever. She ran her hands down his chest, poking her fingers between his shirt buttons. Prime Ministers are always pushed, initially by their own vanity and sense of impregnability, and eventually by the electorate or their own colleagues and political friends. Although not by a King, not for many years.

'Don't worry about your clients, Sally. I'll fix it.'

'Thank you, Francis.' She kissed the back of his neck, the fingers still descending on his buttons as though she were practising a piano scale.

'You understand your job exceptionally well,' he breathed.

'Mrs Urquhart not around?'

'She's visiting her sister. In Fife.'

157

'Sounds a long way away.'

'It is.'

'I see.'

She had run out of buttons. He was still standing, newspapers at his feet, facing the door like Horatius at the bridge, ready to take on any intruders, feeling omnipotent. When he was like this, with her, she knew that nothing else mattered for him. Part of him yearned for the door to burst open and for all of Downing Street to see him with this much younger, desirable woman and to understand what a true man he was. Perhaps he hadn't realized that they had stopped barging in with their interminable messages and Cabinet papers while she was here, always finding an excuse to telephone ahead first, or simply not bothering to come at all. They knew, of course they knew. But maybe he didn't know they knew. Maybe he was already losing touch.

'Francis,' she whispered in his ear. 'I know it's late. It will be in darkness, but . . . You always promised to show me the Cabinet Room. Your special chair.'

He couldn't answer. Her fingers held him speechless.

'Francis? Please . . .'

He hadn't slept again. And he knew he was beginning to get things out of proportion. Ridiculous things like his tooth mug. The valet had changed it, just like that, assuming as they all did that they knew best what was good for him. It had caused an unholy, spitting row, and now he felt ashamed. He'd got his mug back, but in the process lost his equilibrium and dignity. Yet somehow knowing what was happening to him only seemed to make it worse.

The face in the bathroom mirror looked haggard, aged, the crow's feet around the eyes like great talons of revenge, the fire within damped and exhausted. As he studied his own image he saw reflected the face of his father, fierce, intemperate, unyielding. He shivered. He was growing old even before his life had properly started, a lifetime spent waiting for his parents to die just as now his own children waited for him. If he died today there would be a huge state funeral at which millions would mourn. But how many would remember him? Not him the figurehead, but him, the man?

As a child there had been some compensations. He remembered his favourite game dashing back and forth in front of the Palace guard, all the time being greeted with the satisfying clatter of boots being scraped and arms being presented until both he and the guard were breathless. But it had never been a proper childhood, alone and unable to reach out and touch like other children, and now they were intent on depriving him of his manhood, too. He would watch television yet couldn't understand half the commercials. A stream of messages about mortgages, savings plans, money dispensers, new liquids for washing whiter and gadgets which got the paint into those difficult corners and out of the bristles of the brush. It was as though the messages came from another planet. He already had the softest brand of toilet tissue, but hadn't the slightest idea where to buy it. He didn't even have to take the top off his toothpaste in the morning or change a razor blade. It was all done for him, everything. His life was unreal, somehow so irrelevant, a gilded cage of miseries. Even the girls they'd found to help with some of the basics had called him 'Sir', not only when they first met and in public, but later when they were alone, in bed, with nothing else between them other than an enthusiastic sweat while showing him how the rest of the world spent their time.

He'd done his best, everything that was expected of him and more. He'd learned Welsh, walked the Highlands, captained his own ship, flown helicopters and jumped out of planes at five thousand feet, presided over charity committees, opened the hospital wings and unveiled their plaques, laughed at the humiliations and lamentable impersonations, ignored the insults, bitten his lip at the vicious untruths about his family and turned the other cheek, crawled on his belly through the mud and slime of military training grounds just as he was expected to crawl through the mud and slime of Fleet Street. He'd done everything they had asked of him, yet still it was not enough. The harder he strived, the more cruel their jests and barbs became. The job, the expectations, had grown too much for any man.

He looked at the bony, balding head, so like his father's, and the sagging eyes. He'd already seen the morning newspapers, the reports of the debates, the speculation and innuendo, the pont-ification of the leader-writers who either discussed him as if he were known so intimately to them they could peer deep into his soul, or treated him as if he, the man, simply didn't exist. He was their chattel, a possession brought out on display at their con-venience to sign their legislation, cut their ribbons and help sell their newspapers. They wouldn't allow him to join the rest of the world yet deprived him of the simple solace of being alone.

The once clear blue eyes were bloodshot with fatigue and doubt. Somehow he had to find courage, a way out, before they broke him. But there was no way out for a King. Slowly his hand began to tremble, uncontrollably, as his thoughts began to tangle in con-fusion, and the tooth mug started to shake. His damp fingers gripped white around the porcelain, struggling to regain control, yet it was all slipping away and the mug flew off as though possessed, grazed the edge of the bath and bounced onto the tiled floor. He stared after it, captivated, as if watching the performance of a tragic ballet. The mug gave several tiny skips, the handle bouncing this way and that, waving at him, taunting him until, with a final extravagant leap of despair, it twisted over and smashed into a hundred angry, savage teeth. His favourite tooth mug was gone after all. And it was their fault.

January: The Third Week

'Couldn't I have done this at the Cup Final, Tim? You know how I hate football.' Urquhart was already having to raise his voice to make himself heard above the crowd, and the match hadn't even started.

'Final's not until May, and we don't have time.' Stamper's bright eyes darted around the ground. His pleasure was not going to be diluted by the whingeing of his boss; he had been a keen fan since the days he was no bigger than a football. Anyway, it was part of his programme to make Urquhart appear a man amongst the people, a Prime Minister out enjoying himself and keeping in touch. The media would get bored eventually with such spoon-feeding but not, Stamper had reasoned, before March. This was an ideal occasion, a floodlit European Championship qualifying match against arch rivals Germany with passions of victorious wars and World Cup defeats being rekindled on the terraces and in front of televisions throughout every constituency. As he had reminded the recalcitrant Urquhart several times, soccer fans may not have as much money as the crowd at the Opera House, but they have many more votes and Urquhart was there to be seen helping them defend the nation's honour.

A roar engulfed them as a Mexican wave rippled around the ground, the fans throwing themselves from their seats in the image of their forefathers going over the top at the Somme, Verdun, Vimy Ridge and countless other bloody encounters with the Hun. The VIPs' box was littered with an assortment of half-consumed drinks, overweight football bureaucrats and magazines carrying the latest news of twisted ligaments and even more distorted dressing-room gossip. None of it was to the Prime Minister's taste and he sat hunched over, seeming to have withdrawn inside the folds of his overcoat, yet as Stamper leaned over Urquhart's shoulder from his seat in the row behind he discovered his leader engrossed in the screen of a miniature television, less than three inches across. He was watching the evening news.

'She's getting too old for a bikini, if you want my opinion,' Stamper bantered.

The liquid-crystal display shone bright with the image of a paparazzi photograph, slightly shaky with the effect of a gentle Caribbean swell on the long-distance lens, but unmistakably showing Princess Charlotte cavorting on a secluded beach. The tropical colours were brilliant.

'You don't do our Royal Family justice, Tim. She is doing nothing improper. It is not a crime, after all, for a princess to be seen on a beach with a tanned companion, even if he happens to be considerably younger and slimmer than she. Nor does it matter that only last week she was skiing in Gstaad. You simply have no appreciation of how hard the Royal Family works. And I do deprecate the unpleasant British characteristic of envy, that simply because we are sitting here freezing our balls off in January while the country is slipping into recession, we should criticize those who happen to be more fortunate than ourselves.'

'I fear others won't see it in quite the same noble light as you.'

Urquhart wrapped the car rug more tightly around his knees and fortified himself from a thermos of hot coffee amply laced with whisky. He might feign being a young man while astride Sally, but the cold night air stripped away such pretences with little mercy. His breath was condensing in clouds. 'I fear you are right, Tim. More lurid stories about how many holidays she's had in the last year, how many nights she's spent in different parts of the country from the Prince, when she last saw the children. The gutter press will read anything into one harmless holiday snap.'

'OK, Francis. What the hell are you up to?'

Urquhart turned in his seat so that Stamper could hear him better above the noise around the stadium. He took another sip of coffee. 'I've been thinking. The agreement on the Civil List expires shortly and we've just begun renegotiating the Royal Family's income for the next ten years. The Palace have put in a pretty tall bid based

162

on what some would say was an unreasonably high forecast of inflation over the coming years. It's only an opening position, of course, something to bargain with, to make sure we are not too mean with them. It would be all too easy at a time of general belt-tightening to squeeze them, to argue that they should share the burdens along with the rest of us.' He arched an eyebrow, and smiled. 'But I think that would be shortsighted, don't you?'

'Give it to me, Francis. Unravel the workings of that devious mind of yours, because you're way ahead of me and I don't think I'm going to catch up.'

'I take that as a compliment. Listen, and learn, Timothy.' Urquhart was enjoying this. Stamper was good, very good, yet he didn't have the magnificent view of the political lowlands afforded from the window of Number Ten. And he didn't have Sally, either. 'I keep reading in the press that we are moving to a position of constitutional . . . competition, shall we say, between King and Prime Minister, in which the King appears to have considerable if uninformed popular support. If I squeeze him on the Civil List I shall simply be accused of churlishness. On the other hand if I choose to be generous, it will prove I am fair-minded and responsible.'

'As always,' the Party Chairman mocked.

'Unfortunately, the press and public have a simplistic way of looking at the Civil List as rather like a Royal salary. The going rate for the job. And I'm afraid the media will not take kindly to a family which celebrates a huge pay increase by dashing off from ski-slope to sun-blanched beach while the rest of us shiver. Even responsible editors like our friend Brynford-Jones are likely to misunderstand.'

'I shall insist on it!' Stamper shouted above the loudspeaker system introducing the players.

'If it appears the Royal Family is abusing the Government's generosity, I fear that would be more of a problem for the King than the Prime Minister. Little I can do about it. Hope he doesn't find it too much of a distraction.'

The pitch was in brilliant floodlight, the teams lined up, the referee ready, the official photographs taken, the stadium noisy with the clamour of sixty thousand fans. Suddenly the chorus of raucous shouts subsided to a conspiratorial rustle.

'God Save The King, Tim!'

As Urquhart stood with Stamper for the playing of the national anthem, he felt warmer. He thought, above the perfunctory singing of the crowd, he could hear the sound of falling branches.

The King's desk was a mess. Books and copies of *Hansard* were piled along the front edge with pieces of paper sticking out like weeds to mark passages for future reference, the telephone had become submerged beneath a tide of computer print-out bearing the accounts of the Duchy of Lancaster, and an empty plate, which had earlier carried his lunch of a single round of wholemeal bread and smoked salmon, floated aimlessly around. Only the photograph of the children in its plain silver mount seemed immune from the encroachment, standing alone like a desert island amidst stormy seas. Typically, his brow was furrowed as he read the report on the Civil List.

'A little surprising, don't you think, David?'

'Frankly astonishing. We seem to be enjoying the spoils of victory without my being aware we've yet been engaged in combat. It's not what I expected.'

'Could it be a peace signal? There's been far too much gossip about the Palace and Downing Street. Maybe this a chance for a new start. Eh, David?' The voice sounded tired, lacking in conviction.

'Maybe,' Mycroft responded.

'It's certainly generous.'

'More generous than I realized he could be.'

The eyes shot a look of reproach across the jumbled desk. He was not a cynic, he liked to think of himself as a builder who found the best in people. It was one of his most infuriating characteristics, Mycroft had always thought. Yet the King did not disagree.

'It enables us to be generous in return.' The King had risen from his chair and moved to gaze out of the window across the gardens, slowly twisting his signet ring. The new gardens were beginning to

164

show definitive and distinctive form, and he found great solace as his mind filled in the many gaps and created a vista of beauty in front of him. 'You know, David, I've always thought it anomalous, embarrassing even, that our private income from the properties and interests owned by the Duchy of Lancaster and elsewhere remains free of tax. I'm the richest man in the country, yet I pay no income tax, no capital gains tax, no inheritance tax, nothing. And still in addition I get a Civil List allowance of several millions which is just about to be substantially increased.' He turned and clapped his hands. 'It's time for us to join the rest of the world. In exchange for the new Civil List, we should agree to pay tax on the rest of our incomes.'

'You mean a token payment?'

'No, no gestures. The full going-rate on it all.'

'But there's no need,' Mycroft protested. 'There's no real pressure on you, no controversy about it. Once you agree to it you'll never be able to renege. You will be binding your children and your children's children, no matter what Government is in power and no matter how punitive the taxes might be.'

'I have no intention of reneging!' His tone was sharp, a flush in his cheeks. 'I'm doing it because I think it is right. I've been over the Duchy accounts in great detail. Heavens, those assets should provide enough income for half a dozen Royal families.'

'Very well, Sir. If you insist.' Mycroft felt chided. It was his duty to offer advice and sound cautionary notes, and he did not care for being scolded. Even after the long years of friendship he was still not comfortable with the Monarch's flashes of impatience; it's what came of waiting a lifetime yet being in such a hurry, he told himself. And the outbursts were growing more frequent in the few short months since he had been on the Throne. 'What of the rest of the Family? You expect them also to volunteer tax?'

'I do. It would be a nonsense if the King were to pay tax yet more junior members of the Firm were not. People wouldn't understand. *I* wouldn't understand. Particularly not after the sort of press they've managed to organize for themselves recently. I know the media are vultures, but do we really have to offer ourselves up on plates ready to be devoured? A lot more clothing and a little more common sense wouldn't go amiss at times.' It was as close as he would come to personal criticism of his own family, but it had been no secret in the sculleries and laundry rooms of the Palace how incensed he'd been, both with Princess Charlotte's lack of discretion and the media's lack of restraint.

'If you are to . . . persuade them to forgo substantial income, the word needs to come directly from you. You can't expect them to take that sort of idea from me or any other aide.' Mycroft sounded restless. He had been sent before on similar errands to members of the Royal Family. He found that the more junior the rank, the more hostile grew their reception.

The King managed a rueful smile which turned his face down at one corner. 'You're right to be squeamish. I suspect any messenger sent on such a delicate task would return with his turban nailed firmly to his head. Don't worry, David, this one's for me. Brief them, if you will, on the new Civil List arrangements. Then prepare a short paper for me setting out the arguments and arrange for them to come and see me. Separately rather than in a gang. I don't want to be subjected to yet another collective family mugging around the dinner table, not on this one.'

'Some are abroad at the moment. It may take several days.'

'It has already taken several lifetimes, David.' The King sighed. 'I don't think a few more days can matter very much . . .'

The British Airways 747–400 from Kingston arrived ten minutes behind schedule on the approach to Heathrow, unable to make up the delay caused by a picket line of striking passport officers which had stretched around the departure terminal and spilled onto parts of the tropical runway. The flight had missed the pre-arranged landing slot and normally might have had to circle for another fifteen or twenty minutes before air-traffic control found a suitable gap in the queue, but this was not a normal flight and the captain was given immediate permission to land as twelve other flights which had arrived on schedule were shuffled back into the pack. The Princess was waiting to disembark the moment the wheels touched down.

The Boeing had taxied to a terminal in one of the quieter corners of the airport and normally the Princess and her escorts would be driven directly out of Heathrow through a private perimeter gateway. She would be back at Kensington Palace even before her fellow passengers had struggled to the head of the taxi rank. Today, however, the Princess did not drive directly away. First she had to collect the keys of her new car.

It had been a foul few months for all manufacturers of luxury cars and the prospects for the rest of the year looked worse. Trade was tough; sales – and sales promotions – were at a premium. So it had seemed an excellent idea for Maserati UK to offer the Princess a free edition of their latest and most sporty model in the expectation of considerable and on-going publicity. She had accepted with alacrity. As the aircraft drew alongside its arrival gate the managing director of Maserati waited anxiously on the tarmac, keys tied with an extravagant pink bow dangling from nervous fingers, eyeing the clouds. He could have wished for a kinder day, the intermittent drizzle had necessitated copious attention to the bodywork to keep it shining, but there were compensations. The media coverage afforded the Princess in recent days had considerably increased both the size and the enthusiasm of the press contingent lined up beside his car. The publicity value of his shares in the Princess had already increased considerably.

She breezed onto the damp tarmac with a polished white smile and tan which defied the elements. It would take less than ten minutes, a few words of greeting and thanks with the anxious little man in the shiny mohair suit waving the keys, a brief photo-call as the cameras compared her bodywork with that of the fierce red Maserati, and a couple of minutes spent driving slowly round in circles as she discovered the location of the gears and they squeezed off a few feet of promotional video. A breeze, and fair exchange of her time for a growling new £95,000 four-and-a-half litre turbo-charged mechanical Italian beast.

The press, of course, had other ideas, wanting to enquire after her holiday and the whereabouts of her husband and holiday companion, but she was having none of it. 'The Princess will entertain questions only about the car, gentlemen,' an aide had announced.

Why not a Jaguar – because it was American owned. How many other cars did she have – none like this wicked brute. What's the top speed – seventy miles an hour while I'm driving. Hadn't she recently been clocked at over a hundred on the M1 – a sweet smile and a grab for the next question. Would she lean a little lower over the bonnet for the benefit of the cameras – you guys must be joking. The next shower of rain looked imminent and already it was time for a few quick revolutions around the cameras before departing. She climbed in as gracefully as the low-slung bodywork would allow and wound down the window for a final smile at the jackal pack as they closed in.

'Isn't it a bit demeaning for a Princess to flog foreign cars?' a sharp voice asked bluntly.

Bloody typical. They were always at it. Her cheeks coloured beneath her tan. 'I spend my entire life "flogging", as you so snidely put it. I flog British exports wherever I go. I flog overpriced tickets for charity dinners to help the starving in Africa. I flog lottery tickets so we can build retirement homes for pensioners. I never stop flogging.'

'But flogging flash foreign sports cars?' the voice continued.

'It's you lot who demand the flash. If I turned up in second-hand clothes or third-hand cars, you'd be the first to complain. I have to earn my living the same as everybody else.' The smile had disappeared.

'What about the Civil List?'

'If you knew how difficult it was to do everything that's expected of you on a Princess's allowance, you wouldn't ask such bloody fool questions!'

That was enough. They were goading her, she was losing her temper, it was time to go. She slipped the clutch, a fraction impatiently, for the car began to perform inelegant kangaroo hops towards the cameramen who scattered in alarm. Serve the bastards right. The V-8 engine stalled, the man in the shiny suit looked dismayed and the cameras snapped angrily. She restarted, selected a gear and was off. Damn their impertinence. Back at the Palace after only a week away she would be greeted with a small hillock of paperwork which would contain countless invitations, more requests and begging letters from charities and the underprivileged. She would show them. She would answer all the invitations, accept as many as possible, go on eating the dinners and raising the monies, smiling at the old and the young, the sick and the infirm, comforting those who were just plain unlucky. She would ignore the jibes and go on working hard, as she always did, grinding away through the hillock. She had no way of knowing that on top of the unopened pile lay a brief telling her about arrangements for the new Civil List, and that already copy was being prepared for the morning editions attacking a pouting princess in a brand new foreign sports car who complained she was not paid enough.

Misery in a Maserati.

The image of the Princess's glowing brake lights faded from the television as Urquhart hit the red button. His attention stayed fixed on the blank screen for a long time, his half-knotted tie hanging limply around his neck.

'Am I not old enough for you, Francis? You prefer middle-aged nymphomaniacs to good, clean-living young girls like me, is that it?'

He gave her a doleful look. 'I couldn't possibly comment.'

Sally dug him playfully in the ribs; distractedly he pushed her away. 'Stop that or I'll revoke your visa.' But the warning served only to redouble her efforts. 'Sally! We've got to talk.'

'God, not another of those serious, meaningful relationships. And just when I was beginning to have some fun.' She sat on the sofa opposite him, smoothing down her dress. She put her underwear in her handbag, she'd sort that tangled mess out later.

'There will be a storm about those pictures tomorrow. The head-lines will be savage. Alas, it is also the day I've chosen to make the public announcement about the new Civil List. Unfortunate, the announcement sitting alongside those sort of pictures, but . . .' – he smiled a huge, theatrical smile like Macbeth welcoming dinner guests – 'it can't be helped. What I find most distressing is that it will focus attention not only on our hapless and witless Princess but on the whole Royal Family. And that's where I need your help, O Gypsy. Please.'

'I am a stranger in your land, Suh, and my campfire is small,' she mocked in a deep Southern drawl.

'But you have magic on your side. Magic that can take a family so royal, and make it so common.'

'How common?'

'So far as the lesser Royals are concerned? As common as gigolos on a beach. But not the King, though. This isn't all-out war. Just make sure he's not above criticism. Reflect a degree of disappointment. It can be done?'

She nodded. 'Depends on the questions, how you set it up.'

'How would you set it up?'

'Can I go to the bathroom first?' Her dress was now immaculately smoothed, but somewhere underneath she was still a mess.

'Tell me first, Sally. It's important.'

'Pig. OK, off the top of my head. You start with something like: "Have you seen any news about the Royal Family in the last few days, and if so, what?" Just to get them thinking about the photographs without, of course, being seen to lead them on. That would be unprofessional! If they're such bozos that they've not heard a damn thing about the Royals, you can exclude them as dickheads and deadbeats. Then something like: "Do you think it is important that the Royals set a good public example in their private lives?" Of course people will say yes, so you follow up with: "Do you think the Royal Family is setting a better or worse public example in their private lives than in previous years?" I'll bet my next month's income that eight out of every ten will answer worse, much worse or unprintable.'

'The Princess's bikini could yet prove to be as powerful as the sling of David.'

'If somewhat larger,' she added testily.

'Continue with the tutorial.'

'Then perhaps: "Do you think the Royal Family deserves its recent pay increase or do you think, in the current economic circumstances, it should be setting an example of restraint?" Words like that.'

'Perhaps even: "Do you think the number of members of the

Royal Family supported by the taxpayer should remain the same, get larger, or be reduced?" '

'You're learning, Francis. If you put in a question immediately before that to ask whether they feel they get good value for money from the work of Princess Charlotte and a couple of other disreputable or unknown Royals, they'll be warmed up for it and you'll get an even fiercer response.'

His eyes were glittering.

'Only then do you come to the killer. "Is the Royal Family more or less popular, or doing a better or worse job for the country, than five years ago?" Top of the mind the public will say they are still great fans. So you have to bring out their deeper feelings, the concerns they hide away, the sort of things they're not always aware of themselves. Put that question up front, first off, and you'll probably discover that the Royals are only marginally less popular than they were. But ask away after you've given them a chance to think about sand, sex and Civil Lists, and your devoted and loyal citizens will have become a rebellious mob who will string up their beloved Princess Charlotte by her bikini straps. Is that enough?'

'More than enough.'

'Then if you don't mind I'm going to disappear for a little repair work.' Her hand was on the door handle when she turned around. 'You don't like the King, do you. Man to man, I mean.'

'No.' The reply was dry, blunt, reluctant. It only fuelled her curiosity.

'Why? Tell me.' She was pushing at doors he had not chosen to open freely, but she had to broaden the relationship if it were not to descend into empty habit and boredom. It had to be more than simply screwing each other, and the Opposition between times. Anyway, she was naturally curious.

'He's sanctimonious, naive,' came the low reply. 'A pathetic idealist who's getting in the way.'

'There's more, isn't there?'

'What do you mean?' he asked, irritation undisguised.

'Francis, you're halfway to raising a rebellion. You're not planning that just because he's sanctimonious.'

'He's trying to interfere.'

171

'Every editor in Fleet Street tries to interfere yet you invite them to lunch, not to their own lynching.'

'Why must you press it? All this twaddle about his children and the future!' His face revealed anguish, the tone had sharpened and his characteristic control had disappeared. 'He lectures me constantly about how passionate he is to build a better world, for his children. About how we shouldn't build a gas pipeline or nuclear power station without thinking first, about his children. How his first duty as a future King and Monarch was to produce an heir to the Throne – his children!' The flesh around his eyes had grown grey and his lips were spittled with saliva as he grew rapidly more animated. 'The man is possessed about his children. Forever talking about them whenever I meet him. Nagging. Harassing. Whining. As if children were some form of miracle which he alone could perform. Yet isn't it the commonest, most covetous and selfish act of all, to want to recreate your own image?'

She stood her ground. 'No, I don't think it is,' she said softly. She was suddenly frightened by the eyes which were red with fire, looking directly at her yet at the same time staring through her to some torment hidden beyond. 'No, it's not. Not selfish.'

'It's sheer egoism and self-love, I tell you. A pathetic attempt to grab at immortality.'

'It's called love, Francis.'

'Love! Was your child born out of love? Damned funny kind of love that leaves you in hospital with broken ribs and the child in a cemetery plot!'

She slapped him with the full force of an open palm, and knew at once it was a mistake. She should have recognized the danger signs in the throbbing veins at his temples. She should have remembered that he had no children, had never had children. She should have shown pity. Understanding came with a cry of pain as his hand lashed in return across her face.

Immediately he drew back, despairing at what he had done. He collapsed into a chair, the energy and hate draining from him like an hour-glass shedding its last grains of sand. 'My God, Sally, forgive me. I am so very sorry.'

By contrast, she retained a supreme calm. She'd had so much practice. 'Me too, Francis.'

He was panting, the leanness that often gave him the appearance of vigour and youth now turning him into a shrivelled, ageing man. He had breached his own defences. 'I have no children,' he said, gasping for breath, 'because I cannot. I have tried all my life to convince myself that it never mattered, but every time I see that damned man and listen to his taunts, it's as if I am stripped naked and humiliated simply by being in his presence.'

'You think he does it deliberately . . . ?'

'Of course it's deliberate! He uses his talk of love like weapons of war. Are you so blind you can't see?' His anger gave way to contrition. 'Oh, Sally, believe me, I'm sorry. I have never hit a woman before.'

'It happens, Francis.'

Sally stared at this new image of the man she had thought she knew, then closed the door quietly behind her.

A buzz of expectation grew as Urquhart walked into the House from behind the Speaker's Chair, red leather folder tucked beneath his arm, civil servants filing like ducklings into the officials' box at the back of the Chamber. They were there to provide him with instant information should the need arise, but it wouldn't. He had briefed himself very carefully for this one; he knew exactly what he wanted.

'Madam Speaker, with permission, I would like to make a statement . . .'

Urquhart looked slowly across the packed benches. McKillin sat on the other side of the Dispatch Box, double-checking the statement which Urquhart's office had made available to him an hour beforehand. He would be supportive. Such matters were supposed to be non-controversial and, in any event, as Urquhart's personal relations with the King had become the subject of press controversy, so the Opposition Leader's identification with the Monarch had grown. Your enemy, my friend. It's what Opposition was about. The Leader of the small Liberal Party, sitting with his band of eternal

173

optimists towards the far end of the Chamber, was likely to be less enthusiastic. He had seventeen MPs in his party and an ego greater than all the others combined. As a precocious backbencher he had made a name for himself by introducing a private bill to restrict the scope of the Civil List to only five members of the Royal Family and, furthermore, to batter home the message of equality by passing Royal succession down through the eldest child of either sex, and not exclusively the eldest son. It had given him ten minutes of parliamentary time before the bill was thrown out, but several hours of prime time on television and coverage in newspapers which he measured in feet. He had a record to defend; doubtless he would seek to do so with decorum but, as Urquhart glanced further around the House, the Prime Minister noted that decorum had a short shelf-life in politics.

His eyes alighted on 'The Beast of Bradford'. Dressed in his habitual shapeless sports jacket, the colourful and eccentric Member for Bradford Central was already leaning forward in anticipation, lank hair falling over his eyes, wringing his hands and waiting to leap to his feet at the first opportunity. The Opposition MP was a street-fighter who saw every issue as a chance to pursue the class war against capitalism, which he fought with considerable venom sustained by the scars of a factory accident as a working student which had left him with two short fingers on his left hand. An ardent republican, he was primed to self-ignite on issues involving hereditary rights. He was also utterly predictable, which is why Urquhart had ensured that one of his own members, a Knight of the Leafy Suburbs renowned for his bucolic complexion and pugnacious temper, was stationed directly opposite. The Knight had been deputed to 'take care' of The Beast during the statement; what this might involve had been left to The Knight's discretion, which was notoriously fragile, but he was anxious 'to get back into the fray', as he put it, after treatment for a mild heart complaint. He was already glowering across the floor at the Honourable Member for Bradford Central, seated barely six feet away.

'I would like to make a statement on arrangements for future financial support for His Majesty the King during the ten-year period ahead,' Urquhart continued. He paused to look directly at

174

The Beast and smiled condescendingly. The other responded with an audible growl, which only served to broaden the Prime Minister's smile. The Beast's cage was already being rattled.

'The settlement is a considerable and I hope generous one, but is for a full ten-year period during which the vagaries of inflation must be accounted for. Should inflation prove to be less than predicted, the surplus will be carried forward . . .'

''Ow much is the Princess getting?' The Beast snapped.

Urquhart ignored him and continued with his explanation.

'Come on, then. Tell us. 'Ow much are we paying Charlotte to screw around in the Caribbean next year?'

'Order! Order!' Madam Speaker demanded shrilly.

'I was only asking . . .'

'Shut up, you fool!' snapped The Knight, a comment heard by everyone in the Chamber with the exception of the official record takers of *Hansard*.

'Carry on, Prime Minister.'

The atmosphere was already tangled, the temperature rising as Urquhart continued to the end of his short announcement. He had to struggle through growing noise as The Knight continued his private tussle across the floor of the Chamber. The Beast muttered away throughout the brief and supportive response of the Leader of the Opposition who, in a modest attempt to get under Urquhart's skin, was fulsome in his praise of the King's environmental work and social perceptiveness.

'Tell that to this bloody man!' the Knight stormed, waving an accusing finger at The Beast who had just impugned his wife's fidelity. He got a crude gesture involving two amputated fingers in response.

The Liberal leader, when it came to his turn, was less supportive. 'Will the Prime Minister recognize that, although we fully support the valuable work of the Royal Family, its financial affairs leave much to be desired? The Civil List represents but a fraction of the expense to the taxpayer of the Royal Family when you take into account the aeroplanes of the Royal Flight, the Royal Yacht, the Royal Train . . .'

'The Royal Racing Pigeons,' interrupted The Beast.

175

'. . . the costs of which are buried in the budgets of various Government departments. Wouldn't it be better, more open and honest, to consolidate all these expenditures into one budget so that we know exactly what the true figures are?'

'It's a sham. What're you 'iding?'

'I resent the Right Honourable Gentleman's insinuation that I am being neither open nor honest . . .' Urquhart began.

''Ow much is it, then?'

'There is no secret conspiracy on these matters. The Royal Family gives us excellent value for money—'

''Ow much money?'

A handful of others were joining in the interruptions from the Opposition benches. It seemed they might have found a weakness in the Prime Minister's defences and could not resist the temptation to exploit it.

'The figures vary greatly from year to year because of exceptional items . . .'

'Like what?'

'. . . such as refits and modernization of the Royal Trains. Also the Royal Palaces require extensive upkeep which in some years is unduly heavy. It is often very difficult to extract the exact cost out of large departmental budgets.' Urquhart appeared to be suffering from the interruptions. He was noticeably under pressure, reluctant to give details, which only excited his hecklers further. The more he prevaricated the louder became the calls for him to 'come clean'; even the Liberal leader was joining in.

'The House must understand that the statement I am making today covers the Civil List only. On other items of expenditure I am bound by custom, and it would be most improper of me to make announcements about such matters without first consulting His Majesty. We must preserve the dignity of the Crown and recognize the esteem and affection in which the Royal Family is held.'

As Urquhart paused to consider his words the noise levels around him rose sharply. His brow clouded.

'It was only the other day that the Opposition benches were accusing me of treating His Majesty with contempt, yet now they insist that is precisely what I do.' This antagonized his hecklers; the language swilling around the floor became increasingly unparlia-mentary. 'They are a shambolic lot, Mr Speaker.' Urquhart waved a menacing finger at the benches opposite. 'They don't want information, they just want a row!' He appeared to have lost his temper in the face of the constant baiting, and Madam Speaker knew that it would mark the end of any sensible dialogue. She was just about to curtail discussion and call the next business when an explosion erupted in the vicinity of The Knight, who was on his feet.

'On a Point of Order, Madam Speaker!'

'No points of order, please. We've already wasted enough time . . .'

'But that wretched man just told me to go and have another heart attack!'

Accusatory fingers pointed towards The Beast and the pande-monium grew worse.

'Really!' snapped the Speaker in exasperation.

''E's got it wrong, as always,' The Beast was protesting innocently. 'I told 'im 'e would have another 'eart attack, if he found out 'ow much the bloody Monarchy cost. It's millions and millions . . .'

The rest was lost in the storm of outrage from all sides.

Urquhart picked up his folder and started to leave. He looked at the parliamentary benches in turmoil. Great pressure would undoubtedly be brought to bear on him to reveal the full cost of the Royal Family, and he might have to give it. In any event, prompted by the row, every newspaper in Fleet Street would be setting journalists to dig and make inspired guesses, and reasonably accurate figures wouldn't be too difficult to find. A pity, he thought to himself, that last year the King's Flight replaced both their ageing aeroplanes, and modern jets don't come cheap. A still greater pity that it happened to coincide with an extensive refit for the Royal Yacht *Britannia*. The figures even the dimmest journalist would arrive at would be well in excess of one hundred and fifty million pounds, and that was too large a chunk of red meat for even the most loyal editor to ignore. Yet nobody could accuse Urquhart of being unfair or inconsiderate to the King, not personally. Hadn't he done his best to defend the King, even while under considerable pressure? By tomorrow morning's headlines it would be the King himself experiencing the pressure. Then for Sally's opinion poll.

Even for a Prime Minister it had been an exceptional day's work, he told himself.

'Mr Stamper would like a word, Prime Minister.'

'In his capacity as Privy Councillor, Chairman of the Party, Chief Bottle Washer or honorary president of his football club?' Urquhart swung his feet down from the green leather sofa on which he had been propped reading Cabinet papers as he waited in his House of Commons office for a series of late-night divisions. He couldn't remember what they were voting for next. Was it to increase punishment for offenders, or reduce subventions to the United Nations? Something, anyway, which would get the tabloids going and reveal the Opposition in the worst possible light.

'Mr Stamper didn't say,' responded the humourless private secretary, who had still put no more than his head and left shoulder around the door.

'Wheel him in!' the Prime Minister instructed.

Stamper appeared, offered no word of greeting, and made straight for the drinks cupboard where he poured himself a large whisky.

'Looks like bad news, Tim.'

'Oh, it is. Some of the worst I've heard for ages.'

'Not another selfish swine in a marginal seat gone and died?'

'Worse, much worse, Francis. Our latest private polls put us three points ahead. What's even more worrying, for some reason people seem to like you, you're ten points ahead of McKillin. Your vanity will be uncontrollable. Your ridiculous plan for an early election looks as if it could work after all!'

'Praise the Lord.'

'There's something even more fascinating, Francis,' Stamper continued in more serious demeanour. Unbidden he had filled a glass for Urquhart and handed it to him before continuing. 'I've just been having a quiet chat with the Home Secretary. The cock-up theory of politics rules supreme. Seems that little shit Marples has at last

178

got himself caught with his trousers down, late the other night on the towpath at Putney.'

'In January?' Urquhart asked incredulously.

'Absolutely *in flagrante*. With a fourteen-year-old. Apparently he's into little boys.' He made himself comfortable behind Urquhart's desk, his feet up on the Prime Ministerial blotter. He was deliberately pushing his luck, teasing. His news must be particularly weighty, mused Urquhart.

'But lucky. The police were going to charge him so he broke down and told them everything in the hope they'd go easy on him. Lots of names, addresses, gossip, suggestions of where to look if they wanted to find an organized prostitution ring.'

'Castration's too good—'

'And it appears he came up with a very interesting name. David Mycroft.'

Urquhart took a deep swig.

'So all of a sudden our boys in blue have gone coy and are asking for a little informal guidance. If Marples gets prosecuted, he'll implicate Mycroft and all hell will break loose. The Home Secretary's given a nod and a wink that prosecuting the Honourable and Upright Member for Dagenham would not be in the public interest. So we're saved a by-election.'

Urquhart swung his legs down from the sofa. 'What do they have on Mycroft?'

'Not a lot. Just his name and the fact that Marples was tangling with him at some gay club on New Year's Eve. Who knows where that could lead? But they haven't interviewed him.'

'Maybe they should.'

'They can't, Francis. If they go after Mycroft they've got to do for Marples as well, which in turn will do for us all. Anyway, if spending time at a gay club were a crime we'd have to lock up half the House of Lords.'

'Listen to me, Tim. They can have Marples kebabbed on a rusty skewer for all I care. But he wouldn't be charged for weeks, not until after the election, by which time it won't matter a bent farthing. Yet if they can put pressure on Mycroft now, it may be just the insurance policy we need. Don't you see? Pieces for position. Cap-

179

ture the low ground today, in exchange for giving up a player later, when it no longer matters. I think they call it a queen sacrifice.'

'I think I need another drink. Problems like that, so close to the heart of the Palace. If this were to come out . . .'

'How long's Mycroft been with the King?'

'Known each other since they were both spotty youths. One of his longest-serving aides. And closest friends.'

'Sounds distressingly serious. It would be awful if the King knew.'

'And were covering up for Mycroft, in spite of the sensitivity of the work he does. Must know half the nation's secrets in his job.'

'Be even worse if His Majesty didn't know. Fooled, bamboozled, defrauded for thirty years by one of his closest friends, a man he has put into a position of trust.'

'A knave or a fool. A monarch who didn't fulfil his responsibilities, or couldn't. What will the press make of all this, if it gets out?'

'Terrible news, Tim. This is terrible.'

'Worst I've heard in ages.'

There was a long moment of silence. Then, coming from inside the Prime Minister's room, the private secretary heard a sustained, almost uncontrollable bout of gut-wrenching laughter.

'Damn them! Damn them all, David! How could they be so cretinous?' The King hurled one newspaper after another into the air as Mycroft watched the pages flutter down to lay strewn across the floor. 'I didn't want the Civil List increase, but now I'm attacked for greed. And how can it be that only a few days after informing the Prime Minister that I wished the Royal Family to pay full taxes on our income, they report it as if it's his idea?'

'Downing Street's unattributable briefing . . .' Mycroft muttered feebly.

'Of course it is!' snapped the King as if talking with a backward pupil. 'They even suggest I'm caving in to pressure in agreeing to pay tax, that I've been forced into it by the hostile press coverage. That man Urquhart is abominable! He can't help but twist everything to his advantage. If he even stumbled by accident upon the truth he would pick himself up and carry on as if nothing had happened. It's preposterous!'

A copy of *The Times* was hurled to the farthest corner of the room, settling like huge flakes of snow.

'Did any of them bother to enquire after the facts?'

Mycroft coughed awkwardly. 'The *Telegraph*. Their story is fair . . .'

The King snatched the paper from amongst the pile, scanning its columns. He seemed to calm a little. 'Urquhart is trying to humiliate me, David. To cut me to ribbons, piece by piece, without even a chance to explain myself.' He'd had the dream again last night. From the pages of every newspaper he could see staring at him the wide, expectant eyes of the grubby boy with the dribble of crumbs on his chin. It terrified him. 'I will not let them drag me like a lamb to the slaughter, David. I must not permit that. I've been thinking: I must find some way of explaining my views. Get my point across without Urquhart getting in the way. I shall give an interview.'

'But Kings don't give newspaper interviews,' Mycroft protested weakly.

'Not before they haven't. But this is the age of the new, open Monarchy. I'm going to do it, David. With the *Telegraph*, I think. An exclusive.'

Mycroft wanted to protest that if an interview were a bad idea, an exclusive could be even worse, giving all the other newspapers something to shoot at. But he didn't have the strength to argue. He hadn't been able to think clearly all day, ever since he had answered a knock at the door early in the morning to discover a DC and Inspector from the Vice Squad standing on his front step.

January: The Fourth Week

Landless had driven himself, simply telling his staff that he would be uncontactable. His secretary hated mysteries; when he presented excuses she always assumed he was off being grubby with some young woman who had a strong back and weak bank balance. She knew what he was like. Some fifteen years earlier she, too, had been young and grubby with Landless, before things like marriage, respectability and stretch marks had intervened. Such insights into the inner man had helped her become an efficient and outrageously overpaid personal assistant, yet hadn't stopped her being jealous. And today he had told no one, not even her; he didn't want the whole world knowing where he was even before he had arrived.

The reception desk was tiny and the waiting room dull, covered in mediocre early Victorian oils of horses and hunting scenes in imitation of Stubbs and Ben Marshall. One of them might have been an authentic John Herring; he couldn't be positive but he was beginning to develop an eye for such things; after all, he'd bought enough of the genuine article over the past few years. Almost immediately he was being summoned by a young footman in full livery, waisted tails, buckles and stockings, and ushered into a small but immaculately appointed lift where the mahogany shone as deep as the Palace servant's shoes. He wished his mother had been here: she would have loved it. She'd been born on the day Queen Alexandra died and had always believed it somehow tied her in, hinting at a mysterious 'special link', and in later life attending gatherings of spiritualists. Just before his dear old mum had taken her own trip to 'the other side' she had stood for three hours to catch a view through the crowd of Princess Di on her wedding day. She'd only seen the back of the coach, and that for no more than a few seconds, but she'd waved her flag and cheered and cried, and come home feeling she had done her bit. For her it was all patriotic pride and commemorative biscuit tins. She would be wetting herself if she were gazing down now.

'Your first time?' the footman enquired.

Landless nodded. Princess Charlotte had telephoned him. An exclusive interview with the *Telegraph*, implying she had set it up herself. Would he be sure to send someone reliable? And allow the Palace to check the article before it was printed? Perhaps they could have lunch again soon? He was being led along a broad corridor with windows overlooking the inner courtyard. The paintings were better here, portraits of long-forgotten Royal scions by masters whose names had endured rather better.

'You address him as "Your Majesty" when you first go in. Afterwards you can simply call him "Sir",' the footman muttered as they approached a solid but unpretentious door.

As the door swung quietly open, Landless remembered Charlotte's other question. Was the idea a good one? He had doubts, serious doubts, about whether an exclusive interview would be good for the King, but he knew it would be bloody marvellous for his newspaper.

'Sally? Sorry to telephone so early. You haven't been in contact for a day or two. Everything all right?'

In fact it had been nearly a week, and although Urquhart had sent along flowers and two major potential clients, he hadn't found the right moment to call. He shrugged. They'd had a spat, she would get over it. She would have to if she wanted to retain an inside track. In any event, this was urgent.

'How's the opinion poll coming along? Ready yet?' He tried to judge her mood down the phone. Perhaps a little cool and formal, almost as if he'd woken her up. Anyway this was business. 'Something's come up. Word is His Royal Conscience has given an exclusive interview to the *Telegraph* and they're hoping to get it cleared for publication in a couple of days. I haven't any idea what's in it, Landless is sitting on it as though he were hatching an egg, but I can't help feeling that in the public interest there should be a bit

183

of balance. Don't you think? Perhaps an opinion poll, published beforehand, reflecting the growing public disaffection with the Royal Family? To put the interview in context?' He looked out of the window across St James's Park, where, beside the pelican pool, two women were struggling in the grubby morning light to pull their squabbling dogs apart. 'I suspect some newspapers like the *Times* might even infer that the King's interview was a hurried and somewhat desperate attempt to respond to the opinion poll.' He winced as one of the women, her smaller pet lodged firmly between the jaws of a large black mongrel, gave the other dog a firm kick in the testicles. The dogs separated, only for the two owners to begin snarling at each other. 'It would be really superb if the poll were ready for release by, say . . . this afternoon?'

As Sally rolled over to place the phone back in its cradle, she stretched the aches of the night out of her bones. She lay staring at the ceiling for a few moments, allowing the mental instructions to seep from her brain down through her body. Her nose was twitching like a periscope above the sheets, tasting the news she had just received. She sat up in bed, alive and alert, and turned to the form beside her.

'Got to go, lover. Mischief afoot and work to be done.'

*　　*　　*

Guardian, Page One, 27 January

NEW STORM HITS KING
'IS HE A CHRISTIAN?'

A new storm of controversy surrounded the Royal Family last night when the Bishop of Durham, from the pulpit of his cathedral, questioned the King's religious motives. Quoting the King's much-criticised newspaper interview earlier this week in which he revealed a deep interest in Eastern religions and did not discount the possibility of physical resurrection, the fundamentalist Bishop attacked such 'fashionable dalliance with mysticism'.

'The King is the Defender of the Faith and anointed head of our Church of England. But is he a Christian?'

Buckingham Palace indicated last night that the King had simply been trying to emphasize, as King of a country with a large number of racial and religious minorities, that he felt it his duty not to take a narrow and restrictive view of his religious role. But the Bishop's attack seems set to fuel further controversy in the wake of the recent critical opinion poll which showed dramatically falling support for some members of the Royal Family such as Princess Charlotte, and a growing demand to restrict the number of members of the Royal Family who receive their income from the Civil List.

Supporters of the King rallied to his defence last night. 'We shouldn't be enticed into a constitutional supermarket, shopping around for the cheapest form of government,' Viscount Quillington said.

In contrast, critics were quick to point out that the King, in spite of his own personal popularity, was failing to set a clear lead in many areas. 'The Crown should stand for the highest standards of public morality,' one senior Government backbencher said, 'but his leadership of his own family leaves much to be desired. They are letting down both him and us. They are overpaid, overtanned, underworked, and overly numerous.'

'The Royal oak is being shaken,' said another critic. 'It would do no harm if one or two members of the Family were to fall out of the branches . . .'

*   *   *

News began trickling through shortly before four in the afternoon, and by the time it was confirmed the short winter's day had finished and all London was dark. It was a wretched day; a warm front had

185

passed across the capital bringing in its wake a deluge of relentless rain which would continue well into the night. It was a day for staying home.

Staying home had been the mistake, fatally so, of three women and their children who called 14 Queensgate Crescent, a tenement block in the middle of Notting Hill, home. It was the heart of old slumland, which in the sixties had housed streetwalkers and tides of immigrants under the stern eye of racketeers. 'Rachmanism' they had called it then, after the most notorious of the landlord-racketeers. 'Bed and breakfast' it was called in the modern parlance, where the local council housed one-parent and problem families while they searched around listlessly for somewhere or someone else to take over the responsibility. Much of the temporary accommodation provided in Number 14 had changed little in the thirty-odd years since it had been a brothel. Single rooms, shared bathrooms, inadequate heating, noise, rotting woodwork and unremitting depression. When it rained, they would watch the windowsills trickle and the damp brown stains creep even lower as the wallpaper peeled from the walls. But it was better than sitting in the middle of the downpour outside, or so they had thought.

Institutional housing breeds indifference, and no one had bothered to report the smell of gas which had been lingering for days. That was up to the caretaker, and so what if he only turned up when he felt like it. It was somebody else's problem. Or so they had thought.

As dusk had gathered the automatic timer had turned another gear and switched on the light in the communal hallways. They were only sixty-watt bulbs, one per landing, scarcely adequate, but the small spark caused by the electrical contact had been sufficient to ignite the gas and blow the five-storey building right out of the ground, taking much of the neighbouring building with it. Fortunately there had been no one in next door, it was derelict, but remnants of five families were inside Number 14 and of the twenty-one women, children and babies only eight would be pulled out of the rubble alive. By the time His Majesty reached the scene it consisted of little more than a huge pile of bricks, fractured door frames and twisted fragments of furniture over which firemen crawled beneath harsh arc lights. Several persons were believed to have been inside for whom there was still no account. A double bed teetered precariously on a ledge of splintered wood many feet above the heads of the rescuers, its sheets flapping in the squally wind. It should have been pulled down before it had a chance to fall on those below, but the mobile crane was having trouble getting through the rain and rush-hour traffic and they couldn't afford to wait. Someone thought they had heard a noise from the rubble directly beneath and although the infra-red image enhancer showed nothing, many willing hands were tearing at the ruins, lashed by the rain and the fear they would be too late.

As soon as the King had heard the news he had asked to visit the scene. 'Not to interfere, to gawk. But a word to the bereaved at a time such as this can speak louder than a thousand epitaphs later.' The request had gone through to the Met Police Control Room at Scotland Yard just as they were briefing the Home Secretary, who had immediately passed the news on to Downing Street. The King arrived on site only to discover he had unwittingly been involved in a race he had already lost. Urquhart was already there, holding hands, comforting the injured, consoling the distressed, giving interviews, searching for the television cameras, being seen. It made the Monarch look like a man sent onto the field from the substitutes' bench, no better than an able reserve, following in others' footsteps, but what did it matter? This wasn't a contest, or, at least, shouldn't be. Or so the King struggled to convince himself.

For some time the Monarch and his Prime Minister succeeded in avoiding each other as one took briefing and quietly sought out survivors while the other concentrated on finding a dry spot from which to give interviews. But both knew a meeting would have to come. Avoiding each other would be news in itself and would serve only to turn tragedy into farce. The King stood like a sentinel gazing at the devastation from atop a mound of rubble surrounded by a rapidly enlarging lake of slime and mud, through which Urquhart had to trudge to meet him.

'Your Majesty.'

'Mr Urquhart.'

Their greeting had the warmth of a collision of icebergs. Neither looked directly at the other, but chose to examine the scene around them.

'Not a word, Sir. There has already been too much damage done, too much controversy stirred. See, but do not speak. I must insist.'

'No perfunctory expression of grief, Mr Urquhart? Not even to one of your own scripts?'

'Not a wink or a nod, no sideways expressions or exaggerated lowering of the eyes. Not even to an agreed formula, since you seem to delight in untangling every knot we weave.'

The King waved the charge away with a dismissive gesture.

The Prime Minister spoke slowly, with great deliberation, returning to his theme. 'I must insist.'

'Silence, you think?'

'Absolutely. For some considerable period.'

The King turned from the carnage and for the first time looked directly at the Prime Minister, his face frozen in condescension, his hands thrust deep into the pockets of his raincoat. 'I think not.'

Urquhart struggled to avoid rising to the challenge and losing his self-control. He wasn't willing to let the King escape with even a trace of satisfaction.

'As you have seen, your views have been widely misunderstood.'

'Or manipulated.'

Urquhart ignored the innuendo.

'Silence, you say,' the King continued, turning his face into the wind and spray, his nose jutting forward like the prow of some great sailing ship. 'I wonder what you would do, Mr Urquhart, if some damn fool bishop made you the target of such ludicrous misrepresentation. Shut up? Or stand up? Wouldn't you think it even more important to speak out, to give those willing to listen the opportunity to hear, to understand?'

'But I am not the King.'

'No. A fact for which both you and I should be grateful.'

Urquhart rode the insult. Beneath the burning arc lights a tiny hand was spotted beneath the rubble. Brief seconds of confusion and hope, much scrabbling, only for the flicker of anticipation to die amidst the mud. It was nothing but a doll.

'I must make sure, Sir, that I am also heard and understood. By you.' To one side there was a crash of falling masonry but neither stirred. 'Any further public outpourings by you would be regarded as deeply provocative by your Government. A declaration of constitutional war. And no Monarch has taken on a Prime Minister and won in nearly two hundred years.'

'An interesting point. I had forgotten you were a scholar.'

'Politics is about the attainment and use of power. It is a rough, indeed ruthless arena. No place for a King.'

The rain ran in rivulets down their faces, dripping from their noses, creeping behind their collars. They were both soaking and chilled. Neither was young, they should have sought shelter but neither would be the first to move. At a distance onlookers could hear nothing beyond the rattle of jackhammers and the urgent shouts of command, they could see only two men staring face to face, rulers and rivals, silhouetted against the harsh glow of the rescue lights in a monochrome scene washed by rain. They could not distinguish the insolence on the face of Urquhart nor the ageless expression of regal defiance that suffused the cheeks of the other. Perhaps an astute observer might have seen the King brace his shoulders, but surely only against the elements and the harsh fortune that had brought him to this place?

'Did I miss a mention of morality in there, Prime Minister?'

'Morality, Sir, is the monologue of the unexcited and the unexcitable, the revenge of the unsuccessful, the punishment of those who tried and failed, or who never had the courage to try at all.'

It was Urquhart's turn to attempt to provoke the other. A silence hung between them for many moments.

'Prime Minister, may I congratulate you? You have succeeded in making me understand you with absolute clarity.'

'I didn't wish to leave you in any doubt.'

'You haven't.'

'We are agreed, then? No more words?'

When finally the King spoke, his voice had grown soft so that Urquhart had to strain to hear it. 'You may rest assured that I shall guard my words as carefully as you aim yours. Those you have used today I shall never forget.'

The moment was broken as a shout of warning rose above the

scene and men scurried from the rock pile as the wooden ledge shivered, jarred and finally collapsed, propelling the bed into a slow, graceful somersault of death before it was reduced to nothing more than another pile of matchwood on the ruins below. A solitary pillow sagged drunken in the wind, skewered upon the pointed shard of what that morning had been a baby's cot, its plastic rattle still singing in the wind. Without another word Urquhart began the trudge back through the slime.

Mycroft joined the King in the back of his car for the return drive to the Palace. For much of the trip the Monarch was silent, lost in thought and his emotions, eyes closed – affected by what he had witnessed, thought Mycroft. When he spoke, his words were soft, almost whispered, as though they were in a church or visiting a condemned cell.

'No more words, David. I am commanded to silence, or must accept the consequences.' His eyes were still closed.

'No more interviews?'

'Not unless I want open warfare.'

The thought hung between them for several moments which dragged into silent minutes. His eyes were still closed. Mycroft thought it might be his opportunity to speak.

'Perhaps it's not the right time . . . it's never really the right time. But it would be helpful for me to take a few days away. If you're not doing much in public. For a while. There are a few personal things I need to sort out.'

The King's head was still back, eyes shut, words coming in a monotone and squeezed of emotion. 'I must apologize, David. I've rather taken you for granted, I'm afraid. Lost in my own problems.' He sighed. 'With all this confusion I should still have found time to enquire. Christmas without Fiona must have been hell. Of course. Of course you must have a little time off. But there's one small thing I want your help with beforehand, if you can bear it. I want to arrange a small trip.'

'To where?'

'Three days, David. Just three days, and not far. I was thinking of Brixton, Handsworth, perhaps Moss Side and the Gorbals. Work my way up the country. Dine at a soup kitchen in Cardboard City one day, have breakfast at the Salvation Army the next. Take tea with a family living off benefit and share their one-bar fire. Meet the youngsters sleeping rough. You get the idea.'

'You can't!'

The head remained back, sightless, the tone still cold. 'I can. And I want cameras to accompany me everywhere. Maybe I shall live off a pensioner's diet for three days and challenge the press travelling with me to do the same.'

'That's bigger headlines than any speech!'

'I shall say not a word.' He started laughing, as if cold humour were the only way to suppress the feelings that battered him within, so forcefully they had left him a little in fear of himself.

'You don't have to. Those pictures will be top of the news every night.'

'If only every Royal engagement could get such coverage.' The tone was almost whimsical.

'Don't you know what you're doing? It's a declaration of war on the Government. Urquhart will retaliate . . .'

Mention of the Prime Minister's name had a galvanizing effect on the King. His head came up, red eyes open and burning bright, the jaw tightened as if a burst of electricity had passed through him. There was fire in his belly. 'We retaliate first! Urquhart cannot stop me. He may object to my speeches, he may bully and threaten me, but this is my kingdom, and I have every right to go wherever and whenever I bloody well please!'

'When did you have in mind for starting this civil war?'

The grim humour settled on him once more. 'Oh, I was thinking . . . next week.'

'Now I know you're not serious. It would take months to organize.'

'Wherever and whenever I please, David. It needs no organization. I'm not going to meet anyone in particular. No advance notice need be given. Anyway, if I give them time to prepare all I will see is some anaesthetized version of Britain which has been swept and whitewashed just for my visit. No, David. No preparation, no warning. I'm bored with playing the King; time to play the man! Let's see if I can take for three days what so many others have to take for a lifetime. Let's see if I can lose the silk-covered shackles and look my subjects in the eye.'

'Security! What of security?' Mycroft urged desperately.

'The best form of security is surprise, when no one expects me. If I have to get in my car and drive myself, by God I'm doing it.'

'You must be absolutely clear. Such a tour would be war, right out in front of the cameras, with no hiding place and no diplomatic compromise later on to smooth everything over. It would be a direct public challenge to the Prime Minister.'

'No, David, that's not the way I see it. Urquhart is a public menace, to be sure, but this is more about me. I need to find myself, respond to those things I feel deep inside, see whether I am up to the task not just of being a King, but of being a man. I can't go on running away from what I am, David, what I believe. This is not just a challenge to Urquhart. It's more of a challenge to myself. Can you understand?'

As the words hit him, Mycroft's shoulders sagged, the weight of several worlds seeming to bear down upon his shoulders. He felt exhausted from his own lifetime of running, he had no resources left. The man sitting beside him was not just a King, he was more, a man who insisted on being his own man. Mycroft knew exactly how he felt, and marvelled at his courage. He nodded. 'Of course I do,' he responded softly.

'Elizabeth. The toast is burnt again!'

Urquhart contemplated the ruins of his breakfast which had crumbled at the first touch of his knife and showered into his lap. His wife was still in her dressing gown; she had been out late again – 'working hard, telling the world how wonderful you are, darling' – and was only half awake.

'I cannot think in that ridiculous little kitchen, Francis, let alone cook your toast. Sort out the refurbishment and then you can have a proper breakfast.'

That again. He'd forgotten about it, pushed it to one side. There were other things on his mind.

'Francis, what's wrong?' She had known him too long not to catch the signs.

He gestured to the newspapers, announcing plans for the King's visit. 'He's called my bluff, Elizabeth.'

'Will it be bad?'

'Could it be worse? Just when everything was beginning to come right. The opinion polls turning in our favour, an election about to be called. It will change everything.' He dusted the crumbs off his lap. 'I can't go to the country with everyone talking about nothing but poverty and freezing pensioners. We'd be out of Downing Street before you had time to choose new wallpaper let alone get your paste bucket out.'

'Out of Downing Street?' She sounded alarmed. 'It may sound churlish, but haven't we only just got here?'

He looked at her pointedly. 'You'd miss it? You surprise me, Elizabeth. You seem to spend so much time away.' But she usually came back before daybreak, and as she sat there he understood why. She wasn't at her best first thing in the morning.

'Can't you fight him?'

'With time, yes. And beat him. But I don't have time, Elizabeth, only two weeks. The pathetic thing is that the King doesn't even realize what he's done.'

'You mustn't give in, Francis. You owe it to me as well as yourself.' She was struggling with her own toast as if to emphasize what weak, useless creatures men were. She was no more successful than he, and it irritated her. 'I've shared in all the sacrifices and the hard work, remember. And I have a life, too. I enjoy being the Prime Minister's wife. And one day I'm going to be a former Prime Minister's widow. I'll need some support, a little social respectability for when I'm on my own.' It sounded selfish, uncaring. And as she did when she couldn't help herself, she used her most potent weapon, his guilt. 'If we had children to support me, it would be different.'

He stared at the ruins of his breakfast. That's what it had come to. Dickering over his coffin.

'Fight him, Francis.'

'I intend to, but don't underestimate him. I chop off a leg, yet he keeps bouncing back up again.'

'Then fight him harder.'

'You mean like George Washington?'

'I mean like bloody Cromwell. It's us or him, Francis.'

'I've struggled so hard to avoid that, Elizabeth, truly I have. It would not simply be destroying one man but several hundred years of history. There are limits.'

'Think about it, Francis. Is it possible?'

'It would certainly be a distraction from bellyaching about the underprivileged.'

'Governments don't solve people's concerns, they simply try to rearrange them in their favour. Can't you rearrange them in your favour?'

'Inside two weeks?' He examined the determined look in her eyes. She was in earnest. Deadly earnest. 'That's what I've spent all night thinking about.' He nodded gently. 'It might just be. With a little luck. And witchcraft. Make him the issue, the people versus the King. But this would not simply be an election, it would be a revolution. If we won, the Royal Family would never recover.'

'Spare me the pity. I'm a Colquhoun.'

'But am I a Cromwell?'

'You'll do.'

He suddenly remembered they had dug up Cromwell and stuck his rotting skull on a gibbet. He looked at the remnants of charred toast, and was very much afraid she might be right.

PART THREE

February: The First Week

The ringing of the telephone startled him, intruding into the quiet of the apartment. It was late, well after ten, and Kenny had already retired to leave Mycroft working on some last-minute arrangements for the King's tour. Kenny was on stand-by; Mycroft wondered whether the telephone was summoning him to fill a last-minute vacancy on some flight crew, but surely not at this time of night?

Kenny appeared at the bedroom door, rubbing wearily at his eyes. 'It's for you.'

'For me? But who . . . ?'

'Dunno.' Kenny was still half asleep.

With considerable trepidation Mycroft lifted the extension. 'Hello.'

'David Mycroft?' the voice enquired.

'Who's speaking?'

'David, this is Ken Rochester from the *Mirror*. I'm sorry to bother you so late. It's not too inconvenient, is it, David?'

Mycroft had never heard of the man before. His nasal tones were unpleasant, his informality insolent and unwelcome, his concern patently insincere. Mycroft made no reply.

'It's something of an emergency; my editor's asked if I can come on the tour tomorrow, along with our Royal correspondent. I'm a special features writer myself. You moved, have you, David? Not your old number, this.'

'How did you get this number?' Mycroft asked, forcing out every word through suddenly leaden lips.

'It is David Mycroft, isn't it? From the Palace? I'd feel a total fool talking about this to anyone else. David?'

'How did you get this number?' he asked again, the constriction in his throat drying his words. He had supplied it to the Palace switchboard for use only in an emergency.

'Oh, we usually get whatever we want, David. So I'll turn up tomorrow to join the rest of the reptiles, if you'll make the necessary arrangements. My editor would be furious if I couldn't find some way of persuading you. Was that your son I spoke to on the phone? Sorry, silly question. Your son's at university, isn't he, David?'

Mycroft's throat was now desiccated, unable to pass any words.

'Or a colleague, perhaps? One of your high-flyers? Sounded as if I'd woken him from bed. Sorry to have disturbed you both so very late at night, but you know how editors are. My apologies to your wife . . .'

The journalist prattled on with his confection of innuendo and enquiry. Slowly Mycroft withdrew the telephone from his ear and dropped it back into its cradle. So they knew where he was. And they would know who he was with, and why. After the visit of the Vice Squad he had known it would happen sooner or later. He'd prayed it would be much later. And he knew the press. They wouldn't be satisfied with just himself. They'd go for Kenny, too, his job, his family, his private life, his friends, everybody and anybody he'd ever known, even through his dustbins in search of all the mistakes he had ever made. And who hadn't made mistakes? They would be remorseless, unstinting, uncompromising, unspeakable. Mycroft wasn't sure he could take that sort of pressure; he was even less sure he had the right to ask Kenny to take it. He wandered over to the window and glanced up and down the darkened street, searching the shadows for any hint of prying eyes. There was nothing, nothing that he could see at least, but it wouldn't be long, maybe as soon as tomorrow.

Kenny had fallen asleep again, innocent and unaware, his body twisted in the sheets as only young people can manage. All they had wanted was to be left alone, yet it was only a matter of time before others came to tear them apart. As he lay beside Kenny, trying to share his warmth, he shivered, already feeling the exposure. The real world no longer lay beyond Kenny's doorstep, it was forcing itself right inside the room.

*   *   *

Urquhart had arrived back late from the diplomatic reception to find Sally waiting for him, chatting over a plastic cup of coffee with a couple of Protection Squad officers in what passed as their office: a cramped closet-sized room just off the entrance hall. She was perched on the corner of their desk, supported by her long and elegant legs, which the seated detectives were admiring with little sign of reticence.

'My apologies for disturbing you at your work, gentlemen,' he muttered tetchily. He realized he was jealous, but felt better as the detectives sprang to their feet in evident confusion, one of them spilling the coffee in his haste.

'Good evening, Prime Minister.' Her smile was broad, warm, showing no after-effects of their previous meeting's misunder-standing.

'Ah, Miss Quine. I was forgetting. More opinion polls?' He attempted an air of distraction.

'Who do you think you're kidding?' Sally muttered from the corner of her mouth as they made their way from the room.

He arched an eyebrow.

'If they thought you'd really forgotten about a late-night meeting with a woman who had a figure like mine, they'd send for the men in white coats.'

'They are not paid to think but to do as I tell them,' he responded waspishly. He sounded as if he meant every word, and Sally felt alarmed. She decided to change the subject.

'Talking of opinion polls, you're six points ahead. But before you start congratulating yourself, I have to tell you that the King's tour will blow that lead right out of the water. It's going to be one heck of a circus – lots of hand-wringing and talk of compassion. Frankly, not a game where your side fields a strong team.'

'I'm afraid His Majesty is going to have distractions of his own before the week is out.'

'Meaning?'

'His press officer and close friend, Mycroft, is a homosexual. Shacked up with an air steward.'

'So what? It's no crime.'

'But sadly the story is just dribbling out to the press, and in their usual disreputable fashion they will be bound to make him wish he were a simple criminal. There's not only the deceit of his family – apparently his poor wife has been forced to leave the marital home after more than twenty years of marriage in disgust at what he's been up to. There's also the security angle. A man who has access to all sorts of sensitive information, state secrets, at the heart of our Royal Family, has lied his way right through the regular vetting procedures. Laid himself wide open to blackmail and pressure.' Urquhart was leaning on the wall button which would summon the private lift to the top-floor apartment. 'And then, most serious of all, is deceit of the King. A lifelong friend, whom he has betrayed. Unless, of course, you wish to be uncharitable and conclude that the King knew all along and has been covering up to help an old friend. Messy.'

'You're not implying that the King, too—'

'I imply nothing. That's the job of the press,' he responded, 'who, I confidently predict, by the end of the week will be wading in it.'

The lift doors were open, beckoning. 'Then why wait, Francis? Why not strike now, before the King sets off and does all that damage?'

'Because Mycroft is no more than a dunghill. The King needs to be pushed not from a dunghill but from a mountain top, and by the end of his tour he will have climbed about as high as he's going to get. I can wait.'

They stepped into the lift, a small, insalubrious affair which had been squeezed into a recess of the old house during refurbishment earlier in the century. The narrowness of its bare metal walls forced them together and, as the doors closed, she could see the way his eyes lit up, sense the confidence, arrogance even, like a lion in his lair. She could be either his prey, or his lioness; she had to keep pace with him or find herself devoured.

'Some things you shouldn't wait for, Francis.' Match him step for step, hold on to him, even as he slithered towards his own mountain top. She leaned across him to the control panel, and as her groping fingers found the key the lift stopped quietly between floors. Already her blouse was unbuttoned and he was kneading the firm flesh of her breasts. She winced, he was getting rougher, more bruising, his thrust for domination more insistent. He still had on his overcoat. She had to allow it, to encourage and indulge him. He was changing, no longer bothering with self-restraint, perhaps no longer able. But as she wedged herself uncomfortably in the corner of the lift, bracing her legs against the walls, feeling cold metal on her buttocks, she knew she had to go with him as far as she could and as far as he wanted to go; it was the type of opportunity that would not present itself again. It was once in a lifetime and she had to grab it, whether or not he any longer said please.

It was four a.m. and pitch dark when Mycroft crept slowly from the bedroom and began to dress quietly outside. Kenny still slept, his body innocently engaged in a tumbling match with the bed linen, an arm wrapped around a toy bear. Mycroft felt more father than lover, driven by a deep and innate sense of protectiveness towards the younger man. He had to believe that what he was doing was right.

When he had finished dressing he sat down at the table and switched on a small lamp. He needed light to write the note. He made several hopeless attempts, all of which he tore into small pieces and placed atop a mounting pile beside him. How could he explain that he was fractured between his feelings of love and duty towards two men, the King and Kenny, both of whom were now threatened through him? That he was running away because that is what he had done all his life and he knew no other answer? That he would continue running as soon as the King's tour was over – for surely he had three days left before disaster struck?

The pile of torn paper mounted, and in the end he was left with nothing more than: 'I love you, believe me. I'm sorry.' It sounded so pathetic, so insufficient.

He placed the scraps of paper back inside his briefcase, snapping the locks as quietly as he was able, and put on his overcoat. He glanced out of the window to check the street, which he found silent and cold, as he felt inside. As carefully as he could he crept back to place the note on the table where Kenny would find it. As he placed it against the vase of flowers, he saw Kenny sitting up in bed, staring at the case, the overcoat, the note, understanding flooding into his sleep-filled eyes.

'Why, David? Why?' he whispered. He raised no shout, shed no tears, he had seen too many departures in his life and with his job, but accusation filled every syllable.

Mycroft had no answer. He had nothing but a sense of imminent despair from which he wanted to save all those he loved. He fled, away from the sight of Kenny clutching a favourite bear to his chest as he sat forlornly amidst his throne of sheets, he ran out of the apartment and back into the real world, into the dark, past the empty milk bottles, his footsteps on the pavement stones echoing down the empty street. And as he ran, for the first time in his adult life Mycroft discovered he was crying.

Later that day there were tears elsewhere. Tears that hung in the damp night air of winter, that dripped down the mould-covered walls and into the overflowing gullies of the concrete underpass, and clung around the eyes of the old derelict as he stared into the face of his King. The dirt of weeks beneath his finger nails he no longer noticed and the stench of stale urine he no longer smelled, but the King had been aware from several yards away and even more so as he knelt beside the sum of all the old man's possessions – a hand grip tied with sisal, a torn and stain-covered sleeping bag, and a large cardboard box stuffed with newspapers, which would probably be gone by the time he returned the following night.

'How on earth did he get like this?' the King enquired of a charity worker at his elbow.

'Ask him,' suggested the charity worker, who over the years had lost patience with the high and mighty who came bearing their hearts on their sleeves, to express their deeply felt concerns yet who always, without exception, did so in front of accompanying cameramen, who treated the down-and-outs as impersonal objects rather than as people, who peered and passed on.

The King flushed. At least he had the decency to recognize his own crassness. He knelt on one knee, ignoring the damp and the debris which seemed to be everywhere, to listen and to attempt understanding. And in the distance, at the end of the underpass where they had been shepherded by Mycroft, the cameras turned and recorded the image of a sad, tearful man, bent low amidst the filth, listening to the tale of a tramp.

It was said later by those accompanying members of the media that never had a royal press aide worked more tirelessly and imaginatively to give them the stories and pictures they needed. Without interfering with the King or intruding too savagely on the pathetic scenes of personal misery and deprivation, they were faced with abundance. Mycroft listened, understood, cajoled, wheeled and dealed, encouraged, advised and facilitated. At one point he intervened to delay the King a moment while a camera crew found their ideal position and changed their tape, at another he whispered in the Royal ear and got the King to repeat a scene, steam rising from the drains and beautifully backlit for effect by a street light, with a mother cradling a young baby. He argued with police and remonstrated with local officials who tried to insinuate themselves into the picture. This was not to be a caravan of officialdom who would pass by on the other side as soon as the obligatory photographs were taken; this was a man, out discovering his Kingdom, alone with a few derelicts and his conscience. Or so Mycroft explained, and was believed. If during those three days the King slept fitfully, then Mycroft slept not at all. But whereas the King's cheeks became more sallow and his eyes more sunken and full of remorse as the tour passed from day to night and back to freezing day, Mycroft's blazed with the fire of a conqueror who saw justification in every scene of deprivation and triumph in every click of the shutter.

As the King stooped beside the derelict's cardboard hovel to listen, he knew his suit was being ruined by the damp slime which covered everything, but he did not move. He was only kneeling in it, the old man lived in it. He forced himself to stay, to ignore the odours and the chill wind, to nod and smile encouragement as the old man, through the bubbling of his lungs, told his tale, of university degrees, of a faithless marriage which shattered his career and confidence, of dropping out, only to find no way back. Not without the basic respectability of an address. It was no one's fault, there was no blame, no complaints, except for the cold. He had once lived in the sewers, it was drier and warmer down there and no hassle from policemen, but the Water Board had found out and put a lock on the entrance. It took a moment to take in. They had locked this man out of the sewers . . .

The derelict stretched out his arm, revealing a bandage through which some bodily fluid had escaped and solidified. The bandage was filthy, and the King felt his flesh crawl. The old man drew closer, the misshapen fingers trembling and blackened with filth, thick and broken finger nails like talons, a hand not fit even for the sewers. The King held it very tightly and very long.

When at last he rose to move on, there was foul smear on the leg of his suit and his eyes were damp. From the bite of the wind, probably, because his jaw was set firm and angry, but from tears of compassion the press would say. 'King of Conscience' the headlines would shout. The King walked slowly and stained out of the dripping underpass and onto the front page of every newspaper in the country.

Gordon McKillin's advisers had argued the matter through for a full day. The original idea had been to call a press conference, the full works, and deliver as strong a message as possible to ensure that no journalist left with any question unanswered. But the Opposition Leader had his doubts. If the purpose of the exercise was to identify himself as closely as possible with the King's tour, shouldn't he match it in style? Wouldn't a formalized press conference seem too heavy, too intrusive, as if he were trying to hijack the King for party political purposes? His doubt grew into a flood of uncertainty and the plans were changed. The word was circulated. McKillin would be found on his doorstep immediately after breakfast time, bidding his wife farewell in a touching family scene which complemented the informal fashion of the King's tour, and if any cameras or press men happened to be passing . . .

The scrum outside the front door in Chapel Street was appalling and it took several minutes before McKillin's communications adviser nodded that the multitude of cameras was in position and organized. It had to be right; after all, Breakfast TV was carrying it live.

'Good morning, ladies and gentlemen,' he began as his wife hovered shyly in the background. 'I'm delighted to see you all, for what I assume is an early look at our forthcoming announcements on transport policy.'

'Not unless it includes the abolition of the Royal Trains.'

'Hardly.'

'Mr McKillin, do you think the King is right to take such a high-profile tour?' The questioner was young, blonde, aggressive, thrusting a microphone at him as though it were a weapon. Which, of course, it was.

'The King is high profile, in that he has no choice. Of course he is right to see for himself how the underprivileged live. I believe what he is doing is admirable and I applaud it.'

'But Downing Street is said to be very upset; they say that such matters should be left to the politicians,' another voice chimed in.

'When did Mr Urquhart last visit such places himself, for goodness sake? Just because he doesn't have the *nerve*' – in his Highland tongue the word sounded like a military drum roll calling troops to the advance – 'to face the victims of his policies, that is no reason why others should also run away.'

'You wouldn't criticize the King's tour in any respect?'

McKillin paused. Keep the vultures waiting, guessing, anticipating. His chin came up to make him look more statesmanlike, less fleshy around the jowls, as he had rehearsed a thousand times. 'I identify myself entirely with what the King has done. I've always been a firm supporter of the Royal Family, and I believe we should be thanking fortune we have a King who is as concerned and involved as he is.'

'So you're one hundred per cent behind him?'

The voice was slow, emphatic, very dour. 'One hundred per cent.'

'Will you be raising the matter in the House?'

'Och, no. I cannot. The rules of the House of Commons are quite clear in excluding any controversial discussion of the Monarch, but, even if the rules permitted, I would not. I believe very firmly that our Royal Family should not be used by politicians for narrow

205

partisan purposes. So I'm not planning to raise the matter or hold any press conferences. I will go no further than simply expressing my view that the King has every right to do what he is doing, and I join in his concern for the underprivileged, who form such a large part of modern Britain . . .'

The communications man was waving his hands about his head, drawing one arm across his throat. Time to wrap up. Enough said to grab a headline, not enough to be accused of exploiting the situation. Always keep the vultures underfed, wanting more.

McKillin was making his final self-deprecating plea to the cameras when from the street came the noisy rapping of a car horn. He looked up to see a green Range-Rover shuffling past. Wretched man! It was a Liberal MP, a neighbour from farther down Chapel Street who took delight whenever he could in disrupting the Opposition Leader's doorstep interviews. The more McKillin protested about fair play, the louder and more sustained became his neighbour's efforts. He knew it would mark the end of interest in the interview from the Breakfast TV producer, he had perhaps only a second or two of live television left. McKillin's eyes lit up with pleasure, he offered a broad smile and cast an extravagant wave in the direction of the retreating Range-Rover. Eight million viewers saw a politician at his best, for all the world as if he were responding graciously and enthusiastically to the unexpected greeting of one of his most ardent supporters. Serve the bugger right. McKillin wasn't going to allow anything to spoil what was turning out to be an excellent day.

As the producer brought the programme back to the studio, Elizabeth Urquhart dragged her attention away from the flickering screen to look at her husband. He was playing with pieces of blackened toast, and he was smiling.

The coach taking the party of journalists from the Gorbals to the airport on the outskirts of Glasgow swayed as it turned the sharp corner into the car park. Mycroft, standing in the aisle, clung tightly as he surveyed the results of his handiwork. Throughout most of the coach sat journalists who were exhausted but content, their work having dominated the front pages for three full days, their expenses justified for at least another month. Plaudits were offered in abundance to Mycroft for his Herculean efforts on their behalf. Goodwill expressed itself in face after face, genuine and whole-hearted, until his eyes reached the back rows of the coach. There, like truculent schoolboys, sat Ken Rochester and his photographer, alongside another pair from a rival newspaper who had also joined the tour at the last minute. They weren't accredited Royal correspondents but sailed under a flag of journalistic convenience which described them as feature writers. The attention they had been paying him, and the cameras that had been turned in his direction when they should have been pointed at the King, left Mycroft in no doubt as to whom they intended to feature in their next reports. The word was clearly spreading, the vultures were circling overhead, and the presence of competitors would make them all the more anxious to pounce. He had less time than he had realized.

His thoughts returned to the words which had inspired him and others over the last few days, words he had taken directly from the King. Words about the need to find himself, to respond to those things he felt deep inside, to see whether he was up to the task not just of doing his job, but of being a man. The need to stop running. He thought of Kenny. They wouldn't leave him alone, he was sure of that, the Rochesters of this world weren't the type. Even if Mycroft never saw Kenny again, they would treat Kenny as fuel to feed the pyre, destroy Kenny in order to get at him, destroying him in order to get at the King. He felt no anger, there was no point. That was the way the system worked. Defend the free press and damn the weak. He felt numb, almost clinical, distanced even from his own plight, as if he had stepped outside himself and could regard this other man with the objective detachment of a professional. After all, that's what he was.

At the rear of the coach Rochester was talking conspiratorially in the ear of his photographer, who proceeded to squeeze off yet another series of shots as Mycroft stood above the heads of the journalists, like an actor before his audience playing out some great drama of the doomed. By the weekend, Mycroft reasoned. That was all the time he had left. Such a pity it was excrement like

Rochester who would get the credit for the story rather than the court correspondents he had worked with and grown to respect over all these years. As the camera shutter clicked away, he began to find his calmness being steadily eaten away by his acid dislike of Rochester with his curled lip and ingratiating whine. He could feel himself beginning to tremble and he held on more tightly. Don't lose control, he shouted at himself, or the Rochesters will win, tear you to pieces. For God's sake be professional, go out on your own terms!

They were well inside the car park now, heading for the bustle of the departures building. Through his lens, Rochester's photographer saw Mycroft tap the driver on the shoulder and say something which caused the coach to turn aside and park in a quiet lay-by some considerable distance from the terminal. As the coach stopped, Mycroft squeezed out a tight smile for the throng around him. He was right in their midst.

'Before you finish this tour, there's one part of the story you haven't yet got. It might surprise you. It might even surprise the King . . .'

Urquhart sat on the Government Front Bench, shielded only in part by the Dispatch Box, surveying the army of waving hands and wagging tongues before him. George Washington? He felt more like General Custer. The restraint of Opposition shown on McKillin's doorstep had gone as the backbench hounds scented blood. It needed nerve, this job, to withstand the slings and arrows and all the vile taunts of which a parliamentary enemy could think. He had to believe in himself, utterly, to force out any room for doubt which his enemies might exploit. Perfect, absolute, uncompromising certainty in his cause. They were a rabble, not only lacking in principle but also in imagination; he wouldn't be surprised if in their new-found royalist fervour they descended to singing the national anthem, right here and now, in the Chamber of the House of Commons, the one place in all the Kingdom to which the Monarch was denied entry. His eyes lit on The Beast and he smiled grimly. The Beast was, after all, a man true to himself. While others around him roared and waved and stirred themselves to heights of manufactured passion, The Beast sat there looking simply embarrassed. The cause was, to him, more important than victory. He wouldn't cast it aside simply to grasp the opportunity of humiliating his opponent. Bloody idiot.

They were such petty, unworthy specimens. They called themselves politicians, leaders, but none of them understood power. He would show them. And his mother. Show her that he was better than Alistair, had always been better, would always be better than them all. No doubts.

As the first backbencher was called, Urquhart knew what he would say, regardless of the question. But they always asked such predictable questions. It would be the King. And Madam Speaker would object, but he would answer it anyway. Emphasize the principle of keeping the Monarch out of politics. Deprecate their ill-concealed attempt to drag him into partisan warfare. Insinuate that any damned fool could identify problems, the responsible looked for solutions. Encourage them to make as much noise as possible, even if it meant an afternoon of prime ministerial humiliation, to tie themselves as tightly as they could to the King so that they could never unravel the knots. Then, and only then, would it be time to push His Majesty off the mountain top.

'Damn! Damn! Damn!!!' The expletives ricocheted off the walls as Stamper gave vent to his fury, for a moment drowning the television commentary.

Sally and Urquhart were not alone. Stamper sat in one of the large leather armchairs of the Prime Minister's study, agitatedly devouring the news report and his finger nails. For the first time since their relationship had started, she was being shared with someone else. Perhaps Urquhart wanted others to know, maybe she had become a status symbol, another prop for his virility and ego. Or maybe he had simply wanted an audience to witness another of his triumphs. If so, he must be sorely chagrined at the scenes unfolding in front of their eyes.

'In an astonishing finale to the Royal tour this afternoon, the

209

King's press secretary, David Mycroft, announced his resignation,' the reporter intoned.

'I am a homosexual.' The pictures of Mycroft were not particularly clear, there was too much backlighting coming from the windows of the coach, but they were good enough. Surrounded by seated colleagues, sharing news with them as he had done for many years, a player plucking at his audience. This was no fugitive with shifting eyes and sweaty brow, cornered, back to the wall. This was a man in control.

'I had hoped that my private life would remain just that, and not interfere with my responsibilities to the King, but I can no longer be sure of this. So I am resigning.'

'What was the King's response?' a reporter was heard to challenge.

'I don't know. I haven't told him. When last I asked to resign, he refused my resignation. As you all know, he is a man of the utmost compassion and understanding. But the task of the Monarch is more important than any one man, particularly a press aide, and so I have taken it upon myself to relieve him of any responsibility by announcing my resignation publicly, to you. I only hope that His Majesty will understand.'

'But why on earth is being a homosexual a bar to your job?'

Mycroft bent his face into an expression of wry amusement. 'You ask *me* that question?' He laughed as if someone had made a modestly good joke. No animosity, no snarl of an animal at bay. God, it was a fine performance. 'A press officer is meant to be a channel for news, not the target of it. Speculation about my private life would have made my professional duties impossible.'

'Why have you hidden it all these years?' It was Rochester from the back of the bus.

'Hidden it? I haven't. My marriage broke up recently after many years. I was always faithful to my wife, and I am deeply grateful to her for the years of happiness we spent together. But with that break-up came a new understanding and possibly a final opportunity, to be the man that perhaps I always wanted to be. I have made that choice. I have no regrets.'

With apparent utter frankness he had turned the attack. Anyway, most of the people here were old colleagues, friends, nothing could disguise the atmosphere of sympathy and goodwill. Mycroft had chosen his moment, and his interrogators, well.

Urquhart turned off as the TV reporter continued the saga of the Royal aide, whom he described as 'much respected and well liked', against a background of footage from the just-completed tour.

'Selfish bastard,' Stamper muttered.

'I thought you wanted him out,' Sally interjected.

'We wanted him hung, not walking into the sunset with the applause of the crowd ringing in his ears,' snapped Stamper. Sally suspected he was irritated by her presence in what had formerly been an all-male preserve.

'Don't fret, Tim,' Urquhart responded. 'Our target was not Mycroft, but the King. And even as he surveys his realm from the mountain top, the ground beneath his feet is beginning to crumble. Almost time to give him a helping hand. In the small of the back, I think.'

'But you only have a week before . . . Those images of the tour are killing you, Francis,' she said softly, marvelling at his composure.

He looked at her with narrowed, hard eyes, as if scolding her for lacking faith. 'But there are images, dear Sally, and there are images.' A dark smile split his face but his eyes remained like rock. He crossed to his desk, extracting a small key from his wallet before slowly unlocking a top drawer. He extracted a large manila envelope and spilled its contents across the desk. Every action was meticulous, like a craftsman jeweller displaying his most precious stones. There were photographs, perhaps a dozen of them, all in colour, which he sorted through to select two, holding them up so that Sally and Stamper could clearly see.

'What do you think of them?'

She was uncertain whether he meant the photographs or the pair of breasts they prominently displayed. The two photographs, as all the others, revealed the uninhibited charms of Princess Charlotte. The only variation on the central theme was the precise position of her body and the contortions of the young man with her.

'Oh, I say,' breathed Stamper.

'One of the more onerous burdens of being Prime Minister is that one is entrusted with a variety of secrets. Stories that are never told. Such as the tale of a young military equerry to the Princess who, fearing that his favoured position at the side and on top of the Princess was in jeopardy, took out an insurance policy in the form of these photographs.'

'Oh, I say,' Stamper said once more as he rifled through the other shots.

'It was the equerry's bad luck,' Urquhart continued, 'that he should try to encash the policy with the wrong man, an investigative journalist who also happens to be a former operative for the security services. And so the photographs finished up in my drawer while the unfortunate lovesick boy has been told in no uncertain terms that his testicles will be ripped from his body should any copies find their way around Fleet Street.' He took back the photographs, which Stamper had been clinging to perhaps a moment too long. 'Something tells me, Timothy, that I wouldn't wish to be in his predicament in a few days' time.'

The two men laughed bawdily, but Urquhart noticed that Sally seemed not to be enjoying the moment.

'Something bothering you, Sally?'

'It doesn't feel right. It's the King who is doing the damage to you, not Mycroft or the Princess.'

'The limbs first . . .'

'But she's done nothing. She's not involved.'

'Bloody soon will be,' snorted Stamper.

'Call it an occupational hazard,' Urquhart added. His smile was stretching more thinly.

'I can't help thinking of her family. The effect on her children.' An edge of stubbornness was beginning to creep into her voice and her full, expressive lips pouted in defiance.

His response was slow and stonily firm. 'War breeds misery. There are many unfortunate victims.'

'Her only sin, Francis, is to be saddled with a healthy sex drive and an inbred English wimp for a husband.'

'Her sin is getting caught.'

'Only because she's a woman!'

212

'Spare me the collective feminism,' Urquhart snapped in exasperation. 'She's spent a lifetime living off the fat served at the Royal table, and the time has come for her to pay the bill.'

She was about to respond but she saw his eyes flare and pulled herself back. She wasn't going to win this argument and, in pursuing it, she might lose much more. She told herself not to be so naive. Hadn't she always known that a woman's sex was no more than a tool, a weapon, which as often as not fell into the hands of men? She turned away, conceding.

'Tim, make sure these get a good airing, will you? Just a couple for the moment. Leave the rest.'

Stamper nodded and took the opportunity to bend over the desk and rifle once more through the photographs.

'Now, Tim. There's a good fellow.'

Stamper's head came up sharply, his eyes flickering as he looked first at Urquhart, then at Sally, then back to Urquhart. The ember of understanding began to glow in his eyes, and with it rivalry. She was muscling in on his relationship with the boss, and had an advantage not even Stamper with all his guile and gamescraft could match.

'I'll get right to it, Francis.' He gathered up two of the images and looked sharply at Sally. 'Night, one and all.' Then he was gone.

Neither of them spoke for some time. Urquhart tried to appear nonchalant, taking great care to adjust the razor-sharp creases of his trousers, but the softness of the words when eventually they came belied their menace.

'Don't go coy on me now, O Gypsy.'

'She's going to get a very raw deal out of this one.'

'It's them or me.'

'I know.'

'Still on side?'

In answer, she crossed slowly to him and kissed him passionately, forcing her body up against his and her tongue into his mouth. Within seconds his hands were fondling, bruising. She knew his instincts were angry, animal. Roughly he bent her forward across his desk, sweeping his pen tray and telephone to one side and knocking over a framed photograph of his wife. Her skirt was lifted

213

over her back and he was at her, tearing at her underwear, forcing himself inside, kneading the flesh of her buttocks with such intensity that she winced at the bite of his nails. She was prostrate across the desk, her nose and cheek forced flat into the leather top. And she remembered. As a young girl of perhaps thirteen she had taken a short cut through the back alleys of Dorchester on her way to the cinema and there had come face to face with a woman, bent low across the hood of a car. She was black, with bright crimson lips and gaudy eyes which were hard, impatient, bored. The man behind her was fat and white and had sworn at Sally, foul, disgusting words, but he had not stopped. The memory crowded back in all its chilling clarity, as Urquhart's nails dug ever more deeply into her skin and her face was pressed painfully into the scattering of photographs across the desktop. She felt like crying, not in ecstasy but in pain and degradation. Instead, she simply bit her lip.

Mycroft found him on the moors above Balmoral, where he often went when troubled and wanting to be alone, even in the middle of winter with snow on the ground and an easterly wind which had found nothing to obstruct or deflect it since it had gathered strength in the shadows of the Urals two thousand miles away. There were ageless spirits up there, he had once said, which lurked in the crannies of the granite outcrops and sang as they ran with the wind through the rough heather, long after the deer had sought the shelter of lower pastures. The King had seen him coming, but had not offered any greeting.

'I had no choice. *We* had no choice.'

'We? Since when was I consulted?' The regal tone betrayed a sense of insult and personal hurt. The anger – or was it solely the wind? – brought a bucolic flush to his cheeks and his words came slowly. 'I would have stuck by you.'

'You think I didn't realize that?' It was Mycroft's turn for exasperation. 'That's why I had to take the decision out of your hands. It's time to start following your head rather than your heart.'

'You have committed no offence, David, broken no law.'

'Since when did such things matter? I would have become a

214

monumental distraction. Instead of listening to you they would have been sniggering behind their hands at me. You've taken such personal risks to carry your message across without interference and I would simply have got in the way, another excuse for them to sidetrack and confuse. Don't you see? I didn't resign in spite of you. I resigned because of you.' He paused, searching the mists which clung to the moorland around them and burying himself deeper inside the borrowed ski jacket. 'And, of course, there's someone else. I had to think of him, too. Protect him.'

'I feel almost jealous.'

'That I could love two men in such different ways I never thought possible.' Mycroft's hand reached out to touch the other man on the arm, an unforgivable action between man and Monarch, but the words and the freezing wind seemed to have stripped the formality away.

'What's his name?'

'Kenny.'

'He will always be welcome. With you. At the Palace.'

The King placed his hand to cover that of Mycroft, who lowered his head, weighed down by gratitude and emotion.

'Ours was a very private matter, not something for headlines and the baying of hounds, of having his private life turned inside out,' Mycroft explained.

'Such plants rarely grow when showered in innuendo and the manure of publicity.'

'I'm very much afraid this may all have been too much for him. But thank you.'

The wind sighed through the heather, a low, mournful sound as the light began to fade, like demons of the night come to reclaim their land.

'It has all been such an unhappy accident, David.'

'Funny, but I feel almost relieved, released. No regrets. But no accident, either.'

'Meaning?'

'I'm not a great believer in coincidence. It was timed to detract from your tour, meant to damage you as much as me.'

'By whom?'

215

'By whoever had a motive to get at you. And by whoever had the opportunity. By someone who knows the Member for Dagenham and who has the resources to track down a private phone number.'

'It would require someone who could sink very low.'

'The lowest. And he will continue his pursuit of you, have no doubts. There will be more.'

'Then I hope I can find your courage.'

'You already have. All you need is the courage to face up to yourself, that's what you said. To play the man – your own words. Facing up to others holds fewer torments, believe me. But I think you already know that.'

'I shall need your advice, David, more than ever if, as you say, it is all to get worse.'

Slowly at first, then with gathering force, drops of cold-hardened rain began to fall across the two lonely figures. Darkness was encroaching fast.

'Then the best advice I have for you, Sir, is for us to get off this bloody moor before we both freeze to death and save Francis Urquhart the bother.'

February: The Second Week

It took less than a second for the phone to be answered in the foreign-currency dealing room at one of the City's leading finance houses which squatted alongside the Thames, in a site near to where the Great Fire that had destroyed half of London more than three centuries earlier had started. It wouldn't take another fire to ruin the City again, they joked, just another Japanese takeover.

The phones never took long to be answered. The difference between disaster and success could often be measured in seconds, and the chief currency dealer couldn't afford to be caught napping by either the markets or any of the seventeen other currency dealers, all of whom envied his job and the commissions that went with it. He dragged his thoughts away from the ruinously fashionable forty-foot cruiser he had just agreed to purchase to concentrate on the voice at the end of the phone. It was not, however, a deal, but an enquiry from one of his many press contacts.

'Heard any rumours about some scandal at the Palace, Jim?'

'What rumours?'

'Oh, nothing very specific. Simply a buzz that there's something brewing which is just about to blow the Royal Yacht out of the water.' He didn't see the dealer wince. 'My editor's asking us all to check around, bit of a dragnet, really. But something's smelling pretty ripe.'

The dealer's eyes flashed up to his screen yet again, checking the mixture of red, black and yellow figures. Sterling seemed to be fine, all the attention today was on the rouble following news of a fresh outbreak of food riots in Moscow. A cripplingly severe winter seemed to have frozen both the capacity of its leaders and the nerve of its foreign exchanges. The dealer rubbed his eyes to make sure;

217

his eyes ached from the constant strain, yet he didn't dare wear his prescription glasses in the office. His position was all about maintaining confidence and at thirty-seven he couldn't afford the slightest sign of age or physical decline; there were too many waiting eagerly to push him off his seat.

'Heard nothing this end, Pete. There's no activity in the markets.'

'I can tell you, the flies are definitely beginning to buzz at this end.'

'Maybe it's just another load of Royal bullshit being spread about the Royal parks.'

'Yeah, maybe,' responded the journalist, sounding unconvinced. 'Let me know if you hear anything, will you?'

The dealer punched the button to disconnect the line and returned to massaging his eyeballs while trying to figure out how he was going to stretch his already crippling mortgage to cover his latest material indulgence. He was dreaming of naked girls covered in smiles and coconut oil and laid out across glass-fibre reinforced with kevlar when the phone rang again. It was a client who had heard similar rumours and who wanted to know whether to make a quick switch into dollars or yen. More flies. And as the dealer looked once again at the screen, the sterling figures began to flash red. A fall. Not much of one, only a few pips, but it was another hint. Could he afford to ignore them? Hell, he was getting too old for this, maybe he should pack it all in and spend a year sailing around the Caribbean before getting himself a proper job. But not yet, not before he had made one last big hit, to cover the boat and the bloody mortgage. He tuned in his aching brain to the box that connected him to the brokers and their constant dangling of buy and sell prices, pressing the button which put him through.

'Cable?' he enquired. It was dealers' kvetch for the price of sterling, harking back to the days when the two great financial empires of London and New York were connected only by unquenchable avarice and a submarine cable.

'Twenty, twenty-five. Five by ten,' came the crackling response. Even in this age of space travel they still couldn't fix the lines connecting them with the brokers' rooms less than a sparrow's fart away. Or were his ears going, too?

218

He sighed. In for a penny, in for five million. 'Yours. Five.'
The selling had begun.

The door to the editor's office had been slammed shut. It wouldn't make any difference; everybody in the building would hear about it within minutes. The deputy, news and picture editors stood around the chief editor's desk in a formation which gave the impression of Sioux circling a wagon train, but he wasn't giving up without a fight.

'I'm not holding the front page for this. They're disgusting. An invasion of privacy.'

'They're news,' responded his deputy through clenched teeth.

'You know the proprietor's breakfast rule. Nothing on the front page that would offend two old ladies reading the paper over breakfast,' the editor countered.

'That's why there's no one other than old women who read our paper nowadays!'

The editor wanted to shove the words straight back down his pushy deputy's throat, but since they were precisely those he had used in his increasingly frequent rows with the ageing proprietor, he couldn't. He stared once again at the two plate-sized photographs which had already been cropped in red pencil to concentrate the attention away from extraneous features such as the bed, the disarranged pillows and entangled legs, and onto the body and face of the Princess.

'We can't. It's simply obscene.'

Without a word the picture editor leaned across the desk and, with red pencil and ruler, drew two neat lines cutting both photographs just above the nipple. What was left had all been seen before in countless beach photographs of the Princess, but it made no fundamental difference; the expression on her face, the arched back and the tongue in her ear told the whole story.

'What does the Palace have to say?' the editor enquired wearily.

'Sweet bugger all. Since Mycroft publicly deflowered himself they're in something of a mess.'

'First Mycroft, now this . . .' The editor shook his head, conscious that he would be hounded off the society dinner circuit if these went out under his name. He found another burst of resistance. 'Look, this isn't the bloody French Revolution. I will not be the one to drag the Royal Family to the guillotine.'

'There's a real public issue here,' the news editor interjected, somewhat more quietly than the deputy. 'The King involves himself in all sorts of matters, stirring up political controversy, while quite clearly he is ignoring what's going on under his own palace roof. He's supposed to be the personal embodiment of the nation's morality, not running a knocking shop. He's turned out to have more blind eyes than Nelson.'

The editor lowered his head. Sterling had already dipped nearly two cents on the rumours; it was inflicting real harm.

'No one's asking you to lead a revolution, just keep step with the others.' The deputy took up the cudgels once more. 'These piccies are all over town. By morning we might be the only paper not carrying them.'

'I disagree. I don't give a damn about the foreign rags. This is a British affair. Every editor in this town knows the consequences of using these photos. No one's going to rush, not in British newspapers. No.' He braced his shoulders with patriotic pride and shook his head in determined fashion. 'We are not going to use them unless we know for certain that someone else has. It may be throwing away a scoop, but it's the kind of scoop I don't want etched on my gravestone.'

The deputy was about to make some comment that the accountants were already chiselling the circulation figures on his gravestone when the door burst open and the gossip columnist rushed in. He was too excited and breathless to make any sense, his words wrapping themselves in impenetrable knots, until in exasperation he threw his hands in the air and made a dive for the TV remote control on the editor's desk. He punched the button to call up one of the satellite news channels. It was German-owned, run out of Luxembourg and had a footprint that covered half of Europe, including most of Southern England. As the screen came to life they were greeted with the images of an ecstatic Princess Charlotte, nipples and all. Without a further word the deputy grabbed the pictures and rushed off to save the front page.

'Oh, I like this, Elizabeth. I like this a lot.'

It was after one in the morning, the early editions had arrived, and Elizabeth with them. He seemed not to mind, chuckling as he glanced through the reports.

' "This morning the King stands accused of dereliction of duty",' Urquhart read out from the pages of *The Times*. ' "In pursuit of personal popularity and his own political scruples he has laid open not only himself but the institution of the Monarchy to frontal attack. The politicians and press lords who have jumped on his bandwagon in the last few weeks have revealed themselves as opportunistic and unprincipled. It has taken courage to stand firm for constitutional principle, to remind the nation that the Monarch should be neither showbiz nor social conscience, but an impartial and politically uninvolved head of state. Francis Urquhart has shown that courage; he is to be applauded".' Urquhart chuckled again. 'Yes, I do like that. But then I should, my dear. I wrote most of it myself.'

'I prefer *Today*,' Elizabeth responded. ' "An end to Royal tittle and tattle. It's time for them all to belt up and button up!" '

' "Crackpot King",' Urquhart announced, reading from another. ' "HRH should have an urgent word in the Princess's ear, even if he has to jump to the front of the queue to do so . . ." '

Elizabeth was in fits of laughter. She had just picked up the *Sun* with its blaring headline: 'King of Cock-Up'. 'Oh, my dear,' she struggled to respond through convulsions of mirth, 'you really have won this battle.'

He grew suddenly serious, as though someone had thrown a switch. 'Elizabeth, I've scarcely even started to fight.' He picked up the phone, an operator answered. 'See if the Chancellor of the Exchequer is still in the land of the living,' he instructed, replacing the phone very carefully. It rang less than half a minute later.

'How are you, Francis?' a weary and just-woken voice enquired down the line.

'Well, and about to get considerably better. Listen carefully. We

221

have a particularly difficult crisis on our hands which has already set the doves fluttering in the dovecote. We need to take action before they all fly away for good. I believe sterling is about to take yet another precipitous fall. In the circumstances it would be uncivil and unworthy if we were to ask our friends in Brunei to hold on any longer. It would place an important international alliance at risk. You are to call the Sultan's officials and suggest they sell their three billion pound tranche immediately.'

'Christ Almighty, Francis, that will do for the currency completely.' There was not a trace of tiredness now.

'The markets must have their way. It is a matter of great misfortune that the consequences will strike terror into the hearts of ordinary voters as they see the pound plummet and their mortgage rates about to soar. It will be an even greater misfortune that the whole debacle will be blamed on the King's conscience and those who support him.'

There was silence on the end of the phone.

'I make myself clear?'

'Absolutely,' came the quiet answer.

Urquhart looked attentively at the receiver before softly replacing it. Elizabeth was looking at him with unconcealed admiration.

'We must all make sacrifices in battle, Elizabeth.' He placed the tips of his fingers to the point of his nose. Unconsciously he was beginning to mimic the King in some of his mannerisms, Elizabeth thought. 'I'm not quite sure how to put this delicately,' he continued, 'so perhaps I shall have to crave your understanding and be blunt. It does not pay to fight a battle from within glass houses. It would be helpful if you would stop taking such an ardent interest in Italian arias. Your new-found operatic interests could be so easily . . . misconstrued. It might confuse the troops.'

Elizabeth, who had been sipping a glass of wine, replaced the glass gently on the table.

'Government drivers are such a gossipy bunch,' he added, as if by way of explanation and excuse.

'I see.'

'No hard feelings?'

'After all these years?' She inclined her head. 'Of course not.'

'You are very understanding, my dear.'

'I have to be.' She reached for her purse and extracted an earring. It was bold, fashionable, enamelled, costume jewellery from Butler & Wilson in the Fulham Road. One of Sally's. 'The cleaner gave me this the other day. Found it jammed down the side of the Chesterfield. Thought it was one of mine. I'm not sure how to put this delicately, Francis . . .'

He flushed, lowered his eyes, said nothing.

'Sauce for the goose? Even a Canadian goose?'

'She's . . . American,' he responded haltingly.

'Nevertheless.'

'Elizabeth, she is important to me; she has more vital work to do.'

'But not on her back, Francis. Not in a glass house.'

He looked directly at his wife. It had been a long time since anyone had put him in such a corner. He wasn't used to it. He sighed, he had no choice.

'All you have to do, Elizabeth, is to say please. You remember how to say please, don't you?'

'It's getting very messy.'

'It'll get worse.'

'You sure?'

'Never been more certain.'

'How so?'

'Because he can't yet be certain about winning an election; there's more to be done. He needs a few more points on the polls. He can't stop now. Risk a Royal comeback. And . . .' She hesitated. 'And because he's an axeman. His target isn't the Princess, it's the King himself. I'm not sure if he knows any longer when to stop hacking.'

He was silent, pondering. 'Sally, you're absolutely certain about this?'

'About his plans? Yes. About him . . . ?' She could still feel the mangled flesh of her buttocks where his finger nails had dug deep. 'I'm certain.'

223

'Then I have work to do.'

He rolled out of bed and reached for his trousers. Moments later he was gone.

The currency dealer turned over and lay in the luminous blue glow of his digital alarm. Four thirteen a.m. Crap. He wouldn't get back to sleep again now. He'd been unsettled all night, his thoughts jarring between the yacht and the young nurse he'd tried and failed to pull a few hours previously. They had shared a ludicrously indulgent meal at Nikita's; she'd drunk too much cherry vodka and been sick. *Tant pis.*

He flicked on his palm-sized Pocketwatch and checked the miniature screen for the latest state of the markets. Perhaps that's what had been eating away at him. Christ! Sterling was down almost another two hundred points in the Far East and he was beginning to wish he, too, had drunk a little less vodka. He was holding twenty million pounds overnight, and he suddenly felt very exposed. He punched one of the memory buttons on his bedside phone which connected with his branch in Singapore, eight hours ahead. 'What's up?'

'Negara's been selling steadily since the market opened,' an accented voice told him. So the Malaysian central bank was in on the act . . .

'What's Cable in forty?' he demanded.

'Sixty-five seventy.'

Selling at sixty-five, buying at seventy. But no one was buying. Time to join the herd. 'Shit, let's move it. At sixty-five.' He put the phone down, having just sold forty million pounds sterling in the belief the price would continue falling. If it did he would have covered his overnight position, and more. He'd better get into the office early, in case the entire bloody world woke up with a headache and the herd started to stampede. And maybe he would call that very special client who helped with all those unofficial deals on the side. The client wouldn't mind being woken at this hour, not for the size of stakes he played with. And if they got it right, he could stop worrying about the yacht. And that silly nurse.

*   *   *

Evening Standard, City Edition, 9 February

POUND AND PRINCESS EXPOSED

Sterling continued to come under heavy pressure as the London market followed the lead set overnight in the Far East. Dealers expressed concern that the stream of sexual scandal enveloping the Royal Family could cause a full-blown constitutional and political crisis, following the resignation of the King's press secretary last week and lurid photographs of Princess Charlotte published in many of this morning's newspapers.

The Bank of England and other European banks moved to support sterling as soon as the markets opened but could not prevent further speculative selling driving the currency down hard against the bottom of its EC limits. There were reports of a major holder of sterling in the Far East dumping significant quantities of the currency. It is feared that interest rates may have to be raised substantially to prop up the ailing pound.

'This sort of situation is a new one for us,' one dealer commented. 'The markets hate the uncertainty, at times this morning they were in turmoil. The sheiks are saying if Buckingham Palace crumbles, how safe is the Bank of England? The City has the atmosphere of a farmyard before Christmas . . .'

*   *   *

It was a good day for a hanging, McKillin thought. The Chamber was packed beyond capacity with many Members, deprived of a seat on the benches, standing at the Bar, crouching in gangways or crowding around the sides of the Speaker's Chair. The pressure of so many mostly male bodies crushed together gave rise to a heady, boisterous atmosphere, overflowing with expectation. It was said there had been similar scenes at Tyburn when they came to hang some wretch from the three-legged gallows, and that they even paid for the privilege of watching the poor bastard swing.

There had already been a long queue of victims today. The waves of panic rippling through the currency markets had washed over into the Stock Exchange and by lunchtime share prices were off, badly. The cries of pain emanating from those with exposed positions could be heard from all over the City and it was going to spread faster than a lassie's legs at the Edinburgh Festival. The building societies were meeting in emergency session; mortgages would have to be raised, the only question was by how much. It wasn't the King's fault, of course, but people had lost their innocent belief in bad fortune, in catastrophes simply happening, they had to have someone to blame. And that meant that McKillin, too, was in the firing line, reflecting ruefully on his recent public displays of indulgence on behalf of the Royal Family, wincing at one hundred per cent. He had thought all morning of defence through aggression, making a full-scale charge in support of the King, but decided that the King's position was too well covered by hostile guns. The troops behind him were no Light Brigade, and he wasn't Errol Flynn. No point in getting shot in the Trossachs for nothing, much better to fight another day. Some question about human rights, perhaps, high-ground stuff, related to the PM's lightning trip to Moscow which had been announced for the coming week. That would do, give him some distance from the sound of battle, get him out from under the gibbet . . . As he waited, he began to feel sticky with the heat and pressure from the bodies of overfed men crowding around.

He saw Urquhart appear just in time for the three-fifteen p.m. start, forcing his way through the scrum which surrounded the Speaker's Chair and squeezing past the outstretched limbs of other Cabinet Ministers perched untidily along the Front Bench. Urquhart smiled across the Dispatch Box at McKillin, a fleeting parting of thin lips to expose the incisors, the first warning shot of the afternoon's campaign. Behind Urquhart's position sat the Honourable Lady Member for Dorset North, bobbing obsequiously as her master took his seat, wearing a garishly crimson outfit which stood out like a traffic beacon amidst the gloom of grey suits and which would show well on the television screens. She had been practising her expressions of support all morning in front of a mirror. She was a handsome and well-presented woman, early forties, with a voice like a hyena, which rumour had it could reach top C in bed, as even some members of the Opposition claimed to know. She'd never make Ministerial office, but her memoirs would probably outsell the rest.

McKillin leaned back, giving the impression of a relaxed demeanour while he studied the press gallery above his head; over the finely carved balustrade he could see the heads of the scribblers, faces strained in expectation, their pencils and prejudices sharpened. He wouldn't keep them waiting, he would get in there at the first opportunity, show his colours and retire from the field before the real battle started and it all got out of control. Human rights, that was it. Damned good idea.

Already Madam Speaker had called the first question, to ask the Prime Minister his engagements for the day, and Urquhart was giving his standard and calculatedly unhelpful response, detailing a few of his official appointments 'in addition to answering questions in the House'.

'It'd be the first bloody time.' It was The Beast, from his seat below the gangway which he claimed by right of constant occupation. He looked dyspeptic; perhaps his sandwiches and pint of bitter had disagreed with him.

Urquhart gave short shrift to the first question, about a local by-pass, posed by a conscientious constituency member with a small majority, and it was McKillin's opportunity. He leaned forward and inclined his head towards Madam Speaker.

'The Leader of the Opposition.' Madam Speaker's voice summoned him to the Dispatch Box. He hadn't even finished rising to his feet before another voice cut through the bustle.

'You couldn't mistake him for a Leader of the Opposition, the grovelling little shit.'

McKillin felt his cheeks flush with anger, then astonishment. It was The Beast. His own side!

'Order! Order!' trilled Madam Speaker. In an atmosphere charged

227

like this, with so many hot MPs rubbing shoulders and jostling elbows, she knew it was vital to stamp her authority on proceedings from the first moment of disruption. 'I heard that. The Honourable Member will withdraw that remark immediately!'

'What else would you call someone who threw away all his principles and got caught licking the boots of the Royal Family. He's made a complete balls of it.'

Opposition Members sat largely silent, stunned. Government backbenchers, too, were uncertain, not knowing whether to agree with The Beast or to denounce his vulgarity, but knowing it was essential to make as much noise as possible and stir the pot. In the midst of the growing uproar The Beast, his tangled forelock tumbling across his face and his baggy sports jacket unbuttoned and open, was on his feet and ignoring the repeated demands of Madam Speaker.

'But isn't it an undeniable fact—'

'No more!' shrieked the Speaker, her half-moon glasses slipping down her nose as she flushed uncomfortably hot beneath her wig. 'I shall have no hesitation in naming the Honourable Member unless he withdraws his remarks immediately!'

'But . . .'

'Withdraw!' Cries demanding his retraction grew from all sides. The Serjeant at Arms, the parliamentary constable, dressed for the part in executioner's garb of black cloth court dress, complete with silk stockings and ceremonial sword, was standing to attention at the Bar, waiting on Madam Speaker's instructions.

'But . . .' began The Beast once again.

'Withdra-a-a-a-w!'

There was pandemonium. The Beast looked around, seeming unperturbed, as if he could hear none of the noise nor see the flailing hands and Order Papers. He smiled, then at last seemed to appreciate that his game was up for he started nodding his head in agreement. The din subsided, allowing him to be heard.

'OK.' He looked towards the Speaker's Chair. 'Which words do you want me to withdraw? Grovelling? Little? Or Shit?'

The tidal wave of outrage all but drowned Madam Speaker's cries. 'All of it! I want it all withdrawn!' Eventually she was heard.

'The lot? You want me to withdraw the lot?'

'Immediately!' The wig had been shaken askew and she was attempting to readjust herself, desperately struggling to maintain her temper and sense of dignity.

'All right. All right.' The Beast held up his hands to silence the tumult. 'You all know my views about grovelling to their Royal Mightinesses but . . .' – he stared around fiercely at the pack of parliamentary hounds snapping at his heels – 'if you rule I can't say such things, that I've got to retract it, then I shall.'

'Now. This instant!'

There was a baying of approval from all sides. The Beast was now pointing at McKillin.

'Yes, I was wrong. You obviously *can* mistake him for a Leader of the Opposition. The grovelling little shit!'

In the cacophony of shouts from all sides there was not the slightest chance for Madam Speaker to make herself heard, but The Beast didn't wait to be named, gathering up his papers from the floor and throwing a lingering look of insolence in the direction of his party leader before withdrawing himself from the Chamber. The Serjeant at Arms, who could lip-read the Speaker's instructions, fell in beside The Beast to ensure he remained withdrawn from the premises of the Palace of Westminster for the next five working days.

As The Beast's back passed through the doors and beyond, some semblance of order began to be restored to the Chamber. From beneath her wig, still slightly askew, Madam Speaker gazed in the direction of McKillin, her eyes enquiring after his intentions. He shook his head. He didn't want any longer to ask some fool question about human rights. What about his own human rights? All he wanted was for this cruel and exceptional punishment to come to an end, for someone to come and gently cut him down from the parliamentary gallows on which he was swinging, and hope they might give him a decent burial.

'How do you do it, Francis?' Stamper demanded as he strode into the Prime Minister's office in the House of Commons.

'Do what?'

'Get The Beast so wound up that on his own he's more effective at stuffing McKillin than a dozen Barnsley butchers.'

'My dear Tim, you've become such a sad old cynic. You look for conspiracies everywhere. The truth – if you could ever recognize it as such – is that I don't have to wind him up. He comes ready wound. No, my contribution to the fun is more along these lines.' He indicated the television with its display of the latest teletext news. The building societies had finished their emergency meeting and the result of their deliberations was flashing up on the screen.

'Christ. Two per cent on mortgages? That'll go down like a shovel of shit in drinking water.'

'Precisely. See how much concern the average punter has for the homeless when the mortgage on his own semi-detached roof starts burning its way through his beer money. By closing time tonight the King's conscience will seem an irrelevant and unaffordable luxury.'

'My apologies for ever having uttered a cynical remark in your presence.'

'Accepted. Voters appreciate clear choices, Tim, it helps them concentrate. I am presenting them with a choice which is practically transparent. The King may be a rare orchid to my common cabbage, but when the buggers start starving, they'll grab for the cabbage every time.'

'Enough cabbage to give the King chronic wind.'

'My dear Tim, you might say that. On such matters I couldn't possibly comment.'

The King was also seated before his television screen, where he had remained silently watching events since the televising of Prime Minister's Question Time had begun. He had left instructions not to be disturbed but eventually his Private Secretary could restrain his sense of unease no longer. He knocked and entered with a deferential bow.

'Sir, my apologies, but you must know that we are being in-undated with calls from the media, wanting some reaction, some guidance as to your feelings about events in the House of Commons.

230

They will not take silence as an answer, and without a press officer . . .'

The King seemed not to have noticed the intrusion, staring fixedly at the screen, unblinking, his body taut, the veins at his temple a vivid blue against the parchment skin of his skull. He looked ashen – not with anger, the Private Secretary was well used to the flashes of fire which sparked from the King. The stillness suggested more a man on a different plane, driven deep within himself, the strain indicating that the search to find equilibrium had proved futile.

The Private Secretary stood motionless, watching the other man's agony, embarrassed at his intrusion yet not knowing how to dismiss himself.

Eventually the King spoke, in a whisper, but not to the Secretary. 'It is no use, David.' The voice was parched and hoarse. 'It cannot be. They will no more let a King be a man than they would any man be King. It cannot be done – you know that, don't you, old friend . . . ?'

Then there was silence. The King had not moved, still staring, unseeing, at the screen. The Private Secretary waited for several seemingly endless seconds and then left, pulling the door gently behind him as if he were closing the lid on a coffin.

Sally rushed across to the House of Commons as soon as she received the summons. She had been in the middle of a pitch to a potential new client, one of the country's leading manufacturers of processed beans, but he had been most understanding, impressed even, and had assured her of the business. With contacts like that he seemed uninterested in further credentials.

A secretary was waiting for her at St Stephen's entrance to escort her like a VIP past the long queues of visitors and through the security gates, rushing her past several hundred years of history. It was her first time; one day, she promised herself, she would be back and take a calmer look at the glories of Old England, when she had the patience to queue for several hours with all the rest. But for the moment she preferred the preferential treatment.

231

They showed her straight into his office. He was on the phone, pacing around the room in his shirtsleeves, trailing the cord of the telephone behind him, animated, issuing orders.

'Yes, Bryan, I am well and my wife is well. Thank you very much, now shut up and listen. This is important. You will be receiving details of a new poll tomorrow afternoon. A telephone poll following the panic in the markets. It will be a startling one. It will show the Government in a ten-point lead over the Opposition, and my personal lead over McKillin having doubled.' He listened for a moment. 'Of course it's bloody front-page news, why on earth do you think I'm giving it to you? That front-page poll will be supported by an editorial inside your newspaper, something along the lines of "Mortgages and the Monarchy". It will blame the problem with sterling and international confidence four-square on the King and his flawed personality, and those opportunistic politicians who have sought to encourage him in what you will conclude are his grave errors of judgement for seeking to take on the elected Government. Are you listening?'

There was a mild squawking on the end of the phone and Urquhart rolled his eyes in impatience.

'You are to suggest that their unprincipled support for the King has shattered the Opposition and ruined the credibility of McKillin, and even more seriously has cast the country into a constitutional mess which is causing deep economic anguish. Reluctantly you will call for a thoroughgoing review of the Monarchy – restricting its powers, its influence, its size, its income. Take it all down carefully. Yes, I've got time . . .' He paused. 'Now we come to the important bit, Bryan. Pay great attention. Your editorial will finish by concluding that so much economic, political and constitutional uncertainty has been created that it requires an immediate solution. No time for extended debates, parliamentary commissions of inquiry – not while every shareholder and mortgage-payer in the country is swinging on the hook. The matter needs to be dealt with decisively. Once and for all, in the national interest. You are to suggest that the only established means of deciding who governs Britain is to hold an election. Do you understand? An election.' He looked across at Sally and winked.

'My dear Bryan, of course this is something of a shock, that's why I'm giving you the opportunity to prepare. But just between the two of us, until tomorrow. No running down to the bookies to put a couple of quid on an early election, now. Another of our little secrets, eh? You call me, only me, Bryan, day or night, if you have any questions. OK? Bye.'

He turned with an expectant expression towards Sally. She offered back a serious, hard look, almost a scowl.

'So who's supposed to be producing this magical overnight poll of yours, Francis?'

'Why, you are, my dear. You are.'

Her bug eyes sank back into their sockets as if trying to hide. It was after midnight and she had been sitting in front of the computer terminal ever since the last of her staff had departed for the night and left her on her own. She needed space to think.

Preparing a questionnaire had been simple. Nothing fancy or out of the ordinary. And she had on the shelf any number of computer disks with their random digit dialling facilities which would give a spin to the sample and so to the results, to drive the survey up-market or downmarket, give added weight to council-house tenants or the substantial leafy glades of suburbia, question only company directors or the unemployed. The trouble was she had no idea how much the sample needed to be leant on to get the desired result – Urquhart was clearly ahead, but by how much? By however much, it would be more after *The Times* had sounded off. There was so much unease and anxiety around, it was a perfect time to hotwire the bandwagon.

She wandered around her scruffy premises. The overheads were kept low, all the flash was up front in the reception area, all the quality poured into the strategy and the thinking. The mechanical side was low life. She walked alongside rows of open booths, covered in cloth for sound-proofing, where tomorrow the motley collection of part-time staff would gather to sit in front of their individual computer screens, phoning the randomly chosen tele-phone numbers thrown out by the mainframe, mindlessly reading

233

out the required questions and equally mindlessly tapping in the answers. They would not suspect. They were junkies in torn jeans, off-duty New Zealand nurses worrying about missed periods, failed businessmen who had suffered from the mistakes of others and fresh-faced students eagerly waiting to make their own. All that mattered was they were vaguely computer-literate and could turn up at two hours' notice. They had no means of knowing what was happening to the information they gathered, and wouldn't care. She paced along the carpet worn with time and well trodden with gum, examining the polystyrene tiles missing from the corner where the gutter had blocked and backed up, running a finger along the open metal shelves overflowing with computer manuals and telephone directories, and dispatch dockets cast around like sweet wrappers on a windy day. Little natural light penetrated in here to expose the workings of the opinion-research industry. She told clients it was for security, in reality it was simply because the place was a dump. A pot plant had struggled and withered and eventually died, and now doubled as an ashtray. This was her empire.

It had its advantages, this air-conditioned, computerized, paperless empire. A few years ago she would have needed to shift a ton of paper to do what she had been asked to do; now she had to lift no more than a couple of fingers, tap a few keys – the right keys, mind you – and there you had it. Your result. Urquhart's result. But there was the rub. He had been uncompromisingly specific about the figures he wanted, had already given them to Brynford-Jones. No matter how much she toyed with the specs or put a wobble into the weighting of the sample, what was required was more than a little spin. She would have to end up doing what she had never done before, and fiddle the result. Take two figures, one Government, the other Opposition, and work backwards. Not so much massaging as beating them to pulp. If she were found out she would never work again, might even be put away for criminal deception. To lie, to cheat, to steal the opinions of ordinary men and women and abuse them. For Francis Urquhart. Is that what her dreams were all about?

She gazed once more around the room, its walls painted black

234

to disguise the cracks, its mustiness which even the lavatory deodorizers couldn't disguise, its tired-out percolators and second-hand furniture, its corners which overflowed with plastic cups and discarded cigarette packets, its fire alarm system, brick-red amidst the gloom, a relic of the 1970s, which probably wouldn't work even if tossed into Vesuvius. She picked up the pot plant, plucked off its withered leaves, swept away the stub ends, tidied it as if it were an old and rather disreputable friend, then she dropped the whole thing, container and all, into the nearest waste bin. This was her empire. And it was not enough.

The lack of sleep showed in Sally's eyes, and she had hidden them behind spectacles with a slight tint, which only served to emphasize the fullness of her mouth and the exceptional animation of her nose. As she walked in through the doorway of Downing Street one of the doormen nudged a colleague; they had heard talk of her, of course, but this was the first time she had appeared during daylight. And Elizabeth Urquhart was at home, too. They smiled at her encouragingly, both wishing they could find some excuse to frisk her for weapons.

He was in the Cabinet Room. It was different from the last occasion they had been here, in the dark, with nothing but the distant glow of street lamps and the tips of their fingers and tongues to guide them. He still sat in his special chair, but this time a civil servant drew back a chair on the opposite side of the table for her. It felt as though she were a million miles away from him.

'Good afternoon, Miss Quine.'

'Prime Minister.' She nodded coyly while the civil servant made herself scarce.

He waved his arms a little awkwardly. 'Excuse the, er . . . working formality. A busy day.'

'Your poll, Francis.' She opened her briefcase and extracted a single sheet of paper which she thrust across the table. He had to stretch to retrieve it. He studied it briefly.

'Of course, I know these are the figures I asked for. But where are the real figures, Sally?'

'You're holding them, Francis. Ludicrous, isn't it? You didn't have to get me to cheat and fiddle. Ten points ahead, just as you asked. You're home and dry.'

His eyelids blinked rapidly as he took the information in. A smile began, like the fingers of a new dawn creeping across his face. He started nodding in pleasure, as if he had known all along.

'I could have kept my virginity after all.'

He looked up from the piece of paper, a crease across his brow. She was making a point of sorts but damned if he could figure out what. Over a set of figures, one poll amongst the thousands? Selective statistics, the sort of thing Government departments did by instinct? He took out a colourful handkerchief and wiped his nose with meticulous, almost exaggerated care. He wanted to celebrate yet she seemed intent on puncturing his euphoria. That, and the distance between them across the table, would make the next bit easier.

'How are those new clients I sent you?'

She raised her eyebrows in surprise; it seemed such a tangent. 'Fine. Really fine. Thanks.'

'I'm the one who should be grateful, Sally. There will be more in the future . . . clients, that is. I want to go on helping.' He was looking at the figures again, not at her. He was evidently uncomfortable, unsnapping his watch strap and massaging his wrist, easing his collar as if he felt claustrophobic. Claustrophobic? When she was the only other person in the room?

'What is it, Francis?' She pronounced his name in a more nasal manner than usual; less attractive, he thought.

'We have to stop seeing each other.'

'Why?'

'Too many people know.'

'It never bothered you before.'

'Elizabeth knows.'

'I see.'

'And there's the election. It's all very difficult.'

'It wasn't exactly easy fiddling your goddamned figures.'

There was a silence. He was still trying to find something in the sheet of paper on which to concentrate.

'For how long? How long do we have to stop seeing each other?'

He looked up, a flicker of unease in his eyes, his lips stretched awkwardly. 'I'm . . . afraid it must be for good. Elizabeth insists.'

'And if Elizabeth insists . . .' Her tone was scornful.

'Elizabeth and I have a very solid relationship, mature. We understand each other. We don't cheat on that understanding.'

'My God, Francis, what the hell do you think we've been doing here, there, everywhere in this building, even in that chair you're sitting in, if it wasn't cheating on your wife? Or wasn't it personal for you? Just business?'

He couldn't hold her stare. He began fiddling with his pencil, wondering if she were going to burst into hysterics. Not that, anything but that. He couldn't handle hysterical women.

'Not even after the election, Francis?'

'I've never cheated on her, not like that. Not when she has made her wishes clear.'

'But she need never know. Our work together, it's been fantastic, historic.'

'And I'm grateful . . .'

'It's been much more than that, Francis. At least for me. You are like none of the other men I've ever been with. I'd hate to lose that. You're better than the rest. You know that, don't you?'

Her nose was bobbing sensuously, full of sexual semaphore, and he felt himself torn. His relationship with Elizabeth was his bedrock; through the years, it had made up for his sense of guilt and sexual inadequacy, provided a foundation from which he had withstood all the storms of political ambition and had conquered. It had made him a man. By God, he owed her. She had sacrificed as much as he for his career, in some ways more, but it was all beginning to blur as he stared at Sally. She leant forward, her full breasts enticing, offered up still more fully by the support of the Cabinet table.

'I'd be happy to wait, Francis. It would be worth waiting for.'

And wasn't she right. He owed Elizabeth but with her it had never been like this, not raw, uninhibited, dominating lust.

'And there's our work together. We're lucky for each other, Francis. It's got to go on.'

He had never betrayed his wife before, never! But he could feel that irresistible tightness growing within him once more and somehow Elizabeth seemed to belong to another world, the sort of world they had inhabited before he became Prime Minister. Things had changed; the job imposed different rules and responsibilities. He had given Elizabeth what she wanted, the chance to run her own court in Downing Street, did she have a right to ask still more of him? And somehow he knew he would never be able to find another Sally, would have neither the time nor the opportunity. He might be able to replace her mind, but not her body and what it did for him. She had made him feel so supreme, a young man once again. And he could always explain to Elizabeth that it was in nobody's interest to have Sally roaming free, discontented, perhaps vengeful, not now.

'It would be difficult, Sally.' He swallowed. 'But I'd like to try.'

'First time? Give up your virginity, Francis?'

'If you would have it that way.'

He was staring at her breasts, which held him like a rabbit in the beam of a lamp. She smiled, closed the lid of her briefcase and snapped the locks shut as if inside it she had trapped his innocence. Then she rose and walked slowly around the long table. She wore a tight black body stocking in an oversized silk-cotton jacket from Harvey Nicks, an arrangement he hadn't seen before, and as she approached him the jacket was drawn back to expose her full physical charms. He knew he had made the right decision. It was good for the cause, would ensure continued support and security, Elizabeth would understand that – if she ever found out.

Sally was there, beside him. She extended a hand. 'I can't wait. Partner.'

He stood up, they shook hands. He felt triumphant, all-powerful, as though there were no challenge, no dilemma, to which he could not rise.

She was a remarkable woman, this American, practically a true British sport, his smile suggested.

What an utter English prick, she thought.

*   *   *

238

Brian Redhead's beard had grown longer and wispier with the years, but his Geordie bite remained formidably sharp. Why else would he have survived so long as the doyen of early morning radio and continued to attract an endless stream of politicians to be mangled and torn even before their first cup of coffee had time to grow cold? He sat in his studio within Broadcasting House like a hermit in his cave, searching for some intangible truth, the table strewn with dirty cups, disused notes and soiled reputations, glowering at his producer through the murky window of the control room. A huge old-fashioned wall clock with a burnished oak surround hung on the wall, like a British Rail waiting room, the second hand ticking remorselessly onward.

'It's time once more for our review of the morning papers and we have our regular Thursday reviewer, Matthew Parris, to do just that for us. The Royal robes seem to be in something of a twist again, Matthew.'

'Yes, Brian. Our home-bred answer to all those Australian soaps begins another tangle-filled episode this morning, but perhaps there are signs that some sort of ending may be in sight. There are suggestions that we could be losing at least one of the key players, because the latest straw poll carried in *The Times* puts the Opposition ten points behind and it could be the straw that breaks the Opposition camel's back. Not that Gordon McKillin will take kindly to being compared to a camel, or a tramp for that matter, but he must be wondering how soon it will be before he's sent off to live in a Royal underpass. He might find it a lot more comfortable than the House of Commons this afternoon. But it's *The Times* editorial comment which has galvanized the rest of Fleet Street in their late editions. Time for an election to clear the air? it asks. No one doubts that it would not only be Mr McKillin's leadership under public scrutiny, but also the King's. The *Mirror* goes back to basics. "Under the present system he could be the biggest twerp in the kingdom yet still get to reign. To use his own words, something has got to be done." And not all the other papers show as much respect. Have you forgotten the *Sun* headline of just a few days ago which shouted "King of Conscience"? The *Sun*'s editor obviously has, because he's reused the same headline today – except it's been abbreviated to read simply: "King Con". It seems a week is a long time in Royal politics. There's more in the rest . . .'

In a City office a few miles away from Broadcasting House, Landless switched off the radio. Dawn was still a brushstroke in the sky but already he was at his desk. His first job had been delivering newspapers as an eight-year-old, running all the way through the dark streets because his parents couldn't afford a bike, stuffing letter boxes and catching glimpses of negligée and bare flesh through the badly drawn curtains. He'd put on a bit of weight since then, and a few millions, but the habit of rising early to catch the others at it had stuck. There was only one other person in the office, the oldest of his three secretaries who took the early turn. The silence and her greying hair helped him think. He stood lingering over his copy of *The Times*, laid open on his desk. He read it again, cracking the knuckles of each of his fingers in turn as he tried to figure out what – and who – lay behind the words. When he had run out of knuckles he leaned across his desk and tapped the intercom.

'I know it's early, Miss Macmunn, and they'll still be pouring the milk over their wholemeal cornflakes and scratching their Royal rumps. But see if you can get the Palace on the phone . . .'

He had wondered, very briefly and privately, whether he should consult them, take their advice. But only very briefly. As he gazed around the Cabinet table at his colleagues, he could find no patience within himself for their endless debates and dithering, their fruitless searches for the easy way ahead, the constant resort to compromise. They had all arrived with their red Cabinet folders containing the formal Cabinet papers and the notes which civil servants felt might be necessary to support their individual positions or gently undermine those of rival colleagues. Colleagues! It was only his leadership, his authority which prevented them from indulging in the sort of petty squabbles that would disgrace a kindergarten. Anyway, the civil servants' notes were irrelevant, because the civil servants had not known that he was about to hijack the agenda.

There had been no point in seeking opinions; they would have been so pathetically predictable. Too soon, too precipitate, too

240

uncertain, too much damage to the institution of the Monarchy, they would have said. Too much chance they would lose their Ministerial chauffeurs sooner than necessary. Oh, ye of little faith! They needed some backbone, some spunk. They needed terrifying out of their political wits.

He had waited until they finished smiling and congratulating each other at their favourable showing in the opinion polls – *their* favourable showing! He had called on the Chancellor of the Exchequer to recite for them just how wretched it was all going to be, particularly after the chaos in the markets had knocked the stuffing out of business confidence. A tunnel which had been dug deeper and longer than anyone could have expected, the Chancellor recited, with not a flicker of light to be seen and a Budget in the middle of next month which would blow holes in their socks. If they had any socks left.

While they were chewing nauseously on those bones he had asked the Employment Secretary about the figures. School holidays beginning on March 15, some three hundred thousand school leavers flooding onto the market, and employment prospects which looked as welcoming as a witch's armpit. The jobless total would rise above two million. Another election pledge out of the window. And then he had turned to the Attorney General's report about the prospect for Sir Jasper Harrod's trial. From the ague which crossed one or two of the faces he suspected there were other individual donations which had not yet come to light amongst the high and, for the moment, mighty. Thursday March 28 was the trial date. No, no postponements likely, the dirty linen being hung out to dry within days of the first rap of the judge's gavel. Sir Jasper had made it clear he did not wish to suffer on his own.

The colleagues had begun to look as though they were sailing in an overcrowded dinghy through a Force Nine before he put his own twist to their discomfort. A strong rumour that McKillin was considering resignation at Easter. Only that twerp of an Environment Secretary Dickie thought it good news; the rest had recognized it immediately for what it was – the Opposition's best hope of salvation, a new start, a clean break with McKillin's fooleries and failures, a leap for firm new ground. Even the other dunderheads had seen that – all except Dickie. He would have to go, after the election.

Only after silence had hung in the air for many seconds did he thrown them a lifeline, a chance to be hauled towards dry land. An election. On Thursday March 14. Just enough time if they hurried and scuttled to tidy up the parliamentary loose ends and a dissolution which would squeeze them through before the next storms hit and overwhelmed them. Not a suggestion, not a request for opinions, simply an indication of his mastery of tactics and why he was Prime Minister, and not any of the rest of them. A strong opinion poll lead. An Opposition in disarray. A Royal scapegoat. A timetable. And an audience with the King in under an hour to issue the Royal Proclamation. What more could they want. Yes, he knew it was tight, but there was time enough. Just.

'Your Majesty.'

'Urquhart.'

They did not bother sitting. The King showed no signs of offering a chair, and Urquhart needed only seconds to deliver his message.

'There is only one piece of business I wish to raise. I want an immediate election. For March 14.'

The King stared at him, but said nothing.

'I suppose in fairness I must tell you that part of the Government's manifesto will be a proposal to establish a parliamentary committee of inquiry into the Monarchy, its duties and responsibilities. I shall propose to that commission a series of radical restrictions on the activities, role and financing of both you and your relatives. There has been too much scandal and confusion. It is time for the people to decide.'

When he replied the King's voice was remarkably soft and controlled. 'It never ceases to amaze me how politicians can always pontificate in the name of the people, even as they utter the most absurd falsehoods. Yet if I, an hereditary Monarch, were to read from the Testaments my words would still be regarded with suspicion.'

The insult was delivered slowly so that it sank deep. Urquhart smiled patronizingly but offered no response.

'So it is to be outright war, is it? You and me. The King and his Cromwell. Whatever happened to that ancient English virtue of compromise?'

'I am a Scot.'

'So you would destroy me, and with me the Constitution which has served this country so well for generations.'

'A constitutional Monarchy is built on the mistaken concept of dignity and perfect breeding. It is scarcely my fault that you have all turned out to have the appetites and sexual preferences of goats!'

The King flinched as if he had been slapped and Urquhart realized he may have gone a step too far. After all, what was the point?

'I will bother you no longer, Sir. I merely came to inform you of the dissolution. March 14.'

'So you say. But I don't think you shall have it.'

There was no alarm in Urquhart's demeanour; he knew his rights. 'What nonsense is this?'

'You expect me to issue a Royal Proclamation today, this instant.'

'As I have every right to do.'

'Possibly. And then again, possibly not. An interesting point, don't you think? Because I also have rights accorded by the same constitutional precedents, rights to be consulted, to advise and to warn.'

'I am consulting you. Give me as much advice as you want. Warn me, threaten me for all I care. But that cannot prevent you from granting the dissolution I demand. That is the right of the Prime Minister.'

'Be reasonable, Prime Minister. This is my first time at this, I am new to the job. I need to take advice myself, talk to a few people, make sure I am taking the correct constitutional action. I'm sure I could be in a position to grant your request by, say, next week? Not unreasonable, is it? Just a few days?'

'That cannot be!'

'And why not?'

'You cannot expect me to hold an election on Maundy Thursday when those who are not on their knees are flat on their backs for the Easter holidays. No delay. I will not have it, d'you hear!'

The composure had been peeled away; Urquhart's fists were

243

clenched in consternation and his legs braced as if he were about to launch a direct physical attack against the Monarch. Instead of flinching or drawing back, the King began to laugh, a frosty, hollow noise which echoed around the high ceiling.

'You must forgive me, Urquhart. My little joke. Of course I cannot delay your demand. I merely wanted to see how you would react.' The muscles continued to pull his face into the expression of a smile, but behind it there was no sense of warmth. The eyes were like frost. 'You seem to be in something of a hurry. And so, I have to tell you, am I, for your eagerness has helped prompt a decision of my own. You see, Urquhart, I despise you and all that you stand for. The ruthless, relentless, utterly soulless way you pursue your ends. I feel bound to do everything within my power to stop you.'

Urquhart was shaking his head. 'But you cannot delay an election.'

'No. But neither can I accept what I know to be a fact, that you have destroyed my friends, and my family, and now you attempt to destroy me and along with me, the Crown. You know, Charlotte may be a foolish woman but she is basically a kind soul. She didn't deserve what you did to her. But then, neither did Mycroft.' He waited for a second or two. 'I see you don't even feel the need to deny it.'

'I make no comment. You can prove nothing.'

'I don't need to. Only to myself, at least. You see, Urquhart, you have used those I love as a doormat on which to wipe your boots as you wade your way through the sewers. Now you wish to trample on me. I won't allow it.'

'There's nothing you can do. After this election the Crown will never be in a position to play politics again.'

'On that, Prime Minister, we are agreed. It's taken me much anguish to face up to the fact that what I have been doing these last months, the ideals I have been trying to cherish, the interests I wish to propagate, are politics. Sadly, there is no clear dividing line anymore. If I hold a view in public, even about the weather, then it is politics.'

'At last we are making progress.'

'I am. I'm not so sure about you. I have a duty, a divine duty

244

almost, to do everything within my powers to protect the Crown. I have an equally strong commitment to myself and those things in which I believe. But conscience sits uneasily beneath a modern Crown. You have made certain of that.'

'The people will make certain of that.'

'Perhaps. But not on March 14.'

Urquhart wiped a hand across his mouth in exasperation. 'You are wearing my patience thin. It shall be March 14.'

'But it cannot be. Because you must delay the dissolution of Parliament for an unexpected piece of business.'

'What business?'

'For a Bill of Abdication.'

'Another of your silly jokes!'

'I am not noted for my sense of humour.'

'You will abdicate?' For the first time Urquhart began to feel he was losing his grip. His jaw betrayed the slightest quiver.

'In order to protect the Crown and my conscience. And in order to fight you and your kind by every means possible. It is the only way.'

There was no mistaking the earnestness, that had always been the man's weakness, a complete inability to hide his honesty. Urquhart's eyes flickered rapidly as he tried to calculate the political fall-out, and how much damage any delay might inflict on his plans. He would still win, surely? The People's Parliament before the Crown. He would have to squeeze another week's grace out of the calendar, even if it meant Maundy Thursday – a propitious day for giving Kings their comeuppance. Unless . . . my God, he wasn't going to replace McKillin as Leader of the Opposition, was he? No, it was too ludicrous.

'What role do you expect to play in the campaign?' The words were hesitant.

'A modest one. Highlighting the issues of concern to me – of poverty, the lack of opportunities for the young. Urban and environmental squalor. I shall ask David Mycroft for his help. He has a flair for publicity, don't you think?' The King had changed, the habitual tension in his face seemed to have eased, grown softer, no longer plagued by nightmares and self-inflicted guilt. He seemed almost to be enjoying himself. 'But whatever I shall do shall be done entirely properly. I will not engage in personal confrontation or debate with you. Although others, I suspect, will be less fastidious.' He moved to a button hidden behind one of the window drapes and pushed it. Almost immediately the door opened, and in walked Benjamin Landless.

'You!'

'Me.' He nodded. 'It's been a long time, Francis. Seems like a lifetime ago, almost a different world.'

'Bizarre bedfellows, a King and a low-born thug like you.'

'Needs must.'

'I suppose you intend to publish and promote the Royal witterings.'

'Possibly, Francis. But not to the exclusion of other important news.'

For the first time Urquhart noticed that Landless held something in his hand . . . a clutch of papers?

'Photos, Francis. You know about photos, don't you?'

Landless held them out towards Urquhart, who took them as though offered a goblet of hemlock. He studied them in complete silence, unable to engage his tongue even if he had found the words.

'There seems to have been an outbreak of this sort of thing recently, don't you think, Sir?' Landless offered.

'Regrettably,' the King responded.

'Francis, you'll recognize your wife, of course. The other person, the one underneath − sorry, on top in the one you're looking at now − is an Italian. Possibly you've met him. Sings, or some such nonsense. And doesn't draw his curtains properly.'

Urquhart's hands were trembling such that the photographs were in danger of falling from his grasp. With an angry cry he crushed them within his fist and hurled them across the room. 'I'll disown her. People will understand, sympathize. That's not politics!'

The King could not restrain his snort of contempt.

'I sincerely hope you're right, Frankie,' Landless continued. 'But I have my doubts. People will find it very lumpy porridge when they find out about your own outside interests.'

'Meaning?' A haunted edge was creeping into Urquhart's eyes.

'Meaning a particular young and very attractive lady who has not only been seen a lot in Downing Street since you got there, but who has also recently made a huge killing on the foreign exchanges. Anyone might think she knew something – or someone – on the inside. Or will you try to disown her, too?'

The cheeks were suddenly drained, the words tumbling between trembling lips. 'How on earth . . . ? You couldn't possibly know . . .'

A huge bearlike arm was placed around Urquhart's shoulders and Landless lowered his voice to a conspiratorial whisper. As if on cue, the King walked over to a window and turned his back on them, preoccupying himself with the view of his garden.

'Let you in on a little secret, old chum. You see, she's been my partner as well as yours. I have to thank you. Did very nicely out of the currency wobbles, switched out of sterling just in time.'

'This isn't necessary,' he gasped, bewildered. 'You could have done just as well with me . . .'

Landless looked the other man carefully up and down. 'Nope. 'Fraid you're not my type, Francis.'

'Why, Ben? Why are you doing this to me?'

'How many reasons do you want?' He raised his hand to count off the pudgy fingers. 'Because you so obviously enjoyed treating me like shit. Because Prime Ministers come and go, as you'll soon be gone, while the Royal Family endures.' He nodded his huge head in the direction of the King's back. 'And perhaps mostly because he welcomed me, just as I am, Big Bad Benjamin from Bethnal Green, without looking down his nose, when I was never good enough for you or your high and mighty wife.' He twisted over his hand so that it became an upturned claw. 'So I'm squeezing your balls, as hard as I can.'

'Why? Oh, why?' Urquhart continued to moan.

Landless's fist closed tight. 'Because they're there, Francis. Because they're there.' He chuckled. 'Talking of which, I have good news of Sally.'

Urquhart could only raise mournful eyes in enquiry.

'She's pregnant.'

'Not by me!' Urquhart gasped.

'No, not by you.' The voice, which had patronized, now sneered. 'Seems you're not man enough for anything.'

So he knew about that, too. Urquhart turned away from his antagonist, trying to hide the humiliation, but Landless was in full pursuit.

'She's played you for the fool you are, Frankie. In politics, and in bed – or wherever it was. You shouldn't have used her. All that brains and beauty, and you threw it away.'

Urquhart was shaking his head, like a dog trying to rid itself of an unwanted collar.

'She's got new business, new clients, new capital. And a new man. It's a different life for her, Frankie. And being pregnant, too . . . well, you know what women are like about things like that. Or rather you don't, but take it from me. She's an exceptional and very happy lady.'

'Who? Who did she . . . ?' He seemed unable to finish.

'Who did she prefer to you?' Landless chuckled. 'You idiot. You still can't see it, can you.'

Urquhart's whole body had shrunk, his shoulders sagged and his mouth gaped open. He couldn't, wouldn't, take it in.

A look of triumph suffused the publisher's rubbery face. 'I've beat you at everything, Frankie. Even with Sally.'

Urquhart had an overwhelming, primal desire to crawl away, to find a dark place, any place, to bury his humiliation as quickly and as deeply as he could manage, but he couldn't depart, not yet. There was one more thing he had to do first. A final chance, perhaps, to buy a little time. He made an attempt at straightening his shoulders and walked stiffly across the room until he was facing the King's back. His face was contorted with the effort and he drew a deep, gulping breath. 'Sir, I have changed my mind. I withdraw my request for a dissolution.'

The King spun round on his heel, like an officer on parade. 'Oh, do you, Prime Minister? Damned difficult that, I've already set the wheels in motion, you see. Prime Minister's right to demand an election, of course, the Constitution's clear about that. Can't for the life of me remember the bit where it says he's allowed to call one off. Anyway, I'm the one who dissolves Parliament and signs the Royal Proclamation, and that's just what I'm going to do. If you find my actions objectionable on constitutional or personal grounds, I'm sure I can rely on your vote during the abdication debate.'

'I shall withdraw my proposals for constitutional reform,' Urquhart uttered in exhaustion. 'If necessary, I shall make a public apology for any . . . misunderstanding.'

'Decent of you to offer, Urquhart. Saves me and Mr Landless here insisting on it. I would like the apology made when you introduce the Abdication Bill.'

'But there's no need. You win. We can turn the clock back . . .'

'You still don't understand, do you? I am going to abdicate, whether you want that or not. I am not the right man for this task I was born to, I don't have the self-restraint required of a King. I've come to terms with that. My abdication will protect the Crown and all it stands for much more effectively than if I try to muddle my impatient way through the murky constitutional waters. My son has already been sent for and the regency papers are being drawn up. He is more patient than I, younger, more flexible. He will have a better chance of growing into the great King I shall never be.' He prodded his own chest. 'It's the best thing for me, the man.' The finger turned on Urquhart. 'And it is also the best damned way I can devise of destroying you and everything you stand for.'

Urquhart's lip trembled. 'You used to be an idealist.'

'And you, Mr Urquhart, used to be a politician.'

EPILOGUE

There was a knock on the front door, a soft, tentative sort of rapping. Kenny put down his book and went to answer it. The door
opened and there, on the darkened doorstep, wrapped in a new
overcoat against the blustery rain, stood Mycroft.

Mycroft had prepared his explanations and apologies carefully.
With the announcement of the abdication and election, things had
changed. The press had new fish to gut and fry and would leave
them alone, if Kenny could understand. And forgive. But as he
looked up at the other man he could see the pain deep within the
startled eyes, and his words deserted him.

They stood facing each other, each afraid of what the other might
say, not wanting to expose once again the scarcely healed wounds.
It seemed to Mycroft several lifetimes before Kenny finally spoke.

'Are you going to stand out there all sodding night, David? The
bears' tea will be getting cold.'